A Table for Two

"Lister displays a knack for seamlessly weaving evocative descriptions of culinary delights with equally vivid portraits of engaging characters."
—*Kirkus*

"Sizzling chemistry, sparkling banter, and plenty of charm."
—The Romance Dish

"Lister enchants with a tale of two city slickers who find love in a small town. Anyone who enjoys small-town and enemies-to-lovers tropes will be delighted."
—*Publishers Weekly*

"*A Table for Two* is the perfect blend of heart, small-town charm, and a heartfelt romance you won't soon forget!"
—Annie Rains, *USA Today* bestselling author

"Grab your wineglass! *A Table for Two* was everything and more that my romantic heart needed. No one can write a sensually intoxicating romance, layered with love, trust, and emotion like Sheryl Lister!"
—Sherelle Green, *USA Today* bestselling author

A Perfect Pairing

A Perfect Pairing

SHERYL LISTER

FOREVER

New York   Boston

Forever
Hachette Book Group
1290 Avenue of the Americas, New York, NY 10104
read-forever.com
twitter.com/readforeverpub

First Edition: August 2023

Forever is an imprint of Grand Central Publishing. The Forever name and logo are trademarks of Hachette Book Group, Inc.

The publisher is not responsible for websites (or their content) that are not owned by the publisher.

The Hachette Speakers Bureau provides a wide range of authors for speaking events. To find out more, go to www.hachettespeakersbureau.com or email HachetteSpeakers@hbgusa.com.

Forever books may be purchased in bulk for business, educational, or promotional use. For information, please contact your local bookseller or the Hachette Book Group Special Markets Department at special.markets@hbgusa.com.

Library of Congress Cataloging-in-Publication Data

Names: Lister, Sheryl, author.
Title: A perfect pairing / Sheryl Lister.
Description: First edition. | New York : Forever, 2023. | Series: Firefly Lake
Identifiers: LCCN 2023008723 | ISBN 9781538724194 (paperback) |
    ISBN 9781538755303 (ebook)
Subjects: LCSH: Female friendship--Fiction. | LCGFT: Romance fiction. | Novels.
Classification: LCC PS3612.I863 P47 2023 | DDC 813/.6--dc23/eng/20230303
LC record available at https://lccn.loc.gov/2023008723

ISBNs: 9781538724194 (paperback), 9781538755303 (ebook)

Printed in the United States of America

LSC-C

Printing 1, 2023

For those who believe in second chances.

A Perfect Pairing

CHAPTER 1

Natasha Baldwin shoved one of the coveted truffles she'd been saving into her mouth and tried to concentrate on the rich mixture of dark and milk chocolate rather than the irritating voice of her co-worker. The woman had interrupted their boss a good ten times during the weekly staff meeting and it had only been half an hour. She glanced up at the wall clock and sighed. At this rate, Natasha would never get to her appointment on time. "Do you know how long the meeting's going to go, George? I'm meeting with a prospective client in an hour," she said, hoping to speed things along.

George Lambert sent her a grateful smile. "We should be done in about twenty minutes, barring any other interruptions." George had headed up Firefly Lake's real estate office for as long as Natasha could remember. He was fair but also no-nonsense when it came to selling real estate in their town of fewer than two thousand residents. "Moving on to the subject of the upcoming condominium project, I've decided in order to keep confusion to a minimum, there will be one exclusive Realtor. As always, the bigger projects are given to the Realtor with the best sales record for the preceding

1

quarter." He paused and glanced at each of the four people seated around the conference table.

Natasha's heartrate kicked up. She knew she'd sold well, or as well as one could when living in a small town. However, she also knew that at least one of her co-workers hadn't done too bad, either.

"I think you should go by the Realtor with the most experience," Kathleen said, lifting her chin.

Natasha barely stifled an eye roll. Kathleen never missed an opportunity to call attention to the fact that she had been with the company the longest. In Natasha's mind, if Kathleen spent more time building relationships with prospective buyers and less on trying to show up everyone, she might have a point.

George shook his head. "The policy hasn't changed since the doors of this place opened and won't now. Okay, with four sales, the exclusive Realtor will be Natasha Baldwin. Congratulations."

Inside, Natasha did a little two-step dance move, complete with a shimmy, but kept her outward calm and just smiled. "Thank you so much."

"Thanks for all your hard work. We can talk this afternoon when you get back. All right, people, let's get moving." He came to his feet and walked out of the small conference room.

Natasha stood, and the young woman who'd joined the office a year ago congratulated Natasha before leaving.

Kathleen pushed back from the table with such force, her chair hit the wall. She shot Natasha a nasty look and stormed out.

"I would've had you if it weren't for you closing the sale of the print shop two weeks ago. I was *this* close," Brett Henson said with a laugh, holding his thumb and index finger together. "Congrats, Tasha. It's well deserved." He leaned closer and whispered, "Thank goodness it wasn't Kathleen. Some days I think that woman needs to retire." Brett had started working there a few months before Natasha, and the two got along well.

Laughing, she said, "Thanks. I knew you'd done well, too." She couldn't have been happier that the print shop sale had gone through earlier than expected and wholeheartedly agreed with his sentiment about Kathleen. As of late, the woman had a habit of trying to bully prospective buyers into purchasing properties that far exceeded their budgets, and more than one person had complained to George. But Natasha didn't have time to dwell on that mess. She had a meeting and a celebration to think about. "Well, I'd better get going."

"No doubt to solidify your spot as Top Realtor."

"Don't hate. You had to give it up sometime." Until three months ago, he'd been the Top Realtor in Firefly Lake for over two years and always said he loved the friendly competition.

"Yeah, yeah." He straightened from the table and followed her to the door. "I'll see you later."

Natasha threw up a wave and almost floated to her desk. She grabbed her iPad, stuffed it into her tote, and headed to her car.

It took less than fifteen minutes to arrive at the house that had been one of the original homes built behind Crystal Lake. The place where, as a child, she imagined living in the stately two-story home with its wrap-around porch, large backyard, and open layout. Natasha got out of the car, and her gaze roamed over the property, which had seen better days. A smile curved her lips as she recalled the countless hours she'd spent with Mrs. Ward. The older woman had two sons but had always wanted a daughter and welcomed having tea parties and allowing Natasha to help "decorate" the different rooms. Natasha could trace her love of interior design to Mrs. Ward and this house. Retrieving her cell from her tote, she sent a text to her best friends, Dana Stephens and Terri Rhodes, to share her good news and invite them to a dinner celebration.

A moment later, Dana replied: *As long as you don't expect me to cook, I'm free any night this week.*

Natasha chuckled and sent back: *Lol! No, I'll throw a little something together. It won't be as good as Serenity's, but it'll be edible.* ☺

A friend of hers since childhood, Dana had never liked cooking, but she could make the best margaritas or any other mixed drink. Natasha did okay in the kitchen, but nothing fancy. She left that to their other friend, Serenity Cunningham, who'd started what the friends lovingly called Serenity's Supper Club. They got together at least twice a month and caught up over great food, wine, music, and lots of laughter. However, since Serenity had just gotten married and was on her honeymoon, they were on their own.

Terri's response popped up: *I'm free tonight. Hubby is working late, and I'm in need of some supper club fun!*

Natasha: *Great! Tonight around 7 at my place.*

Dropping the phone back into her tote, she turned at the sound of a car pulling into the driveway. A broad grin spread across Natasha's face as she watched the tall, lean frame of the man exit the car and start toward her. She met him half-way, and he grabbed her up in a bear hug.

"It's so good to see you, Tasha."

Laughing, she said, "Put me down, you nut. It's good to see you too, Chase." Two years her senior, Chase Ward had been greeting her this way since she was a kid.

He set her on her feet and glanced over at the house, his smile fading.

"I'm so sorry about your mom."

"Thanks. Never thought we'd be selling this place. It's been in our family for over fifty years, but with Mike working overseas and me in the military, we just don't have time for the upkeep or worrying about trying to rent it out. And neither of us has plans to move back." Chase shook his head. "I didn't know it had gotten this run-down since I was here. I fixed a few things the last time, but now it looks like the house is going to need a complete overhaul to sell." He hadn't been home in over two years.

Natasha could feel his pain. His mother had suffered a major stroke a couple of months ago and was also in the beginning stages of dementia. Chase planned to move Mrs. Ward to a care facility near his home in North Carolina, where his wife would easily be able to keep an eye on her. She ran a comforting hand down his arm. "Well, come on and tell me what you want done."

They climbed the four steps that led to the wide porch. "Definitely need to get this porch fixed. There are several places where the wood is loose or buckling," he added, pointing to a few spots.

She fished her iPad out of her tote, opened the document

she'd started, and added a notation. After he unlocked the door, Chase gestured for her to go first. As soon as she crossed the threshold, a blast of stale heat greeted her. Swiping at a few spiderwebs, she stepped into the short entryway and followed Chase as he slowly took in the large formal living room.

He walked over to the fireplace, picked up a family photo on the mantel, blew some of the dust off, and stared at it for several seconds before putting it back in its place. "Okay, let's get this done."

It took over an hour for Natasha and Chase to walk through the two-story, four-bedroom, three-bathroom home and document all the things he wanted repaired, restored, and updated. "How long are you going to be here?" she asked as she headed for her car.

"Until next Tuesday. My wife gets in tomorrow, and we'll clear everything out. Are you going to talk to Mr. Davenport about making the repairs?"

"Yes. I'll stop by on my way back to the office." Charles Davenport owned the only construction company in town. "I'll call and let you know when he can start."

Chase hugged her and kissed her cheek. "Thanks for everything, Tasha. And thanks for visiting Mom and keeping me updated on her condition."

"You know how much I love Ms. Velda."

A smile curved his lips. "Yeah, you were the daughter she always wanted. She spoiled you rotten."

Natasha shrugged and started down the steps. "It's not my fault you and Mike never wanted to have tea parties or help redecorate."

He laughed. "Right. That was never gonna happen, so I'm glad she had you."

"See you later." She was still smiling when she got into her car and drove back to town.

She parked in the small lot at the end of the block and walked two doors down to Davenport Family Construction. Inside, she spoke to the receptionist, then took a seat to wait while the woman went down the hall to the back offices. A moment later, she returned and gestured for Natasha to follow her.

"Hey, Natasha." Mr. Davenport came around his desk and embraced her. "Have a seat. What's going on?"

"Hey, Mr. D." She took the offered chair and said, "I wanted to talk to you about getting on the schedule to fix up Ms. Velda's house. Chase and Mike have decided to sell."

He shook his head. "I wondered what they were planning to do. It breaks my heart to see her going down like this." Leaning forward, he tapped a few keys on his computer. "I can put you on the schedule for next Tuesday. Will eleven o'clock work?"

She pulled up her calendar on her phone. "Yep, that'll be fine." Since Chase and Mike didn't live in town, Chase had entrusted Natasha with the task of overseeing the repairs, and she'd promised to keep him updated.

"Okay. How're your folks doing?"

"They're doing well. Both keep talking about wanting to retire, saying they've had enough of working for the government."

Mr. Davenport chuckled. "I can't blame them. I might like to do the same. Sleeping in, fishing—"

7

"And taking all those trips Mrs. Davenport's been talking about." Everyone in town knew about the multitude of travel brochures his wife had. She showed them around every chance she got.

"Yeah, that, too." He stroked his chin thoughtfully. "On second thought, maybe I'd better stick around here a while longer and earn a little more money. No telling where that woman will have me going."

Natasha hopped up from her seat. "On that note," she said laughingly, "I'm out of here. And your secret is safe with me." She gave him an exaggerated wink. He loved his wife to distraction, and Natasha knew he'd been teasing. They were still laughing about it as they sauntered toward the front.

"I don't believe it," he whispered and stopped abruptly.

She glanced over her shoulder to see what had captured his attention and froze.

What is he doing here?

Mr. Davenport rushed past her and engulfed Antonio Hayes in a crushing hug, but she couldn't get her feet to move or her mouth to form a sentence. The tall, lanky, hand-some basketball player who'd captured her heart at age fif-teen had grown into a man with heart-stopping good looks and well-defined muscles that bulged with every move-ment. When Antonio finally looked her way, his gaze held the same iciness it had the last time their paths had crossed. Well, not exactly crossed. She'd seen him from a distance when he came home a few years ago and thought it was time they cleared the air. He'd seen her coming, turned, and went the other way, but not before glaring at her. Obviously, noth-ing had changed. Not wanting him to know how much he rattled her, she pasted a smile on her face. "Hey, Antonio. It's good to see you."

"Natasha." Antonio turned back to Mr. Davenport.

Okay, she didn't expect him to greet her the same way he'd done his godfather, but she figured it had been a long time since their breakup, they were both adults now, and he would at least be somewhere in the vicinity of cordial. Instead, the startling gray eyes that had captivated her the first day she'd seen him in their ninth-grade algebra class now bored into her like a turbulent thunderstorm. "Um, I know you two probably want to catch up, and I need to make a quick stop at the post office. I'll see you later." Natasha made a beeline to the exit.

"I guess you're still sending letters."

She paused and stared at Antonio for a brief moment, her guilt rising all over again. Yes, she'd sent him a letter ending their relationship during their first year of college, and yes, she regretted not taking his calls to explain how insecure she'd been feeling after he started missing their weekly calls. Her gaze went to Mr. Davenport, who divided a wary glance between them and shook his head. She could only imagine what he thought. Emotions rising, Natasha said nothing as she rushed out the door. In their small town, one would think it difficult not to run into each other, but Antonio had made sure it never happened. He'd also never stayed around more than a couple of days those few times he returned, except when he'd helped build his grandmother's cottage. She only hoped this time would be the same. Natasha couldn't take seeing him and knowing he still hated her after all these years.

CHAPTER 2

Antonio Hayes had expected to run into Natasha at some point now that he'd decided to return home, but not less than twenty-four hours after his arrival. The skinny, beautiful girl he'd fallen in love with as a teenager had morphed into an even more gorgeous woman, with enough curves to keep a man busy for days. But the only thing he'd be busy doing was staying as far away from her as possible. Not an easy feat, seeing as how they lived in a small town.

"You all right, son?"

He turned back to his godfather, whose intense and knowing gaze almost made Antonio squirm. "Yeah, I'm good, Uncle Charles."

"Well, come on back, and you can fill me in on why you really came home."

Shaking his head, Antonio chuckled and did just that. On the way, he noted that not much had changed in the place since the last time he'd been there a few years ago. "I see everything's the same."

"If it ain't broke, don't fix it," Charles said, dropping down heavily in his chair.

"How've you been doing? Dad told me about your blood pressure being up." Antonio studied the man who'd been a second father to him and taught him everything he knew about construction. Aside from gaining a few pounds, adding some gray strands in his hair, and having a line or two bracketing his light-brown face, he looked okay.

He waved him off. "I'm fine. Doctor put me on some meds and told me I need to keep the stress down."

"And are you?"

"As much as I can. I'm not pulling those twelve- and fourteen-hour days anymore."

"Good. You need to learn to delegate more."

Uncle Charles grunted. "I delegate just fine. What I really need to do is retire so I can sit on my deck or go fishing more often with your father."

Antonio smiled. "He did mention enjoying retirement." His father and Uncle Charles had a friendship that spanned more than fifty years. Too bad Antonio couldn't claim the same. Most of the guys he'd hung out with in school had moved away, and he could count the number of them he'd kept in close contact with on one hand and still have fingers left over. His older brother, Nathaniel, was Antonio's confidant.

"I knew I should've listened and retired when he did last year."

Laughing, he said, "Dad was more than happy to turn the optometry practice over to Nate. So, when are you planning to retire?"

"Soon, hopefully. What are your plans now that you're back? And are you staying this time?"

"Not sure yet, and yes, I'm staying." He'd contemplated moving back several years ago, but knowing Natasha had returned home instead of staying in Los Angeles, as she'd dreamed, he had changed his mind. "To answer the rest of your question, I'd planned to relax for a few weeks before deciding my next steps." As an investment manager in a top New York firm for the past decade, he'd amassed a nice financial portfolio, which afforded him the opportunity to take some much-needed time off. While there, he'd rarely taken vacations and often worked fifty or sixty hours a week. Now, at age thirty-four, with a failed marriage, he wanted—no *needed*—a change. Antonio had been close to burnout and missed his family—he especially wanted to be near his ailing grandfather and watch his niece grow up. He just had no idea what that looked like at the moment. "I thought about starting my own investment firm, but I'm not sure that's something I really want to do. I could always help you out with a few projects," he added with a grin.

Uncle Charles nodded. "Good. Then I might be able to retire sooner than later."

Antonio's eyebrows knitted together in confusion. "What does my returning home and helping you with a few things have to do with you retiring?"

He leaned forward and clasped his hands on the desk. "I'm sixty-one years old, and I'm tired. My boys have no interest in taking over the business, and after pouring my life into this company, I don't want to see it go under. Besides, it's the only construction company in town, and there's no way I want to see some big corporation come in and take over and change what we've got here in Firefly Lake."

Antonio nodded. He understood his godfather's viewpoint. There had been several instances when some big company tried to push for a major expansion of homes to "bring more people in," as they put it. However, their tight-knit community shut them down every time. While they were good with some growth and had technology to rival big cities, the town's residents enjoyed having no traffic, being able to easily access what they needed, and Antonio's least favorite part, knowing everyone's business. He leaned back and folded his arms. "So, what are you going to do?"

"I'm hoping you'll agree to take over."

He jerked upright. "Wait. What?" His heart pounded, and he shook his head. Surely he hadn't heard correctly.

"You heard me. I want to transfer the business to you."

Antonio lifted a hand. "Why me? Unc, I haven't worked in construction since I left. I've been in finance since I graduated."

A grin kicked up in the corner of Charles's mouth. "Maybe not, but I know about you volunteering with Habitat for Humanity. Didn't you just say you'd help me out? And why not you? It's your dual engineering and business degrees from Syracuse that make you the perfect choice."

Antonio fell back against the chair, stunned. Sure, he'd once dreamed of owning his own construction business, but things were different back then. Then, it was supposed to be him and Natasha—he'd build the houses and she'd use her interior design degree to decorate them. Since their relationship imploded, he had shoved the fantasy into the deep recesses of his mind and locked the door.

"I love you as if you were my own son, and I know you'd do me proud."

Inhaling deeply, Antonio struggled to maintain his composure. That his godfather trusted him with his life's work was humbling.

"How about you think on it for a few days before giving me your answer?"

"Thanks." He stood. "I'll let you know within a week."

Rising to his feet, Charles extended his hand. "Sounds like a plan. Here's the key to the place. Stay as long as you need. Oh, and you're more than welcome to come by for dinner tonight. Marcie would love to see you."

"I appreciate that. Mom's cooking tonight, but tell Aunt Marcie I'll stop by soon." Uncle Charles had built four two- and three-bedroom homes to accommodate his out-of-town family that visited during the holidays, citing the need to maintain the peace and quiet of his own house. Antonio would be renting one of the two-bedroom houses. And not a moment too soon. Ever since he stated his intention to move home, his mother had been steadily trying to let him know about all the available single women in town. He'd spent last night with his parents, and she'd continued her campaign. However, he wasn't interested. He'd been part of the heartbreak club twice, and he was done.

* * *

Natasha decided on something simple for dinner—chicken and shrimp fajitas with cilantro rice and peach cobbler and ice cream for dessert. After setting the cobbler on a trivet to cool, she heard the doorbell and went to answer the door. She smiled at Terri. "Hey, girl. Come on in."

"Hey. Ooh, it smells so good in here, and I'm starving." Terri followed Natasha to the kitchen. "It was so busy in the emergency room today, I was only able to eat six bites of my salad and guzzle half a bottle of water. *And* I had to do an extra three hours to cover for another nurse."

"Well, have a seat and relax." She gestured to the bar and pushed a small cutting board filled with cheese, crackers, and sliced apples in front of her friend. "I figured you'd be coming straight from the hospital, so this should hold you until dinner. Dana is on her way, and she'll be making margaritas."

"Hallelujah!" Terri said as she bit into a cracker topped with smoked cheddar.

Laughing, Natasha turned on the stovetop grill, then retrieved the plate holding the seasoned chicken breasts and shrimp skewers and a bowl filled with sliced bell peppers and onions. She placed the meat on the preheated grill and added olive oil to a sauté pan for the vegetables. Serenity had turned her on to the flavored oils, and Natasha had become hooked immediately.

"Oh, this hits the spot." When the doorbell rang again, Terri hopped off the stool. "I'll get it. I don't want you to risk burning dinner."

Natasha laughed, shook her head, and checked the food cooking. She didn't know what she'd do without her friends. As excited as she'd been earlier, seeing Antonio had put a damper on her day. Admittedly, time had been good to him. He was even more handsome than in high school—smooth walnut skin, close-cropped black hair, and a slim, muscular build. Even though the temperatures hovered in the low

15

sixties, he'd forgone a jacket and worn a fitted tee that let her know he still kept up with his workout regimen. She turned the meat and checked the rice. Seeing it was done, she turned off the burner.

"I'm here and ready to get the party started," Dana said, setting a tote bag on the counter. "Oh my goodness, you made peach cobbler!"

"Don't get too excited. It's canned peaches and store-bought refrigerated crust. I call it my shortcut peach cobbler. And the ice cream is from Splendid Scoops." She added the veggies to the platter with the shrimp.

Terri held up a hand. "Hey, I'm not complaining. We all know who the real cook is in this bunch. I do hope we'll still be able to get our supper clubs in now that Serenity and Gabriel are married. I need this."

"We all do," Natasha said, giving Terri's shoulders a quick squeeze. "As much as Gabriel loves food, I don't think we have to worry about that." After removing the chicken and placing it on a plate, she retrieved the condiments from the refrigerator and set them on the bar. "I'll let the chicken rest for a couple of minutes before I slice it, and then we can eat."

"I'll get the drinks ready, and we can toast your good news, Tasha. Today we're having pineapple margaritas," Dana said.

"Yum," Terri said around a mouthful of cracker. "Okay, let me stop eating these so I'm not too full for my real food." She pushed the board away and wiped her hands on a napkin.

Natasha pulled out plates, cloth napkins, and silverware to set the table, but Terri stopped her.

"Girl, you don't need to set the table. We can eat right here."

Dana poured the drink into three glasses and handed Natasha and Terri each a drink. "I agree." She lifted her glass. "To Tasha. Congratulations on this great opportunity, and may you reach a hundred percent sales by opening day. I know Kathleen is going to try to tell anyone who stands still long enough to listen why she should've been the one."

Terri nodded. "Yes, girl. Here's to getting *all* the sales."

Natasha touched their glasses. "Thanks, and she already tried during our meeting this morning but got shut down quick." She sipped the blended cocktail. "Oh, this is so good, Dana."

"Hey, we all have our gifts. Mine is fixing cars and bartending."

"And playing that piano," she said, setting her glass on the bar. "I'm going to slice the chicken. Terri, can you warm up the tortillas?"

"Sure."

The women went about their tasks, and after bringing all the food to the bar, they settled in for the meal.

A few bites in, Dana said, "Did you know Antonio is in town, Tasha?"

Natasha froze with her fajita halfway to her mouth. She sighed. "Yeah. I saw him, and he still hates me."

"Hey, what happened between you two was a long time ago. I'm sure he doesn't hate you."

She recalled his frigid stare and greeting, then the snippy comment. "You're wrong. He still does." It bothered her more than she cared to let on, and she had no idea why. They'd both moved on, and although she considered him "the one

17

who got away," she had no fantasies of them reuniting. Or even being friends.

Terri held up a hand and divided her gaze between Natasha and Dana. "Wait. What did I miss, and who is Antonio?"

"We dated in high school and broke up our first year of college. More specifically, I broke up with him because of my own insecurities." She didn't want to get into the details at the moment, even though all the negative comments from her so-called friends saying she could never hold on to a guy like him rose in her mind. Natasha pushed them aside. "This is supposed to be a celebration, so no more talk about Antonio. Hopefully, he'll be gone in the next couple of days like always, and I won't have to worry about running into him."

"We are celebrating." Terri held up her glass, and a smile curved her lips. "I'm just curious because your whole face changed at the mention of his name."

She rolled her eyes. "My face didn't do anything."

Terri leaned close to Dana and whispered loudly, "What does he look like?"

Dana chuckled. "Fine, with a capital *F*—tall, muscular build, and gray eyes that had every girl in school falling at his feet. It didn't hurt that he was the school's star basketball player whose scoring record still stands to this day," she added with a mock toast.

Natasha couldn't dispute one word of Dana's description of Antonio. She'd had a hard time keeping her eyes off him earlier, despite the tension between them.

Terri fanned herself. "Well now."

"Well now nothing. It's been over for a long time. Can we talk about something else? Y'all are killing my celebratory mood." She picked up a stray red pepper and popped it into her mouth.

"You're right," Dana said. "No more Antonio talk because I really want some of that peach cobbler."

They all laughed and continued eating while catching up. After finishing the meal and letting the food settle, the women filled bowls with cobbler, topped them with ice cream, and carried the dessert to the family room.

Terri fell back against the sofa and let out a soft moan. "Okay, I know you said this was canned peaches and store-bought crust, but it's so good. I'm definitely going to need this recipe."

Dana chuckled. "I'm just coming over to get more. Y'all know baking is *not* my forte." She worked as a mechanic in her father's garage and was a classically trained pianist, offering private lessons on the side.

"Don't count on this being a regular thing," Natasha said with a smile.

"I won't. And I know I said I wasn't going to bring him up again, but do you have any idea how long Antonio will be in town this time? Last time he stayed about three weeks to help build that cottage for his grandmother at the back of his parents' house."

Glaring at her friend, she said, "No, I do not." And she didn't care.

CHAPTER 3

I don't know why you're moving into one of Charles's rentals when you can just stay here until you decide to purchase a house. It doesn't make sense to waste money like that."

Antonio sighed inwardly. From the moment he'd told his mother about his plans, she'd been on a rant. However, he hadn't lived at home since leaving for college when he was eighteen, and he had no intention of going back. Staying over last night after he'd arrived in town had been enough. He picked up a bowl holding mashed potatoes and followed her to the dining room table. "I'm not wasting any money because he isn't charging me." Antonio smiled at his grandmother as she entered. She'd been asleep when he got in. "Hey, Grandma," he said, bending to kiss her smooth brown cheek.

Nora Hayes hugged him with a strength that belied her petite stature. "Oh, baby, I'm so glad you're home." She held him away from her and studied him critically. "You look good."

Chuckling, he pulled out her chair. "Thanks, and you're as beautiful as ever." A moment later, his father said the blessing, and then they all filled their plates. Along with the mashed potatoes, his mother had prepared fried pork chops, sautéed cabbage, and oven cornbread. The tantaliz-ing smells made his stomach growl. It had been more than two years since he'd eaten his mother's food, and he took ample portions of everything.

"You get settled in at the house?" his father asked.

"I still have some boxes to unpack, but I've taken care of the things I'll need right away." Antonio stuffed a forkful of potatoes into his mouth and stifled a groan. When he chewed into a tender chop, he did moan. "This is so good, Mom."

"You never could resist those pork chops. Who knows, maybe you'll find a nice young lady I can pass my recipe on to, and she can cook them for you," she added sweetly, smil-ing his way.

He choked on the lemonade going down his throat. "Mom."

"A few of the young ladies have been asking about you, especially Claudia Jennings."

His grandmother snorted. "Darlene, you have got to be kidding me." She waved a dismissive hand. "That girl changes men like it's open enrollment. What is she on . . . her third or fourth marriage now?"

"Mama," his father started, fighting a grin.

Antonio wasn't so successful and laughed until he had tears. "Open enrollment, Grandma?"

"Don't *Mama* me, Fred. You know I'm right." Pointing her fork Antonio's way, she said, "You don't need that kind of drama in your life, baby. I know things didn't work out the first time, but the second time will be the charm, trust me." She winked and went back to her food.

Second time? He'd tried the marriage thing once, and all he'd gotten in return was a bunch of lies and a broken heart.

No, he didn't plan to open his heart to another woman. Instead of commenting, he continued eating.

A few minutes later, his father cleared his throat. "Son, now that you're back, what are your plans? The town could use a good financial planner and investment manager." He shrugged. "Maybe you can open your own firm."

Antonio sent his father a grateful smile for the subject change. Frederick Hayes had always run interference for Antonio and his older brother when their mother went on one of her tangents. "Maybe." He briefly debated whether to tell them about his godfather's offer, then decided to share. His family had always been close, and he valued their opinions. Sometimes. "Actually, Uncle Charles is talking about retiring and offered me the business."

"He's been talking about that since I retired."

"He said that was one of his reasons. Apparently, you being able to go fishing whenever and not being a slave to an alarm clock has him a little jealous."

A wide grin covered his father's face. "Hey, what can I say? I love being able to get up when I want. What about his boys?"

"They aren't interested." He'd mulled over the proposal all day, and the more he thought about it, the more he liked the idea.

"I think it's a fabulous idea," Grandma Nora said. "You've been building things since you could hold a hammer in your hand."

"I haven't made a decision one way or another." Antonio wiped his hands on a napkin and finished his drink. "But I'm really considering it."

His mother patted his hand. "I think you should take him

up on his offer, honey. It's always been your dream. Most people don't get a blessing like this dropped in their laps, so I wouldn't think about it too long."

"I won't."

Grandma Nora made a move to stand, and his father helped her up. "Well, this old woman is tired. Antonio, how about you escort me to my cottage?"

Antonio grinned and rose to his feet. "I'd love to." He extended his arm and, after bidding his parents good night, walked her out the kitchen's side door to the small one-bedroom cottage out back he'd helped build a couple of years ago. Once inside, he asked, "How's Grandpa?"

She eased down into her favorite recliner. "Most days not so good, but every now and again he remembers me. Calls me his beautiful flower just like he did when we first started dating." A wistful smile curved her lips.

He shook his head. His grandfather had been diagnosed with Alzheimer's disease a few years ago and had gotten to the point where he needed full-time care. "How often do you get out to see him?"

"Not as often as I'd like. With the place being almost an hour away, it's hard. When he was at the hospital here, I could go every day."

"I'm sorry." Antonio hunkered down in front of her. "Let me know the next time you want to go, and I'll take you."

She cupped his cheek. "I'd appreciate that. What you need to do is take Charles's offer, and then you can build one of those fancy care centers here. I know what you're capable of doing, and I heard about those homes for low-income families you were helping to build."

He laughed and dropped his head. "I don't know about all that, but we'll see." His family knew him well. He couldn't remember a time when he wasn't trying to build or fix something. Most kids had a fort made of blankets and used baseball bats or sticks to hold them up, but not Antonio. At twelve years old, his had been an actual building with two rooms, a table, a pair of chairs, a bookshelf, and a mounted cabinet filled with his favorite snacks. His father had even purchased a mini fridge. A smile curved his lips. Those had been some good times. Just as quickly, his smile faded, thinking about the times he and Natasha had their "dates" there.

Too young to truly date, they had used studying together as a cover. Sure, they'd gotten some studying done, but most often, stealing kisses had been at the top of their agenda. She had been the first and only girl allowed in his private space. Rising to his feet, Antonio scrubbed a hand across his forehead. He needed to stop thinking about her. She'd walked away from their relationship, leaving only a letter, and he still had no idea why. *It doesn't matter*, he told himself. Grandma Nora called his name, drawing him out of his trip down memory lane.

"Oh, and I hope you're going to stay away from Claudia." She made a face.

"I will." He planned to stay away from every woman, but he kept that to himself.

"Good. You've grown into a wonderful young man, and I'm proud of you. There are going to be lots of women who'll try to turn your head." She placed her hand on his chest. "But you pay attention to the only one who turns your heart. And we both know who she is."

He let out a nervous chuckle and stood. "I have no idea who you're talking about, and I don't think I want to know." He kissed her temple. "I'm going to head out."

"Okay. Love you, baby. And you know exactly who I'm talking about. I know she broke your heart, and both of you probably could've done things differently, but the good Lord gives us youth to make those mistakes. If we're fortunate, we grow into adulthood and get a second chance to do things right. It doesn't happen all the time, so don't throw away the opportunity," she added pointedly. "Lock the door on your way out, would you?"

"Love you, too, and I will." Antonio left and headed for his car, knowing full well she'd meant Natasha. She'd always told him they belonged together. At one time, he'd thought the same, but he wasn't buying the second chance speech. He'd call his godfather first thing in the morning to accept his offer. The busier he was, the less time he had to think about Natasha or any other woman his mother tried to parade in front of him.

* * *

Friday evening, Natasha waved at some of the people she knew while weaving her way through the crowd to find a seat for the town hall meeting. Apparently, there was an update on the big condominium project, and it would be the perfect time to pitch her idea. She'd called the mayor's office earlier in the week to get on the agenda.

"You're looking beautiful tonight, Tasha."

She shifted slightly and groaned inwardly. She'd gone out

with Evan Brooks a few times, but they didn't click...at least on her end. But that hadn't stopped him from continuing to ask her out. "Hey, Evan. Thanks."

"Still waiting on you to say yes to going out with me again." Evan wiggled his eyebrows and gave her his most charismatic smile.

"We've already talked about this, and we agreed that we'd be better off as friends."

"That was last year. I was hoping your feelings might have changed now."

She shook her head. "You're a really nice guy, but nothing has changed. Sorry."

He shrugged. "Can't blame a guy for trying to be with one of the prettiest women in town."

Natasha smiled. "Flattery will get you nowhere, Mr. Brooks."

He laughed. "See you around, Tasha."

She watched him make his way through the crowd and sighed. Maybe there was something wrong with her. There had been two other guys interested in her as of late, but neither of those relationships had worked out, either.

"Hey, girl."

She spun around and let out a squeal. "Serenity!" The two women hugged as if they hadn't seen each other in months. "Oh my goodness. When did you get back?"

"Yesterday."

Giving her friend a once-over, she said, "You look so good and relaxed."

Serenity gave her a saucy smile. "That's what happens when you spend a week in Paris and another in the Bahamas with a sexy man." They broke out into a fit of laughter, then quickly covered their mouths, still giggling.

Natasha fanned herself. "You'll have to give me *all* the details. Where's Gabriel?"

She scanned the room. "He went to find Nana."

A moment later, Dana and Terri joined them, and another round of excited chatter ensued. Natasha shared her good news about the condo project.

"Oh, girl, we're going to have to celebrate. Give me a few days to get myself together, and we'll have a supper club dinner. Then I can tell you about how much fun being married is," Serenity whispered conspiratorially with a wink. The women howled. "Let me go find my husband, and I'll catch up with you next week." She sashayed off.

"I'm so glad she decided to give Gabriel a chance," Terri said.

Natasha and Dana nodded, still smiling. When Gabriel first came to town last summer, he'd planned to stay only a few months, and Serenity had been leery of starting a relationship with him. The two started off on the wrong foot, but things had worked out for them, and Natasha couldn't be happier. At least one of them had found her forever man.

The mayor stepped up to the podium and asked everyone to take their seats.

The three women found a spot midway in the community center's large auditorium.

Once everyone had quieted, the council's secretary read the previous meeting's minutes, and then the treasurer gave a financial update. The transparency was one thing Natasha loved about her hometown.

When it came time for new business, Mayor Brewer returned to the microphone. "I met with the real estate development company slated to begin the condo project and we couldn't agree, so we won't be using them." People began talking at once, shouting questions. He held up a hand. "Let me finish. No, we aren't scrapping it. They wanted to build a six-hundred-unit multi-building complex when we asked for something on a much smaller scale, as in no more than thirty or forty."

"And who did they plan on moving into those homes?" someone called out.

"They wanted to bring in folks from the surrounding big cities, at least a thousand."

"I don't think so!"

"No way!"

Mayor Brewer cut in. "Exactly, which is why I told them to take a hike and didn't sign the papers. I know we're all for a little tourism, but something that large scale doesn't fit with the small-town charm we all love." Cheers went up. He waited until it was quiet again before continuing. "I've already talked with Charles over at Davenport Construction, and they'll be taking on the project instead. I also understand that Natasha Baldwin will be the exclusive Realtor on this, so congratulations."

Natasha smiled and nodded her thanks as the room erupted in applause. Her emotions swelled.

Dana leaned over and whispered, "See, everybody knows you're the best one for the job." They shared a smile and tuned back in to the mayor.

"Mr. Davenport, do you have anything to add before we move on?"

"Yep." He stood. "I'm going to be retiring in two weeks, and I'll be handing the business over to Antonio Hayes. Stand up, son. Effective immediately, he'll be handling all the current and upcoming projects."

Natasha gasped and whipped her head around. *No, no, no.* If he was taking over the construction company, that meant he'd be staying for good. Antonio stood, and their gazes met. His expression was unreadable, but his eyes held the same frost they had during their first encounter.

"Dana did not lie," Terri said quietly. "That brother is *definitely* fine with a capital *F*. Rich brown skin and built like an African god...*mercy*! And with all these women staring at him like they want to put him on a plate and devour him, I guess she wasn't lying about that, either."

Natasha was still trying to process this grand announcement, and she couldn't care less about those women.

Dana nudged Natasha. "Looks like you and Tony are going to be seeing a lot of each other."

"This is a small town, but it's still big enough for us to stay out of each other's way," Natasha countered.

"Obviously you've forgotten you'll be working with him to fix up the Ward place to sell."

She had forgotten. "This can't be happening," she muttered while rubbing her temples. It took several minutes for the crowd to settle down.

"It's good to have you back, Antonio," the mayor continued. "Do you have anything you'd like to say?"

Whereas there was buzzing all around the room previously, now Natasha could hear a pin drop. Apparently, not one person wanted to miss what he had to say. She told herself not to look his way, but ten seconds in, she lost the battle.

"I'm going to do my best to continue the legacy of Davenport Family Construction. And it's good to be home," Antonio added as he reclaimed his seat.

His gaze brushed Natasha's once more before he turned away. She fell back against her chair. How in the world were they going to work together? But he'd just said he'd continue Mr. Davenport's legacy, so that would include any dealings they might have, which meant every time she needed someone to fix up a potential home for sale. With the way he apparently still felt about her, she didn't see how they'd be able to occupy the same space, let alone cooperate on a joint task. Then again, the company employed several other people. Hopefully, he'd assign one of them to all her jobs. A nudge in her side interrupted Natasha's mental tirade. "What?" she asked Dana.

"The mayor is calling you."

She snapped her head to the front. "I'm sorry, what was that, Mayor Brewer?"

"You had a question about the new condo project?"

Yes, but that was before I found out I'd have to work with Antonio. She hesitated, knowing her suggestion would obligate her to spend even more time with him. However, with all eyes on her, she had no choice. Slowly rising to her feet, she said, "I wanted to make a suggestion to have a few of the units furnished. It would be ideal for college graduates who want to return but can't afford to purchase a house, or for those college students who want to stay in town, but live on their own." It would also help Natasha establish herself as an interior designer and, hopefully, allow her to finally pursue her true passion.

"Sounds like a good plan to me," a woman called out. "I've been trying to figure out a way to keep my granddaughter here."

Several other people echoed the sentiment, and the mayor held up a hand. "Let's put it to a vote. All in favor say 'aye.'" A loud chorus went up. "All opposed say 'nay.'" A smattering of voices chimed in. "The ayes have it. Natasha, since this was your idea, I'll trust that you'll be able to put your interior design degree to good use in getting it done. Get on Antonio's schedule to hammer out the details."

Natasha's response lodged in her throat, and all she could do was nod initially. Finally, she found her voice. "I am hoping to utilize my interior design skills for the project." A few minutes later, the meeting was adjourned. Several women made a beeline to Antonio, smiling up at him as if he were royalty.

Serenity approached. "So, is that the Antonio I think it is?"

"Yep, that's him." As her college roommate, Serenity knew all about the breakup and had been there for Natasha during that devastating time.

"Looks like it's going to get pretty interesting in this little town. Good thing Ms. Adele doesn't live on your street."

Natasha skewered her friend with a look. The older woman lived across the street from Serenity and was the town's biggest gossip. "I don't want interesting." And she certainly didn't want anyone in her business. Already there were a few people directing sly smiles her way. *This is so not good. At. All.*

CHAPTER 4

Im glad you're back, Antonio."

"Do you need help moving into your place?"

"I can bring you dinner *anytime*."

The last statement came from Claudia, and his grandmother's words flashed in his mind like a neon sign. Antonio tried to create some space between him and the women surrounding him. "Thanks, but I'm fine. If you'll excuse me, I need to speak to the mayor before he leaves. Have a good evening, ladies." Without waiting for a reply, he pivoted on his heel and strode across the room, wondering what he'd gotten himself into.

Apparently, his godfather left out a lot about his new job, particularly with regard to Natasha. He spotted her talking to Dana and two other women he didn't recognize. But then, he'd been away so long, he had no idea about the town's newcomers. A few more people stopped to welcome him home before he could take five steps. After a minute or two of polite conversation, Antonio turned and froze. Natasha stood less than two feet in front of him. She closed the distance between them.

"Antonio—"

"We don't need to talk until the building goes up."

She sighed. "Look, I'm sor—"

He held up a hand. "Aside from this project, we have nothing to say to each other." He opened his mouth to tell her that even then, he'd prefer to handle most of their communication by email, but Mayor Brewer rushed over with a wide grin and his hand extended. The man had been on the town council when Antonio left home and, according to his mother, was elected mayor six years ago.

Mayor Brewer smiled at Natasha. "Great idea, Natasha."

"Thanks. Um . . . I'll let you two talk." She glanced up at Antonio with what looked like regret, then walked away.

Antonio watched her go and told himself it was too little, too late for any regrets or apologies.

"Welcome home, Antonio."

"Thanks." The man pumped Antonio's hand so hard, he thought it would fall off. "If you're not busy next week, I'd like to get on your calendar to discuss the condo project."

"Come by my office on Monday afternoon around two, if that fits your schedule."

He nodded. "I'll be there."

"Well, let me go find my assistant before she leaves and tell her, so I don't add something else to my schedule. The old mind isn't what it used to be. See you later."

Antonio chuckled and watched him navigate through the throng of people who'd stood around in groups talking while taking advantage of the refreshments that were always provided for the meeting.

"Glad you're back home, little brother."

He spun around and saw his brother, Nathaniel. "I was wondering when I'd see you." The two men embraced. Although two years younger, at six four, Antonio eclipsed Nate's height by three inches and never let him forget it. "I figured you would've been at dinner Monday."

"Mom invited us, but I had to work late and April had a teacher's meeting." Nathaniel's wife taught third grade.

Antonio opened his mouth to ask about his four-year-old niece, Noelle, then saw her running in his direction.

"*Uncle Tony!*" she squealed, launching herself at him.

Smiling, he bent and caught her up in his arms and kissed her cheek. She wrapped her little arms around his neck and held on tight. "How's my baby girl? I can't believe how much you've grown." She had just turned two the last time he'd seen her, but he made a point to FaceTime her weekly so she wouldn't forget him. He'd missed her tremendously, and seeing her beautiful smile had been one of his reasons for returning home.

"Good. I'm four now." Noelle held up four fingers close to his face. "Are you going to come to my house before you go on the airplane back to your house?"

He laughed. "Yep, I'm coming to your house. And I'll tell you a secret."

Noelle's eyes lit up. "What? I won't tell nobody." She leaned her ear closer.

"I'm going to live here now."

"Yay! Daddy, Uncle Tony is gonna live here. He's not going on the airplane."

Antonio and Nate broke out in laughter, and Nate said, "I thought you said you weren't going to tell anyone?"

She slapped a hand over her mouth and giggled. "Oops."

Antonio patted her back. "That's okay. I'm sure everybody already knows."

"Especially all the single women," Nate said with a chuckle. "I see you still have them chasing you."

He shook his head and sighed. "Mom mentioned something about it." He was certain his mother had spread the news of his return the moment he told her.

"And Natasha?"

"I don't want to talk about it. It's bad enough I'll have to work with her on this new project."

Nate studied Antonio. "Let's go outside and talk."

They started toward the exit, and his mother intercepted them. "Oh, there's my baby." She plucked Noelle out of Antonio's arms and showered the little girl's face with kisses. "Nate, Arlene wants to see her. I'll bring her back in a minute."

"Tony and I are going outside for a minute. If I'm not back, take her to April."

"Okay." She started back across the room.

Antonio and Nate found a spot on the side of the building. "There's nothing to talk about."

"Man, clearly you're still not over her if just the mention of her name pisses you off."

"I've been over her, and I'm not pissed off." Okay, maybe he was a little annoyed. His plan to come home, reconnect with his family, maybe spend some time working with his godfather on a few houses, and think about starting his own business had morphed into something entirely different in less than a week.

"Tony, you two were kids when you broke up. The only way you're going to be able to move forward is to forgive her. Did you ever ask her why?"

"Aside from trying to reach out to her when I first got the letter, no." And it had been eating at him for years. As far as forgiving her, he thought he'd already scaled that hurdle and put it behind him. Yet seeing her again brought back all the hurt and confusion from all those years ago.

"Maybe it's time you did. You're most likely going to have to partner with her more often than not since she's one of a handful of Realtors in town."

Just great. Antonio dragged a hand down his face. "We both have a job to do, and we'll get it done. The end. We don't need to be friends, just professionals."

Nate shook his head. "I hate to tell you this, but you two will always be more than that. You forget I remember what happened. I was there and know how much you were hurt when she ended the relationship."

Of course he'd remember. Nate had been the first person Antonio called when he received Natasha's letter and couldn't reach her. His brother had been the one to help him get through one of the worse times in his life. Antonio felt the pain as if it had happened yesterday. Nate was wrong. The only thing Antonio and Natasha could ever have between them was a working relationship. Nothing more.

* * *

Monday afternoon, Natasha walked the one block to the mayor's office. She'd been surprised when his assistant called and asked her to attend a meeting to discuss her suggestion about the furnished units but elated that Mayor Brewer seemed to be excited about moving forward, and so soon. Now that the local construction company would be handling everything, she figured they'd get the ball rolling much sooner.

Natasha climbed the four steps to the town's government building, which housed the mayor's office as well as the town's manager, treasurer, and attorney. She made her way down the hall and greeted the mayor's administrative assistant. "Hi, Mrs. Rogers. I'm here for a two o'clock appointment with Mayor Brewer."

"Hi, Natasha. Have a seat. He's finishing up a conference call and will be with you in just a moment." The woman had to be in her sixties and had been a fixture in the mayor's office for as long as Natasha could remember.

"Thanks." She sat in one of the quartet of chairs in the spacious area. While waiting, she pulled out her iPad and made some notes about styles and budgets. This would be her first major interior design project, and she couldn't wait. However, she knew it would be at least a year before the construction was completed. And she'd be working with Antonio...again. Hopefully, by then they would at least be cordial.

She glanced up when the door opened, and Antonio's tall frame filled the entryway. *What is he doing here?* Then it dawned on her. He was probably there for the same meeting. When the mayor said the two of them needed to meet, she didn't think he meant this soon.

"Well, if it isn't our star basketball player. Come on over

here and give me a hug." Mrs. Rogers jumped from her chair, hurried around her desk, and engulfed Antonio in one of her famous bear hugs.

"How are you?"

"Doing well for an old lady. You're looking even more handsome these days. Natasha, look who's here," she said with a wide smile.

"Hey, Antonio." Natasha tried to muster up a polite smile.

"Hey."

Mrs. Rogers divided her gaze between Natasha and Antonio. "I remember when the two of you were dating. You were like two peas in a pod. I think it's wonderful that you two will be working together on this. Antonio, have a seat. George should be just about finished with his call."

Natasha wanted the woman to stop talking. Mrs. Rogers was so intent on her trip down memory lane, she totally missed that she was the only one excited about the reunion. Antonio took the chair farthest from Natasha and stared straight ahead. *How in the world are we going to be able to pull this off?* She also had to talk to him about fixing up the Ward place.

Mayor Brewer came out and extended his hand. "Natasha, Antonio. Good, you're both here. Come on in."

She and Antonio stood, and he gestured for her to go first. When she passed him, the scent of whatever cologne he wore floated through her nose. The man still smelled good. Inside the large room, she jumped slightly when Antonio pulled out a chair for her. "Thanks," she mumbled. This time, he had to sit so close she could feel the heat of his body, and it had an unexpected effect on her. No way could she still be attracted to him. It had been years, and she'd moved on, as had he. Yet the way her body reacted said something entirely different.

Mayor Brewer leaned forward and folded his hands on the desk. "Let me just start by saying I'm glad things fell through with the real estate development company. I'm far more comfortable investing in our own. The only reason we approached them in the first place is because Charles didn't want to take it on. I guess I should've asked if you're willing to lead the project, Antonio."

"He briefly mentioned the project after I accepted his offer but didn't go into many specifics. However, I am ready to take it on, and I took the liberty of drawing up a couple of designs after getting more of the details," Antonio said. He pushed a couple of buttons on his iPad and angled it to where they all could view it.

"Charles was right. You're the perfect person to continue his legacy," the mayor said with a wide grin.

Antonio smiled, and Natasha's pulse skipped. She'd always loved his smile. Turning her attention to the screen, she listened as he explained each one. Although she'd heard he had a career as an investment manager, clearly he hadn't forgotten anything related to construction. He'd done a design that offered four clusters of units. A couple of the buildings would have units on two levels, while the others were laid out side by side on one level. "I really like this one," she blurted without thought. Antonio turned his piercing gaze on her, and she braced herself for whatever he planned to say.

"Thanks. I like this one the best, too. It gives the residents options. Before I left the meeting on Friday, a few of the seniors asked whether there would be space for them if they wanted to downsize. I figured it would be easier to have just one level and position the units a little away from the others."

"Smart thinking," Mayor Brewer said. "They'd be away from the noise of the younger crowd. When can you start?"

"Ideally, I'd like to start as soon as possible. I estimate it'll take a year or so to complete, depending on the weather. The more we get done before winter, the better."

"I agree. Natasha, were you thinking about having all the furnished units in one building?"

Natasha angled her head and studied the layout. "Since this is for forty units, what do you think about having at least ten of them available to be furnished? We could either furnish them beforehand or have a few selections for prospective buyers to choose from. Once that design is chosen, it'll be off the market. My vote would be for the latter."

"Almost like an exclusive," the mayor said, leaning back in his chair, nodding and stroking his chin. "I think ten is a good number, and I like the idea of being able to choose the style."

Antonio shifted in his seat. "I agree."

Smiling, she made notes on the document she'd started.

"Let's talk budgets," Mayor Brewer said, opening a file. He went over what the town had decided, taking time to answer questions. Thirty minutes later, he closed it. "Do either of you have any other questions?"

Natasha shook her head. "Not right now."

"None for me," Antonio said.

"Then that covers everything. Let's schedule another

meeting in six weeks right before you break ground, Antonio." They discussed and finalized a date and time. He stood, and they followed suit. The mayor shook their hands. "I appreciate you stepping up to handle this. You two are the perfect pair to bring the town's vision to life."

At one time she'd thought the same, but that was then. Pasting a smile on her face, Natasha said, "Thank you for entrusting me to handle the interior designs. I'll have some layouts ready for our next meeting."

Antonio echoed her sentiment, and they filed out. He held the door open for her as she exited the building, but he hadn't said another word to her.

"Do you have a minute, Antonio?" she asked when he started down the steps.

He paused and faced her, annoyance lining his features. "If this is about another apology, you can save it."

Natasha sighed inwardly. Apparently, he'd only been putting up a good front for the mayor. *So much for that.* "Um, I don't know if Mr. D mentioned it to you, but he was supposed to meet with me at the Wards' home tomorrow to determine the work needed so the family can put it up for sale. But now that you're taking over, I wasn't sure if he's still going out on appointments."

"He isn't, but I can meet you out there to take a look next Thursday around one, if you can make it. Or you can always just send me a letter listing the needed repairs."

Natasha would most likely have to move around a couple of things, but it couldn't be helped. She ignored his sarcastic comment. He was never going to let it go. "No, that's fine. I'll see you there next Thursday." She was a little bummed at having to wait an additional week because she wanted to get this first meeting done. He nodded, loped down the steps, and headed up the block. *He still has that sexy stroll.* Shaking off the thought, she made her way back to the office. At least this time he'd said more than two words to her, even if his tone had been a little terse. Progress. They might be able to make it to cordial associates after all. His last words came back to her. Then again, maybe not.

CHAPTER 5

The following Thursday, Natasha walked into Ms. Ida's Home Cooking and searched for Serenity.

"Hi, Ms. Bernice. Did Serenity come in yet?"

"Hey, baby. Yes, she's sitting over to the right, next to the window. Are you having your usual Caesar salad with shrimp?"

She spotted her friend and smiled. "Thanks, I see her. And no, I think I'm going to have something else today." That the woman knew what she typically ordered meant Natasha frequented the place way too often. But the food tasted so good she couldn't help it. And today she was starving. The glorious smells made her mouth water and her stomach growl. She'd only eaten a boiled egg and yogurt for breakfast. Weaving her way through the tables, she waved at a couple of people, then slid into the booth onto the bench opposite Serenity. "Hey, girl. Sorry I'm late. My last showing went longer than expected." Natasha picked up her menu. The family-style restaurant served everything from breakfast staples like pancakes and waffles to sandwiches and comfort foods, including chicken and dumplings and beef stew.

Serenity waved her off. "Don't worry about it. I just got here myself. After being away for two glorious weeks, it's been tough getting back into the swing of things."

"And, of course, all the patients wanted to hear about your honeymoon," she said, laughing. Serenity worked as a nurse in the town doctor's office.

"Every last one of them."

A server came over to take their order. While Serenity ordered a salad, Natasha opted for fried catfish nuggets, macaroni and cheese, and green beans. She waited until the young woman left before continuing with her conversation. "Okay, I want *all* the honeymoon details."

Serenity brought her hand to her chest and let out a contented sigh. "The first week in Paris was amazing. We ate our way through the city, and of course I had to pick up a couple of dessert recipes to try out."

"That's perfect for you and Gabriel, since you're both foodies."

"You know he actually googled all the places beforehand, so we wouldn't have to waste time once we got there. My husband is serious when it comes to food."

Natasha laughed. "I know. Remember the brownie incident?"

"Oh, you would bring that up. We've more than made up for all the animosity we had at the beginning. I actually made him a batch yesterday," Serenity added with a sly grin.

"Please tell me you saved me at least one." Gabriel was known to devour an entire pan of the thick, rich dessert. Serenity held up a Ziploc bag, and Natasha all but snatched it out of her hands. "Bless you, my sister. This is going to be my afternoon snack. Oh, and I'm going to need some of those boozy berries for two clients." Last year Serenity had made chocolate-dipped strawberries that had been soaked in champagne or whiskey, and Natasha thought they would make a good gift when she closed on a home. She'd been right, and it had become her signature to present buyers with an elegant gift box filled with a few of the champagne-infused treats.

"I'll make them this weekend, and you'd better not eat them all before they're dipped this time," Serenity added pointedly.

"Okay, okay, but you know they're my weakness, so I'm counting on you to make a couple of extra—one milk and one white chocolate, please. Now, back to the honeymoon. How was the Bahamas?"

"Simply divine. We lay on the beach, chilled on our balcony, had a private dinner in a gazebo over the water, a couple's massage... The nights were even better... *divine*." She waggled her eyebrows.

Natasha fanned herself. "All right now. See, you're making me wish I had a sexy brother to help me *indulge*." They burst out in laughter.

"Speaking of sexy brothers, have you seen Antonio since the meeting?"

Her smile faded, and she sighed. "We met with the mayor on Monday to discuss the condo project." She paused when the server returned with their plates.

"Can I get you ladies anything else?" she asked.

"No, thank you," they chorused.

"Okay, enjoy, and holler if you need anything." She moved on to the next table.

"He didn't look any happier to see me, but I did get a whole sentence this time," Natasha said, picking up the conversation. She added hot sauce to her fish and popped one of the smaller pieces into her mouth. An involuntary moan slipped out.

"That good, huh?"

"It is." She forked up one and handed it to Serenity.

"Oh, this is good. I might have to call in an order to go and pick it up when I get off. Now, what do you mean you got a whole sentence this time?"

She told her about the first encounter with Antonio, how he'd all but shut her down at the town meeting and his refusal to listen to her apology. "And now we have to work together. I'm meeting him at Mrs. Ward's house after I leave."

"I was so sad to hear about Ms. Velda. She was the sweetest lady when she came in for her appointments. As far as you and Antonio, I'd think he'd be over what happened after all these years."

"Him mentioning the letter, and more than once, says he's not. But you know what's really crazy?" She glanced around to make sure no one was listening. This would be just the kind of thing that would spread like a wildfire. "I think I'm still attracted to him, and that doesn't make sense. I haven't seen him in years, and it's been even longer since we've spoken. Not to mention how irritating he's being."

"I don't think it's crazy at all. Irritating or not, he was your first love, and you two were planning to get married after graduating from college, so I can totally see some of those feelings coming back. And as yummy as he is, it would be crazy if you didn't have them."

"I guess." But she really didn't want those emotions to creep back in because nothing would come of it. The constant taunts from some of the girls in her high school class flashed in her mind. *You'll never be able to keep him. I don't know what he sees in you. He can do so much better than a nerd.* Natasha pushed the negative thoughts aside and continued eating and catching up on everything that had happened while Serenity was gone. Natasha had planned to save half her food for dinner, but she was obviously hungrier than she thought because only crumbs remained on her plate. At least she'd have her brownie for later.

"Well, I need to get back for the afternoon rush. Call me later and let me know how it goes with Antonio."

"I will." They paid the bill and went their separate ways. On the way out, she ran into another of her would-be suitors who asked her out every time their paths crossed. She'd gone out with Reginald Payne once three months ago, and it had been all she could do to get through the dinner date. The man had barely said two words the entire time they were out, despite her trying to engage him in conversation. She refused to put herself through that kind of torture again. She called out a greeting and threw up a wave but didn't break stride. Natasha saw his crestfallen expression and felt bad. She hoped he found someone, but that woman wouldn't be her.

As Natasha got closer to the house, butterflies danced in her belly. "It'll be fine," she mumbled. "You do your job, he does his, and then you leave. Simple." She could do this.

Antonio was already there, leaning against his car, when she drove up. He glanced up from his cell, straightened, then shoved the phone into his pocket.

"Hey. I hope I didn't keep you waiting long." She walked over to where he stood.

"No. I've only been here a couple of minutes."

She nodded. "How've you been?"

"Fine. So, what needs to be done?"

Natasha growled under her breath. He was not going to make this easy. She pulled out her iPad, opened the file, and headed up the walkway to the porch. "The wood on the porch needs to be replaced all the way around."

Without a word, Antonio climbed the steps and walked the length of the area that ended on both sides of the house, stopping here and there and testing spots with the toe of his boots.

She followed him around one side and saw him leaning over the rail to see the back of the house. "The deck needs replacing, too." Still nothing. He just made notes on his iPad. "Do you want to go out back or see the inside first?"

He gestured toward the front.

Rolling her eyes, she walked off. *No, I'm not doing this today.* Natasha stopped abruptly and whirled around. Antonio plowed into her. Not even her anger could dampen the effect of feeling his hands around her waist and his hard, warm body against hers. Arousal hummed through her veins. Natasha quickly tried to pull back.

"What are you doing?" he said, steadying her. "I could've hurt you."

"You already have. How long are you going to give me the silent treatment? I've tried to apologize several times, and it's been *years*," she said, her voice rising with each word.

"I'm not giving you the silent treatment, and I'm over the

past. We're here to do a job, and that's it. Are we going inside or what?"

She ignored his question, folded her arms, and glared up at him. "No? Then what do you call it? And those little shady comments about me still sending letters... what would you call *that*? Yes, we have to do a job, but you acting like a butthead isn't going to make it easier."

Antonio frowned. "A butthead? Seriously? Look—"

Natasha jabbed a finger in his chest. "No, you look. You need to learn how to accept an apology, *Antonio Jamal Hayes*! I was barely eighteen and I know I messed up, and I tried to tell you I was sorry, but you never, *ever* listened." Her voiced cracked. *I am* not *going to shed one more tear over this man.* Waving a hand, she said, "You know what, I can't do this right now." She rushed around to the front and down the steps to her car.

He hurried after her and placed a staying hand on her arm as she opened her car door. "Tasha, wait."

She shook her head, got into the car, and drove off, angry at herself for allowing him to get to her. With no real destination in mind when she left, Natasha decided to go to the one place that always gave her solace.

Ten minutes later, she parked at Summerhill Creek, grabbed the blanket she usually kept in her trunk, and trekked through the trees to the small hidden inlet she'd found as a teen. Because she knew she'd be doing a lot of walking at the house, she'd worn comfortable shoes and slacks, and she was grateful now for the forethought. Natasha dropped down on the blanket, inhaled deeply, and let it out slowly, hoping for the peace she always felt out here. She closed her eyes and listened to nature's sounds—trees rustling in the gentle breeze, water rushing in the creek, birds calling to one another. Pulling the Ziploc with her brownie out of her purse, she bit off a piece and savored its rich, chocolaty goodness. Maybe because they'd been close friends long before dating, Antonio's aloofness really bothered her.

She tried to see it from his point of view, knowing that she'd hurt him. But she'd been hurt, too. Every missed phone call had chipped away at the confidence she'd had that their relationship would survive the distance until they graduated. And hearing a female voice answer Antonio's phone had been the final straw. Looking back, she probably should have confronted him then. However, in her mind, all the naysayers had been right. She couldn't hold on to him. Sighing, she broke off another piece of brownie and shoved it into her mouth. "So much for us being able to work together," she muttered.

* * *

Antonio stood in the same spot minutes after Natasha roared out of the driveway and muttered a curse. Walking around the house with her had conjured up memories of them doing the same thing whenever he built something. She used to follow him and give pointers on whatever needed to be fixed or adjusted and plan how it should be decorated. It also didn't help that she looked good in the gray slacks that hugged her shapely backside and a long-sleeved, button-down black blouse that revealed a hint of the smooth mahogany skin above her breasts, causing his body to react. Angry that she could still get to him after all this time, he'd thought it best not to say much. Yes, she had apologized, and he thought he'd accepted it and moved on, but after this . . . he obviously still had some things he needed to deal with inside.

Calling him by his full name let him know just how angry he'd made her. The only other time she'd used his government name was during an argument when they were dating over something he couldn't even remember now. It had taken a week to get back into her good graces. His brother's words played loudly in his head: *The only way you're going to be able to move forward is to forgive her.* Admittedly, Antonio tended to be short on forgiveness—something he'd been working on—but his problem, he finally realized, centered on forgetting. Forgetting how much she'd meant to him. Forgetting all the plans they'd made. And forgetting how much he'd loved her. He blew out a long breath. She was right, however. He'd acted like an ass, and he owed her an apology.

He fished his cell phone out of his pocket and called her, but it went directly to voicemail. A second call to her office went unanswered, and the receptionist told him Natasha wasn't due to return for another hour. "Where did she go?" She had been upset when she left, and although they weren't on the best terms, he still didn't want anything bad to happen to her. He thought for a moment about where she might go, then jumped in his car. Growing up, Natasha went to only one place when she was upset or worried about something. Antonio took a chance that it hadn't changed and headed in that direction.

A short while later, he spotted her car in the far corner of the lot and smiled. *Some things stay the same.* After parking,

Antonio got out and surveyed the area. With towering trees, the mountains rising in the distance, and crystal-clear blue-green waters, Summerhill Creek still took his breath away. A gentle breeze blew across his face, and he inhaled deeply. He'd missed being home.

Antonio stood there a moment longer, then made his way to the hidden inlet. He hadn't been there in close to two decades, but he remembered how to get there by heart. As soon as he cleared the trees, he saw her sitting with her head down, which made him feel even worse. He must have made a sound because she turned his way, a scowl lining her beautiful face. Natasha met his gaze briefly before turning away.

"What are you doing here?"

He sauntered over and lowered himself next to her. "I came to make sure you were okay."

Natasha snorted. "Like you care."

"I guess I deserve that."

"What you deserve is for me to never speak to you again, but you caught me on a good day."

A soft chuckle escaped his lips. "Lucky me." They sat silently for a minute, and then he said, "I'm sorry. You were right. It has been a long time, and I'll work on my attitude." He had to in order for him to move forward and not stay stuck in the same cycle of heartbreak. When he'd decided to move back, he'd honestly believed seeing her around town wouldn't trigger those emotions that had taken him years to get over. He'd been proven wrong in spades. And seeing the tears in her eyes and hearing the anguish in her voice unexpectedly got to him. But, then, Antonio could never stand to see her cry.

She whipped her head in his direction and studied him as if determining the truthfulness of his statement. Seemingly satisfied, she nodded. "I know it's probably too late, but no matter what you think, I didn't mean to hurt you. Your heart wasn't the only one broken," she added softly, focusing on something in front of her.

Antonio really wanted to ask her why she did it, but they seemed to be headed toward some sort of fragile truce, and he didn't want to mess it up. However, he knew they'd need to have that conversation sometime soon. "How about we table the past and focus on the here and now?"

"That's not a problem for me, but are you sure you'll be able to do it?"

Not really, but he didn't want to fight with her anymore today. "Yep. So how about we go back to the house and you can show me what we need to do?" They sat a moment longer in comfortable silence, reminding him of how it used to be whenever an issue arose between them. No matter what, they had always been able to work out their differences, and he hoped he could get himself together so it could happen now. He studied her as she stared out at the water, his old memories and emotions rising. Before his action could register with his brain, he leaned over and kissed her cheek. Antonio couldn't decide who was more shocked, him or her. *What the hell . . . ?* He cleared his throat, hopped up, and extended his hand. He'd promised Uncle Charles he'd keep the same level of integrity the business always had, and he'd do whatever it took to make it happen. Minus impromptu kisses or anything else. He chalked the impulsive act up to some deep automatic response from how it used to be with them.

Natasha hesitated briefly, then placed her hand in his as he helped her up.

"And I'll try to refrain from acting like a *butthead*." Antonio slanted her an amused look. He still couldn't believe she'd called him that. Natasha had never been afraid to say what was on her mind. Apparently, that hadn't changed either.

"I'll go with that."

A smile lit her face and hit him squarely in the chest. Not good. A working relationship he could handle. But nothing else.

CHAPTER 6

Saturday afternoon, Natasha activated the speakerphone function on her cell and continued the conversation with her mother while she changed clothes. She'd been trying, unsuccessfully, to get her off the phone for the past ten minutes. However, Natasha couldn't get a word in edgewise as her mother continued her rant. "Mom," she interrupted, "I had planned to call and let you know about my good news this weekend. Things have been a little busy." Not to mention the shock of seeing Antonio again.

"I just don't know why I had to hear it from Bernice instead of you," her mother fussed.

She rolled her eyes and pulled on her jeans. "Mom—"

"And she also told me Antonio is back for good and that he's taking over Davenport's construction company."

"Yes, he's back." Although her parents had relocated to Arizona to be near her paternal grandmother two years ago, Glenda Baldwin still knew all the Firefly Lake gossip, and most times, before Natasha.

"And how is it going? She said you two will be working

together on those new condos the town is building, and I remember how hurt you were when you two broke up."

Complicated. Confusing. "It's going okay. I won't have anything to do until it's completed, and that won't be for at least a year. But there's another house we're doing now."

"Oh?"

"Chase is putting Ms. Velda's house up for sale, and it needs a lot of fixing up."

"And Antonio is going to be the one doing it," she finished.

"Yes, with a small crew." Since their truce a few days ago, Antonio had been a little more open and had even smiled at her once or twice. She still couldn't forget the soft kiss on her cheek. It had caught her totally off guard, and for a moment she'd been transported back to the times when that kiss promised things would be okay whenever something upset or bothered her. He'd seemed just as shocked, and by the way he jumped up right afterward, clearly he'd regretted it.

"Natasha!"

She was so lost in her thoughts, Natasha had completely forgotten about her mother. "I'm here."

"Are you okay? You're not over there daydreaming about Antonio like when you were younger, are you?"

"Um, yes, I'm fine, and no." Daydreaming wasn't the right word. More like trying to figure out how they'd keep the relationship on a smooth and even keel. "Mom, I really need to get going. I'm already late for our supper club meetup."

Her mother laughed. "Oh, all right. That Serenity can cook. Tell her, Dana, and Terri I said hello."

"I will."

"Oh, and can you please let me know about anything else going on with you before the rest of the town hears?"

She smiled. "Yes, Mother. Tell Dad hi. Love you both."

"Love you, too, baby."

Natasha shook her head and ended the call. After lacing up her sneakers, she grabbed her purse and keys and left.

Dana and Terri were already there when she arrived. "Sorry I'm late. My mom called fussing because Ms. Bernice told her about the condos before I did." She hugged each woman, then asked Serenity, "Where's Gabriel?"

"Next door. He said he'd let us have our girls' night alone this time." Gabriel and Serenity had decided to keep Gabriel's house and use it for their families and friends who came to visit.

"More like he didn't want to hear us discussing your honeymoon," Dana said, lifting her glass of wine in a mock toast.

Natasha poured herself a glass. "Exactly. His ears are going to be burning."

"Poor Gabriel," Terri said.

"Poor Gabriel what?" Gabriel said, walking into the kitchen, smiling.

The women all jumped and spun around.

"You aren't supposed to be here. How are we going to talk about you behind your back if you're in the room?" Natasha teased. The four women laughed. She quickly pulled a peach tablecloth from her tote, spread it on the dining room table, then added matching napkins and a spring bouquet with ivory, orange, and yellow flowers.

He chuckled. "Like I said last year—y'all are some cold sisters. Love the table setting, by the way."

"Aw, you know we love you, Gabe." She hugged him. "And thanks."

He shook his head. "Mm-hmm, whatever." Wrapping his arm around Serenity, he placed a gentle kiss on her lips. "You think I could get a plate, baby?"

Serenity stroked his cheek. "For you, absolutely, my love."

"You two are so cute," Terri said. "Hurry up and fix your plate and go, Gabriel, so we can get all the juicy details." She shooed him, bringing on another round of laughter.

After piling food onto his plate, Gabriel said on his way out, "Try not to singe my ears, ladies."

Serenity gestured to the plates on the bar. "Okay, let's eat."

Everyone added servings of the honey-glazed salmon, mashed red potatoes, and roasted broccoli, then gathered around the dining room table. Serenity started the music, and lively conversation ensued.

"Girl, I have missed this," Terri said. "I feel like it's been forever since we've been together. And this salmon..." She swooned in her chair.

Dana bobbed her head to Leela James singing about having a good time. "I agree, and Leela's lyrics are right on point."

Natasha did a little chair dance with her arms in the air while belting out the words, especially the part about not being able to wait to hook up with her crew. This was Natasha's crew, her ride-or-die sisters, and she didn't know what she'd do without them. Serenity leaned over and, using her fork as a microphone, joined in. Halfway through the song, they went back to the delicious food.

Serenity took a sip of her wine. "How did it go with Antonio on Thursday?"

Natasha swallowed a bite of broccoli before answering. "Let's just say it started rocky and ended in a truce." She told them about her blowup and leaving, then him following her to her private spot to apologize. "After the apology, he kissed me on the cheek, but I don't think he meant to do it because he was up and ready to go so fast, I almost didn't believe it had happened."

"Hmm," Dana said, scrutinizing Natasha. "I have to say I'm shocked, and I'm curious about how all this is going to play out with you two having to spend so much time together."

"There's nothing to play out. We're both professionals hired to do a job. The end."

"You forget that I grew up here. Girl, everybody here was just waiting for the wedding date."

Natasha pushed the potatoes around on her plate. She'd been waiting for the same thing until it seemed Antonio wasn't as into the relationship as she thought. "That was a long time ago, Dana. We can't go back."

"I don't know the details, but you can only go forward." Terri shrugged. "Who knows what can happen now that he's back in town. Although, with all the whispering from the women in this town, you may have to get in line," she added with a smile.

"I'm not trying to be in the line. I'll settle for us just being friendly." She'd heard about the line of women vying for his attention, but so far, according to the rumor mill, he hadn't reciprocated. Not that she cared . . . or should care.

* * *

Early Monday morning, Antonio drove to Seaside Meadows Park for a run. Back in New York, he'd spent more time using the treadmill at a high-priced gym than outside. But this place, with its tranquil lake, tree-lined trails, and blooming flowers, made it his favorite spot to jog. Most of his friends and colleagues couldn't understand why he'd want to move back to such a small town, but this was home, and he had space to breathe. Things didn't move at the speed of light, and people were more laid-back.

He took a few minutes to stretch. Ten years ago, he could jump out of the car and hit the trail without worrying about his muscles tightening and getting sore. Now, at almost thirty-five, it was a different story. Once he finished, Antonio stuck in his earbuds, cranked up the music, and started running at a slow, easy pace. As he picked up speed, he mentally went over his schedule for the upcoming week. When he'd taken on the construction company, he thought Uncle Charles would be there daily to help with the transition. But his godfather's definition of *transition* meant popping in for an hour or so twice before retiring, leaving Antonio to jump in with both feet for his first two weeks on the job. He had promised to come in today, however. Antonio was glad to see that many of the same men he'd worked alongside during his teen summers remained. It made things easier than if he'd had to start from scratch.

Antonio reached the incline and powered up the hill. His legs were on fire because he hadn't done anything remotely close to exercising in over three weeks while preparing for the move, but he made it to the top, reversed his course, and went back to his starting point. After stretching and cooling down near the lake, he drove home to shower and change before heading into town.

"It's about time you showed up," Antonio said to his god-father when he entered. "How're you going to just leave me hanging?"

Uncle Charles's booming laughter filled the room. "Man, after sleeping in that first day, then going fishing with your daddy, I'm hooked. It was hard coming back after these three weeks of being off, so you're lucky I didn't just send you an email."

"You just ain't right, Unc." He took the chair across from the desk. "Okay, what's on the agenda today?"

"Not much. Closing out a couple of finished projects and making a list of the three new ones. Now that it's just about spring, folks are fixing up their houses to get ready for sum-mer. One owner is looking to sell. You've already been out to the Ward place, right?"

"Yep, last Thursday."

"How did that go with Natasha?"

"It went."

"Is that why she left in a huff after five minutes with you?"

Antonio lifted a brow. Being in a big city where he could get lost for so long, he'd completely forgotten how nosy small-town people could be. Obviously, someone on the street had seen them. "I'll admit we had a rocky start, but we're fine now."

"Good. She's a sweet girl." He glanced over the glasses perched on the edge of his nose. "But then you already know that. Regardless of what happened between you two back then, Natasha is still a good woman. You could do worse," he added, refocusing on the papers in front of him.

Here we go again. "I don't plan to do anything. We'll have to meet here and there to deal with whatever projects come up, and that's all." Even if there was still a lingering attraction, one he sensed wasn't one-sided, he planned to ignore anything not business related.

"So, what really happened with your big-city wife? Fred said something about you growing apart, but I want to hear it from you."

Antonio didn't want to discuss his ex-wife now or ever. He'd met Lori Metcalf through a mutual friend at a business conference, and the two had struck up a conversation. Subsequently, they met for drinks and dinner a couple of times. Six months later, they'd started dating exclusively and married a year later. She claimed it had been love at first sight, but less than a year into their marriage, Lori received a major promotion and began to pour all her time into the job. He'd been excited for her success and had done everything to support her dreams, but he also wanted their marriage to flourish. After a while, he was the only one giving. From her canceling their dates to decreased intimacy, the deep, emotional connection Antonio hoped to build seemed to fizzle out right before his eyes, leaving him, once again, with a broken heart. And although she expressed wanting children while they dated, it ended up being one more thing in their relationship to be put on hold.

He had no issue with women changing their minds— their bodies, their choice—he just wished she'd let him in on her plans. Despite his best efforts to reclaim the closeness, the two of them continued to drift apart. They had become nothing more than roommates toward the end, and shortly after their second anniversary, it was over. Now, two years later, she'd left him a voicemail saying she wanted to talk to him. He had no idea what she wanted, but what they had was long over, and Antonio wasn't eager to put his heart on the line again for her or anyone else.

"Are you going to sit there all day and frown or answer my question?"

"We wanted different things, and in the end it was better for her to find what she wanted with someone else. There's nothing else to talk about." He gestured to the papers. "So, are you going to fill me in?"

Uncle Charles stroked his chin. "Hmm, if you say so." He slid the folder across the desk and, for the next three hours, went over every detail of the business. After finishing, he said, "I think I'm hungry now. I haven't done this much manual labor in a while."

Antonio smiled. "Where do you want to go? My treat."

His eyebrows lifted. "Yeah? That fried chicken at Ms. Ida's is calling my name."

"Then Ms. Ida's it is." Instead of driving, the two men walked the block and a half to the restaurant.

"You sure are getting a lot of attention," Uncle Charles said with a chuckle as a third young woman called out a greeting to Antonio. "I never have this many people notice when I walk down here by myself."

"Whatever you say." He figured after being here for close to a month, the novelty of him being back home would wear off soon. At least he hoped so. Some days he almost felt like an exotic exhibit in a museum. The mouthwatering smells hit his nose as soon as they entered the restaurant, and Antonio's stomach growled. He hadn't been here in over a decade and planned to make up for it today.

"Oh my word! Antonio Hayes. Get over here and give me a hug." Ms. Bernice rushed around the hostess platform and engulfed him in a hug that nearly cracked his spine.

"Hey, Ms. Bernice." The petite woman had been a fixture in the restaurant since he was a kid and had gone to school with his mother.

She held him away from her, gave him a once-over, then smiled up at him. "Welcome home, baby."

"Thanks."

"Hey, Charles." She grabbed two menus and led them to a table. "Lana will be over to take your order in a minute. Charles, you want your usual lemonade?"

"That would be good. Thanks."

"What can I get you, Antonio?"

"Sweet tea, please." He scanned the menu and had a hard time deciding what to order. He did plan to get the peach cobbler to go, then stop by Splendid Scoops on his way home later for some vanilla ice cream to go with it. By the time Lana brought the drinks, he'd finally decided on chicken and waffles. Antonio took a big gulp of his tea and groaned. He hadn't had sweet tea that tasted so good in years.

"While we're waiting, I want to talk to you about your work habits," Uncle Charles said.

He laughed. "I just started, Unc. They can't be that bad already."

"No, they aren't, but I don't want you to do like I did for so many years—putting in hours way above and beyond what's called for and neglecting the things that are important. Learn balance early, son. I know in the cutthroat world of finance and being at that big investment firm meant long, hard hours, but your health will be better for it."

More hours than he could count, if he were truly honest with himself. Sure, it put him on the fast track to becoming a senior investment manager, but he'd always been exhausted, and it limited the time he spent doing things he loved, like using his skills for Habitat for Humanity and mentoring high schoolers interested in business and finance. That had been part of his reasoning for the move. "I won't. Believe me, I've had enough of sixty- and seventy-hour work weeks." Not including the many business functions he'd attended.

"Glad to hear it."

His godfather dispensed more words of wisdom from his many years in the construction business, and Antonio considered himself blessed to be able to have someone sharing his mistakes, so he wouldn't have to make the same ones. Even though he'd spent the last several years in finance, he'd kept up with his construction licensing, so it was one less thing he had to worry about. He'd also attended a few conferences, made some connections, and met two guys he now considered good friends.

Lana returned with their food. "Do you need anything else?" She divided her gaze between the two men. When they both said no, she smiled and departed.

Two bites in, Antonio knew he'd need to do an extra workout. Along with the thick Belgian waffle that covered the entire plate, he had two pieces of golden fried chicken and scrambled eggs.

"Mmm, they serve the best fried chicken," his godfather said around a mouthful.

"I'm telling Aunt Marcie."

He lifted a brow. "And if you do, you'll never be invited for another dinner again."

Antonio laughed so hard he almost choked. "That's just wrong."

"So is you trying to get me put out of the bedroom and onto the sofa."

Still chuckling, Antonio said, "Wouldn't want you to have to spend your first days of retirement on the sofa, and I love her cooking, so we'll just keep this between us."

"Smart boy."

Over the meal, they laughed and talked about everything from the business to sports and politics. When they finished, Antonio asked for the bill.

"Ms. Bernice said it's on the house," Lana said.

"Tell her I appreciate that." He shouldn't have been surprised because the woman had a big heart. She'd even sent him care packages while he was in college. "I'd like to order the peach cobbler to go."

"Sure thing. Be right back."

"I'm gonna start hanging out with you more," Uncle Charles said with a grin. "Free food, lots of attention..."

He just shook his head. It didn't take long to get the dessert. On the way out, Antonio thanked Ms. Bernice again. "That hit the spot."

"Sure did. Think I'll go home and take a little nap. It feels good to leave someone else in charge." Uncle Charles started whistling as they walked back to the office.

He opened his mouth to ask a question but paused when he saw Natasha leaving from the craft store three buildings down and heading in their direction.

"Hey, Mr. D and Antonio," Natasha said when she reached them.

They returned the greeting, and Antonio's gaze drifted down her body. She wore another pair of slacks and a pullover sweater that hugged her curves, and he couldn't take his eyes off her.

"Lunch at Ms. Ida's?"

"Yep," his godfather answered. "You done for the day?"

"I wish. I needed more boxes and ribbons before getting back to work."

"What are you planning to do with them?" Antonio asked.

Natasha smiled. "They're for the treats I give my clients when they close on a home."

"That's pretty cool. I'm sure they appreciate it." Although he'd told himself he and Natasha only needed to maintain a business relationship or maybe something along the lines of being friendly, parts of him wanted to know more about what she'd been doing over the years. And he was still staring at her. Out of his periphery, he could see his godfather's wide grin and shook himself.

She glanced down at her watch. "I have to get going. See you guys later. Antonio, are we still meeting at the house tomorrow?"

"Yes. I'll see you then."

"Okay." She threw up a wave and strutted off.

Antonio willed himself not to turn around but lost the battle within seconds and watched until she rounded the corner.

"Well, now. Looks like a reunion is in the air."

"There's not going to be a reunion. We're happy with things the way they are." Or so he kept telling himself.

"But you'd both be happier with more."

He didn't even want to think about the implications of *more*.

CHAPTER 7

It is only Tuesday," Natasha mumbled as she leaned back in her office chair and closed her eyes. At this moment, she'd give anything for a long, hot candlelit bath with soft music playing. The one good thing was that she'd finished her friend's interior design project. The purple and cream contemporary-styled bedroom had turned out better than she'd expected, and Daphne had promised to spread the word. In the meantime, Natasha hoped she'd be able to have a few more hours of rest this week.

Since she'd arrived three hours ago, she'd sent and responded to multiple emails, updated her website and social media pages with current listings, gone out to do a pre-offer home inspection and written up the offer, and met with an appraiser at another home. All before eleven o'clock. She planned to drop off the berries to her two clients who'd closed on new homes before she met with Antonio to take measurements of the things Chase wanted updated or replaced.

She sat there for a few more minutes and wondered which version of Antonio she'd see today. The last two times he'd reminded her of the sweet guy she'd fallen in love with all those years ago. Natasha had often imagined what her life would be like if she hadn't made the decision to end their relationship. Or at least tried to talk to him about how she was feeling. But like most teenagers, she'd bought into the *if-he's-not-calling-you-he's-calling-someone-else* nonsense her girlfriends kept whispering in her ear whenever she came home for a visit until the sound became a megaphone. It also didn't help her insecurities that they kept saying how Antonio was going to make it big, while she'd be nothing more than a small-town girl who couldn't compete with the classy women in his world. In the end she ruined a great relationship.

Natasha really couldn't blame Antonio for his hostility, especially when she had never really explained the why. She knew they'd have to clear the air about it at some point, but she didn't want to mess up the tenuous truce of sorts they had going on. Sitting up, she straightened her desk, made sure she had everything in her tote, and headed to the staff breakroom for the berries she'd put in the refrigerator. Serenity had also made Natasha a dozen for herself, and she couldn't wait to dig in tonight when she got home, along with that bath. The dipped strawberries were her weakness, and it would take a herculean effort not to eat all twelve in one sitting.

"Hey, Brett."

Brett turned from doctoring his coffee. "Hey, Tasha. On your way out?"

"Yep. As soon as I grab these strawberries." She opened the fridge and reached for the two boxes. "You were here before me. When did you— Who the hell did this?" Someone had taken a strawberry from each box and bit into the rest. She slammed the door.

Frowning, he came over. "Oh, wow. That's disgusting. You know, come to think of it, I saw Kathleen eating a chocolate-dipped strawberry about an hour ago. Or more like shoving it into her mouth when she saw me coming."

"No doubt her trifling ass did this." If she could get away with it without the police being called, Natasha would march down to the woman's office and snatch her. She was so mad, her hands shook and her heart raced. Thinking she might need to start collecting evidence—it seemed Kathleen's campaign against Natasha was ramping up—she dug her cell phone out and snapped a few photos. Afterward, she tossed the boxes in the trash and took a couple of deep breaths to calm her anger. It didn't help.

"Good idea taking the pictures, but you really should let George know. She has a bad habit of taking what doesn't belong to her, and he's warned her before."

Natasha massaged her temples. "It would be her word against mine, since I can't prove she did it."

Brett placed a comforting hand on her shoulder. "Like I said, *I* saw her eating one. There's no place around here that sells them, so she'd have to explain where she got it. Even more so if she's smelling like champagne at eleven thirty in the morning. That'll bring on a whole other set of trouble." He angled his head thoughtfully. "Hmm, maybe this will be what we need to get her butt out of here."

They shared a smile. "I'll deal with it after I get back. Thanks, Brett." She went back to the refrigerator to retrieve her lunch bag to replace the berries with hers. One more strike against Kathleen. Thankfully, she'd just stocked up on the boxes and ribbon yesterday. "See you later."

After filling the boxes, she decided to take the remaining strawberries with her. They were in a cooler bag with a cold pack and the weather was cool, so she figured they'd be fine for a couple of hours.

She was still fuming when she made it to the Ward house, but she tried to put on a good face. Antonio drove up right behind her. "Hey. Good timing."

Instead of responding, Antonio scrutinized her for a lengthy moment. "What's wrong?"

"What are you talking about?" Obviously, she hadn't done as good a job hiding her frustration as she'd thought.

He came and stood right in front of her and folded his arms. "You forget that I know you ... better than most people. Time and our issues haven't changed that. So, again, what's going on? Talk to me, Tasha," he added quietly.

Natasha didn't want to admit how much his soft plea moved her. Despite everything, he was right. He did know her. Slumping against the car, she said, "I have a co-worker who's tap-dancing on my last nerve." She shared the past issues of Kathleen trying to one up her or conveniently moving things from designated areas so Natasha couldn't find them. "But today she ate two of the chocolate-dipped strawberries I give to my clients when they close on a house and took bites out of the rest, then put them back in the refrigerator."

He stared at her in disbelief. "Wait. What? And they sell chocolate-dipped strawberries here now?"

"No. Serenity made them for me. She loves to cook, and last year she was trying something new and soaked some strawberries in champagne and others in whiskey. I thought the champagne ones would be a great gift for my clients, so I pay her to make some for me."

Antonio's eyebrows knitted together. "Serenity? Your college roommate or a different person?"

She couldn't believe he remembered Serenity had been her roommate. They had "met" over the phone. "Yes, it's her. She moved here a few years ago."

"Oh, but back to this woman who's giving you trouble. You really should talk to your boss."

"I will. I'm even angrier because I had to replace the ones she messed up with mine. I'll be fine. I'm going to go sit in the back for a few minutes before I get started. If you need me for anything before then, come get me."

"I'm really sorry she messed up your day. If you want, I can pay Serenity to make you more."

The sincerity in his voice made her heart skip a beat. She reached for his hand and gave it a gentle squeeze. "Thanks for the offer, but you don't have to do that." It wasn't until he squeezed her hand back that she realized what she'd done and quickly, but gently, let him go. Even after all these years, their hands still felt like they belonged together. "Um...I'll be out back." Natasha adjusted the tote on her shoulder and hurried off. *Why am I having these thoughts about us?* She pushed the thoughts aside and reminded herself that nothing had changed. She and Antonio were not destined to be together.

* * *

Antonio's gaze followed Natasha until she was out of sight. Seeing her so upset bothered him, and he didn't stop to analyze why. The more time they spent together, the more they seemed to slip into their old camaraderie. Back then it had been one of the things he loved about her. Their relationship was easy and drama free. It probably stemmed from the fact they'd been friends first. Even now, despite all that stood between them, he felt those old emotions creeping back in and had no idea how to make them stop.

He turned at the sound of a car pulling up. Time to get busy.

"Hey, boss."

"What's up, Todd?" Antonio grabbed his laser measuring tape and iPad out of the truck. "We can start with the porch and back deck. Both need to be rebuilt."

Todd followed Antonio up the steps. "It's hard to believe they're selling. The Wards have owned this property for decades."

"I know." Chase and Nate graduated together and had been good friends. Mike was three years older. "You take the front and the left wrap side, and I'll get the right and the deck." Antonio went one way and Todd, another.

When he got to the deck, he saw Natasha sitting on the swing Mrs. Ward had built at the far edge of the yard, facing the water. Memories of them sitting together in that same spot rose in his mind unbidden, one in particular. She'd had her sweet sixteen party here. Near the end, they'd sat together, and after gathering his courage, he'd asked her to be his girlfriend. Antonio recalled the relief he had felt when she agreed. He'd given her a necklace with a heart charm he had purchased using money saved from his summer job with Uncle Charles.

She hadn't moved by the time he finished his measurements, and he warred within himself whether to go over and see if she was okay. His feet started moving before he could decide. "You okay?" he asked when he reached her.

"I'm getting there." Natasha patted the space next to her. "Have a seat."

He lowered himself next to her, then, using his foot, started an easy sway. Neither spoke for the first couple of minutes.

She reached into her tote and pulled out a container. "I had planned to have these tonight, but I need one now."

Antonio leaned closer and saw she had four large chocolate-dipped strawberries. They looked professionally made. "These are the ones Serenity made?"

"Yep. Gorgeous, aren't they? If she retired from nursing today, she'd give Ms. Ida's a run for her money."

She bit into one and snaked her tongue out to catch the juice. The sight instantly aroused him, and he had to turn away.

"These are my weakness. It's like the perfect pairing." She held out the container. "Here, try one. Oh, and don't forget these have been soaked in champagne."

"Are you sure? I know you already had to give most of them to your clients."

"I'm sure. I usually don't share them," she said laughingly, "but you offered to buy me more, so I'll make an exception. This time."

Antonio chuckled and reached for one covered in milk chocolate. "I appreciate your generosity." He bit into it, chewed for a moment, and had to admit she was right about it being the perfect pairing. The subtle champagne taste took it over the top. "Okay, these are good. I've never had them with the alcohol." He polished the rest in two bites.

"You should taste the ones in whiskey. They're potent, but oh so good." Natasha took another bite. This time a small piece of white chocolate lingered at the corner of her mouth.

He reached up and brushed it off without thinking. She jumped slightly. "You had a piece of chocolate there." Their eyes locked, and the air around them shifted. His gaze lingered on her lips, and he leaned his head closer. Was it his imagination, or did she do the same? Their lips were inches apart, and if either of them moved...

"Hey, Tony, I'm heading inside," Todd called out.

Natasha gasped sharply and shot up from the swing. "I...I need to get started, too. I'll meet you inside." And she was gone.

Antonio dragged a hand down his face. One second longer and they would've kissed. *What am I doing?* They were supposed to be working on becoming friends again, but every time she came into his line of sight, the things he wanted to do to her didn't land anywhere near the *friend zone.* He sat there a while longer to get his libido in check, then went inside. Natasha and Todd were standing in the living room, discussing baseboard molding.

"She's pretty good at this interior design thing," Todd said, gesturing toward Natasha.

"She always has been." Antonio recalled her working

alongside Mrs. Ward, redecorating a few of these rooms. It seemed to be something they both loved, and Natasha always dreamed of living in this house or one like it.

She glanced at him over her shoulder but didn't respond.

"Todd, if you'll take the stairs, I'll finish up in here with Natasha," he said, his eyes never leaving hers. The moment the words left his mouth, he wanted to call them back. With everything swirling around inside him, he really should be staying as far away from her as possible, interacting only when necessary. Yet curiosity got the best of him. Antonio wanted to know what she'd been doing since college and why she was in Firefly Lake selling real estate when she had always dreamed of opening her own interior design business in Los Angeles. Had there been someone special in her life at some point? And why hadn't she taken a trip down the aisle like him?

As soon as Todd climbed the stairs, Natasha said, "We need to stay focused on the house and nothing else."

"I agree. For now. We're going to have to talk about *us* at some point, though." However, Antonio wasn't quite ready to reopen those wounds.

CHAPTER 8

He almost kissed me." Four days later, Natasha still couldn't believe it. Since then Antonio had been the perfect gentleman, but she didn't know how to take the back-to-business attitude he'd reverted to or the contrasting heated looks he'd thrown her way each time they were together. She'd woken up this morning and decided she needed to talk to someone and drove over to the auto shop to see Dana.

Dana smiled. "And did you push him away?"

"I should have," she mumbled, pacing in front of Dana as she worked on a car Saturday morning.

"Which means you wanted to kiss him, too."

"Yes. No! I mean...Shoot, I don't know." Despite her words, Natasha had been curious. Would it be the same as before? Better? She stopped and threw her hands up. "It's Antonio, the first guy I kissed. The first guy I—"

"Just stop right there. TMI, girl, T-M-I. But seriously, I think it would be cool if y'all got back together."

Natasha dropped her head. "It's never going to happen, Dana," she said resignedly. "He's gone back to acting all businesslike, but sometimes I catch him staring at me with

78

looks that could melt my clothes. I don't know if I'm coming or going."

"Sounds like he's having the same problem. Maybe you should put each other out of misery and give it another go. You won't know where this lingering attraction leads unless you try."

"Even if the chemistry is still there, it won't matter once we have that conversation about why I broke it off in the first place."

Dana wiped her hands on a rag and leaned against the car. "Which I'm sure you plan to tell him soon. I know the girls here gave you hell about not being good enough for him, but I just never believed he would cheat on you."

"Thinking back, I should have handled things so differently, but I let my insecurities get the best of me."

"Does Serenity know? I mean, you were roommates, so I figured you talked to her, at least."

"She knows most of it, just not all the drama that happened in high school." Serenity's support during that time had cemented their friendship.

"Well, I'm sure you and Tony will work it out."

"I hope so." It needed to be soon because she couldn't take being so close to him, beginning to want him again, and knowing he would hate her all over again.

"We'll make sure to have plenty of tissues and wine on hand."

She laughed and gave Dana's shoulders a squeeze. "I love you, girl. I'm so glad you're my friend."

"I love you, too. Now hurry up and talk to Tony so I can get the scoop."

Natasha shook her head. "I can't with you. How long are you going to be here?"

"As soon as I close this hood and wash my hands, I'm out. I only came in on a Saturday morning because my dad had to go pick up some parts and he promised the customer the car would be ready today."

"How about lunch at Ms. Ida's?"

"You ain't said nothing but a word. I'm starving."

"Good. I'll be in the waiting area." While seated, she thought about Antonio. As much as she didn't want to admit it, she wondered what his kisses would be like now. The kisses they shared had been of two teens who fancied themselves in love and, having nothing to compare them with, she'd thought no one could do it better. But they were both grown now and had been with other people. She'd heard he'd gotten married, and since he had returned alone, she assumed things hadn't worked out. Natasha wanted to ask about it but figured she should leave it alone unless Antonio wanted to share.

"I'm ready," Dana said, approaching. "Are we walking or driving?"

"It's not too cold, so we can walk, and I'll pick up my car on the way back." Today the temperature had hit the mid-sixties with a slight breeze, which made it perfect for walking the block and a half to the restaurant. Obviously, several other people had the same idea, as the sidewalks were fairly crowded.

"Next time we're driving," Dana said. "By the time we get there, I'll be starved to death."

They made it to Ms. Ida's a couple of minutes later, and as

soon as she crossed the threshold, she saw Claudia Jennings. The woman's dislike of Natasha went all the way back to junior high school. Natasha never understood why and didn't much care. It got worse once she and Antonio started dating. As the head cheerleader, Claudia believed she should have first dibs on all the star athletes or cute boys, and once she'd settled her sights on one, every other girl was supposed to defer to her wishes. Natasha hadn't gotten the memo—okay, she'd gotten it; she'd just chosen to ignore it. And nothing had changed. Determined to take the high road, she said, "Hey, Claudia."

"Natasha." Claudia turned up her nose and strode past Natasha and Dana.

Dana rolled her eyes. "She still irks my soul. Out here acting like she's God's gift to men, discarding them on a whim and going through them like water in a colander."

Natasha and Dana shared a look and burst out laughing. "Truth!" The hostess seated them and left menus. They decided to share the huge appetizer platter for two, which included chicken wings, ribs, mini quesadillas, and fries.

Dana's cell rang. She dug it out of her pocket and groaned. "It's Paula. Let me go take this." Paula was the receptionist at the auto shop.

The waitress brought their drinks, and Natasha thanked her.

"Hello, Natasha."

She turned, smiled, and stood. "Mama Nora. Ms. Della." She hugged both women. "How are you two ladies doing?"

"We're good for old women," Mama Nora said with a little laugh.

Ms. Della snorted. "Speak for yourself, Nora. I'm not old. I'm *experienced*." That brought on a round of laughter.

Mama Nora took Natasha's hands. "I'm so happy about all your successes, baby."

"Thanks, Mama Nora." She loved Antonio's grandmother as if she were her own. Natasha had been close to Antonio's entire family, but after their breakup, she'd stayed away because she'd felt so bad. However, Mrs. Hayes and Mama Nora told Natasha that they didn't hold anything against her, that they'd all made mistakes when they were young. It made her appreciate those ladies even more. "Are you two just getting here? You're welcome to join us. Dana went to take a call."

"Oh, no. We've already eaten and are just waiting for our ride."

Mama Nora's face lit up, and Natasha glanced over her shoulder to see what had captured the woman's attention. Her pulse skipped when she saw Antonio heading in their direction. The man looked good in anything, but there was something about seeing him in jeans and a tee that stretched taut across his sculpted chest and emphasized his well-defined biceps that did something to her. Always had.

"Ladies." Antonio kissed his grandmother and Ms. Della. "Hey, Tasha."

"Hi."

"I think you forgot someone," Mama Nora said with a twinkle in her eye, dividing her gaze between Antonio and Natasha.

Out of her periphery, Natasha saw several patrons staring

their way, and she knew that if he kissed her, it would be all over town before he made it to the exit.

Antonio hesitated briefly, then placed a soft kiss on Natasha's cheek.

Unlike that first brief, impulsive kiss, this time his lips lingered against her cheek, sending warmth flowing through her and making her heart race. Both Mama Nora and Ms. Della had wide smiles.

Mama Nora brought a hand to her heart. "Della, didn't I tell you these two were meant to be together?"

Ms. Della nodded. "I agree. And they say the second time around is always better."

Natasha did her best not to look at Antonio but failed. His expression appeared to be somewhere between shock and irritation. She let out a nervous chuckle. "Oh, Antonio and I are just friends."

"Right," Antonio chimed in. "Just friends. Are you ladies ready?"

Mama Nora patted Natasha's cheek and divided a knowing glance between Natasha and Antonio. "Mm-hmm, baby. Whatever you two say. Oh, Natasha, I'll be having a birthday party in a few weeks, and I expect you to be there." She looked up at her grandson. "Antonio will give you all the details once they're finalized. Actually, Antonio, you'll bring her, right?"

"Ah . . . sure."

What else would he say to his grandmother? Natasha swore the woman was playing matchmaker. *Not good. So not good.*

* * *

Antonio had a death grip on the steering wheel as he drove his grandmother and Ms. Della home. When Grandma Nora called and asked him to take them to and from the restaurant, he figured it would be an easy pickup and drop-off, but nothing had gone as planned since he stepped foot back in his hometown. And this latest fiasco seriously had him contemplating taking off and spending a couple of days in the Bay Area, maybe Oakland or San Francisco.

The two women chatted as if they didn't have a care in the world, while his gut swirled with emotions he hadn't felt in a long while. The attraction between him and Natasha seemed to be growing steadily, and he didn't know how to make it stop. His matchmaking grandmother and her best friend weren't helping. How could he still harbor the hurt and mistrust that had built over the years but want her more each time he saw her? And the kiss... It had been nothing more than a little peck on the cheek, but the alluring fragrance of whatever perfume she was wearing—something sweet, yet warm and soft—had reached out and wrapped around him like a favorite blanket. Antonio had spent the last several days trying *not* to think about her or that almost kiss, and this little stunt just put her back front and center. Who was he kidding? She'd never vacated that position in his mind, had occupied his every waking moment and starred in his nightly dreams.

Ms. Della giggled. "They still look so cute together."

He glanced in the rearview mirror briefly at Ms. Della, who smiled at him and sighed. Not only had his grandmother and her matchmaking best friend roped him into that kiss, but Antonio now had to worry about it spreading like wildfire across town. Usually, the town's gossip didn't faze him, but this time he'd rather not have everyone in their business, trying to "help" them get back together.

"Oh, they sure do, Della. You know I've always thought of Natasha as a granddaughter, and now that Antonio's back, I may just get my wish," his grandmother said, talking as if he weren't in the car.

"That would be something. It would set all these little hussies trying to chase after him straight. I never could understand a woman throwing herself at a man. Now, ain't nothing wrong with a little flirting here and there, but some of these girls are just plain fast."

"I know what you mean. I'm so happy he chose Natasha. She's nothing like them, and just as sweet as they come."

I'm not choosing anybody. Antonio started to comment but changed his mind, thinking it best to sit this conversation out. So far he'd been tasked with bringing Natasha to a birthday party he knew nothing about, and he didn't want to risk whatever his grandmother might have in mind next. *Nope, I'm going to just keep my mouth closed and drive.*

"Antonio, have you met my grandson, Gabriel, yet?" Ms. Della asked.

"No, ma'am."

"Well, I'm sure you will. He and Serenity just got back from their honeymoon. You know she's Natasha's best friend."

"Natasha mentioned that," he said carefully, not letting on that he knew Serenity.

His grandmother shifted in her seat to face him. "It was such a beautiful wedding, too. Hopefully, there will be another one soon," she added pointedly.

Antonio's gut clenched and he could feel her stare, but he refused to look her way or reply to her comment. The sooner he dropped them off, the better off he'd be. He found himself driving just a little faster to reach his destinations. When he got to Ms. Della's house, he hopped out of the car, helped her out, and walked her to the door.

"One down, one to go," he mumbled to himself. The moment he got in the car, his grandmother started up again. He cut the normal six-minute drive to his parents' house to four and a half.

"Thanks, baby."

Normally, he'd say "anytime," but today he only said, "You're welcome." He got out and went around to her side.

"Ooh, these old bones are stiff," she said as he gently eased her out.

Antonio smiled. "You're not that old, Grandma."

"Seventy-eight is old enough. That reminds me, don't forget you're bringing Natasha to my party."

"I'm sure you'll remind me." As they started around the side of the house, his mother came out the front door. "Hey, Mom."

"Hi, son. What's this I heard about you kissing Natasha in the middle of Ms. Ida's restaurant?"

He groaned. *Just great. This is all I need.* "It wasn't anything like that. A peck on the cheek and nothing more. Ask Grandma. She was there. I greeted her and Ms. Della the same way."

His grandmother waved a hand. "It was nothing, Darlene." Then she said quietly to Antonio, "Nothing like the one you two will share on your wedding day." She tossed him a bold wink and strutted past him. "See you later, and thanks for the ride."

He stood there wondering how things had gotten so out of control in a matter of minutes. His mother's voice reclaimed his attention.

"Well, does this mean you two are back together, because Helen Marks mentioned that her daughter, Leticia, asked about you?"

He headed to his car. "No, we are not together, and I'm not interested in Leticia or any other woman, so if you could pass the word, I'd appreciate it. I'll talk to you later."

Antonio's cell chimed with a text message as he slid behind the wheel. He dug it out and read the message from his brother: *I heard about the lip-lock with Natasha in Ms. Ida's. Damn, man, you couldn't wait and do it in a more private place?*

He leaned his head against the steering wheel and muttered a curse. Packing up and moving sounded like a really great idea right now.

CHAPTER 9

"This is not funny, y'all!" Natasha folded her arms and slumped further down in the chair. Somehow, the simple peck on the cheek from Antonio had turned into a full-blown passionate kiss, with rumors of them being back together and on their way down the aisle. *Sometimes I hate living in a small town.* And her besties, the ones she expected to have her back, couldn't stop laughing. She'd called and asked them to come over to lend a little moral support but almost regretted the decision. To get her mind off the rumors swirling around town, they'd gone to the craft store and picked up some yarn to hand crochet blankets. A client had given Natasha one as a gift and shared the how-to video. At the time, she thought it would be something fun to do with her girls. But she was so frustrated, she kept having to redo her stitches. "And, Serenity, you weren't laughing last year when Ms. Adele said Gabriel spent the night at your house."

Serenity tried to hide her smile. "You got me there, but, girl, this is hilarious. I can't believe all those people sitting there who *saw* the kiss in real time are not correcting all this foolishness." She held up a perfectly done row. "This is kind of cool. They'll make great gifts for Christmas."

"Exactly," she muttered. And, yes, the blanket would make a good gift—if she could ever get it done. Ms. Ida's had been fairly crowded, so there were a good thirty or forty people who knew the truth. And she didn't even want to think about how Antonio felt.

As if reading her mind, Terri asked as she finished her last row and spread the blanket on the floor, "Have you talked to Antonio since it happened yesterday?"

"No. We're finally able to deal with each other without the past creeping in, and I have no idea how he's going to react. It's still a little awkward at times, as if we're both afraid of messing up the truce of sorts we have going." Though she hoped it wouldn't happen, Natasha could see him reverting back to the silent, annoyed man he'd been at the beginning. Antonio had never liked having his business spread and made a concerted effort to keep a low profile. He had only tolerated the attention that came with his popularity as a star basketball player. But this... "The worst part was Mama Nora and Ms. Della were all smiles."

Dana laughed. "With the way she kept smiling at the two of you, Mama Nora couldn't have been more obvious that she's playing matchmaker." Dana had returned from her phone call right after the kiss.

"Yeah, I got that impression." She opened her mouth to say something else and her cell rang. When she saw her mother's name on the display, she groaned. "It's my mother." And she already knew what she wanted. Sighing, she connected. "Hi, Mom. No, Antonio and I are *not* back together, it was *not* a passionate kiss, and we did *not* sneak off afterward. He only came to Ms. Ida's to pick up his grandmother and Ms. Della, and he greeted them with a kiss on the cheek. Since I was standing there talking to them, he did the polite thing and kissed my *cheek*, too. Now, did I cover everything?"

"Well, goodness, you don't have to be so snippy about it. Actually, I kind of hoped there was some truth to it. Antonio always was a nice young man."

Natasha rolled her eyes. "Really, Mom? We just had this conversation a few days ago. Nothing has changed."

"Oh, okay. I'd better go to call Bernice back and set her straight."

"Thanks, Mom, and can you tell her to please pass that piece of truth along?"

Chuckling, her mom said, "I will. Can't say I miss that part. I'll talk to you later, baby."

She said her goodbyes and ended the call, then tossed the half-done blanket aside. "I need wine."

Terri raised her hand. "I vote for wine tasting in Napa or Sonoma."

"You ain't said nothing but a word." Natasha stood. She loved her besties.

* * *

Antonio and his crew were behind schedule on at least three projects. The turn of the calendar this year proved that April really did bring showers. As a result, they'd been limited to inside jobs, and he'd spent the first three days of the work week doing paperwork, rearranging and making the space his own. Uncle Charles had officially retired after their lunch a week ago, and Antonio swore the man had almost skipped to his car. Antonio's father and godfather had already made plans to go fishing again.

He lifted his head at the sound of a knock on his open door and smiled at his assistant. "Hey, Leah. What's up?"

"Nate is here to see you."

"He can come on back, thanks. You know you don't have to walk back here. We have an intercom system," he added with a chuckle.

"I know, but this way I can at least get some steps in. I'll send Nate back."

A minute later Nate stuck his head in the door. He stood and they shared a one-armed hug. "How's it feel to be the sole owner of Davenport Construction, little brother?"

"Feels pretty good. The only drawback..." Antonio gestured toward his desk. "Paperwork. I'd rather be at a job site than sitting in an office. Have a seat," he said, rounding the desk and reclaiming his seat.

Nate took the chair across from Antonio. "You always did love being outside. I don't know how you handled being cooped up inside for the past decade."

He had been good with numbers and had landed the job right out of college. As much as he'd wanted to return home and work with his godfather, as planned, coming back meant running into Natasha. And at that time, Antonio couldn't handle it. Hell, he'd barely handled it the first time he'd seen her a few weeks ago. She was a big part of the reason he'd stayed away—from his family, the career he really wanted. And he realized that part of his issues stemmed from built-up resentment toward her. Thankfully, he'd been working through it and had released most of the past anger and hurt. "I did what I needed to do at the time. It paid well, and I have a nice portfolio to show for it." He shrugged.

"And so do I, thanks to your advice," Nate said with a grin. "With all the money you have stashed away, I'm surprised you decided to rent from Uncle Charles instead of buying something outright."

Antonio leaned back in his chair and angled his head thoughtfully. "I considered it, but I wasn't sure where I wanted to live." He did know he wanted a house that overlooked one of the lakes. The other reason he didn't purchase a home right away was that he didn't want anyone in his business, and that's exactly what would happen. He was still trying to correct the lies from the past weekend.

"Nah, probably more like you didn't want to have to deal with all the women who'd be campaigning to be the next Mrs. Antonio Hayes."

"You know I can't stand you, right?" His brother had always been able to read Antonio. He'd hated it then and liked it even less now. "Don't you need to go look in somebody's eyes or something?"

Nate roared with laughter. "Actually, I don't have an optometry patient for another hour. Plenty of time to get deep into your business. So, how are things going with you and Natasha after the big kiss?".

"I haven't talked to her. We were supposed to meet yesterday but canceled because of the weather." He'd thought about calling to see how she was handling all the gossip, but he needed a little distance to analyze his own feelings.

Antonio still hadn't figured out what to do, but in order for them to move forward toward friendship or . . . *something*, they had to have the conversation he'd been avoiding.

"Come on, Tony. I know you're not still holding a grudge against her. I thought you said you've been working together fine."

"We have. It's just that, I mean . . ." He ran a frustrated hand over his head. "I don't know."

Nate studied Antonio. "You still care about her." When Antonio didn't respond, he said, "It's not a bad thing, bro. You two have history, so it's to be expected. Who knows, this could be a second chance for both of you. Maybe there's a reason things didn't work out with Lori."

"Yeah, there is a reason," Antonio shot back bitterly. "She led me to believe we wanted the same things, when all she wanted was status and money." He came to his feet. "I need to go check on some things. No telling how long the weather will hold." And the last thing he wanted to do was rehash old hurts about his ex.

His brother stood slowly and nodded. "Check on Natasha. You aren't the only one affected by this rumor." He pivoted and walked out.

He braced his hands on the desk, lowered his head, and blew out a long breath. Any mention of Lori still made him feel a certain way. Straightening, he headed out front. "Leah, I'm going out to the Ward place to see if I can get a few things done before it starts raining again. Call me if anything comes up. If I'm not back by four, go ahead and take off."

"Got it. It's not forecasted to rain again until tonight, so you should be good ... hopefully. If I don't see you later, have a good evening."

"You too." Antonio really liked working with Leah. She had a good head for business, and the first thing he'd done when he'd taken over from Charles was give her a promotion from receptionist to executive assistant.

As soon as he stepped outside, the pressure eased in his chest. The drive to the house took less than ten minutes, and he was surprised to see Natasha's car parked in the driveway. When he didn't find her inside, he walked around back, but he still didn't see her. As he retraced his steps to the front, movement out of the corner of his eye caught his attention. Natasha stepped out of one of two sheds several feet away and dusted off her pants. She spotted him and threw up a wave.

"I didn't know you were coming out here today," Natasha said, coming toward him.

He met her halfway. "Thought I'd see if I can get the rest of the deck done before it starts raining again." He and Todd had gotten about halfway done. "What are you looking for?"

"Chase called and said his mom is asking about her photo albums. He thought he'd packed up everything but must have forgotten them. He asked if I would check the sheds."

"Need some help?"

She shrugged. "Sure. I didn't see anything in the smaller one," she said as she headed for the larger one he knew Mrs. Ward had turned into what now would be considered a "she shed."

A short time into their search, the light tapping against the roof let him know he wouldn't be finishing the deck today. Within minutes, the light rain turned into a downpour.

Natasha peered through the window. "Great. My umbrella's in the car."

"Guess we'll have to hang out here until it stops," he said, opening one drawer, then another. When she didn't say anything, he glimpsed over his shoulder and met her gaze. "Problem?"

"I'm not sure. If people found out we were here together...alone, it'll give them more to talk about. And knowing how you still feel about me, I couldn't take it."

Antonio crossed the room to where she stood, the sadness and uncertainty in her eyes making him want to wrap her in his arms. The attraction between them had been growing steadily, and he had no idea what to do about it. At this point he wasn't even sure he wanted it to stop. "And exactly how do I feel about you?"

"You're still angry about—".

He put a finger to her lips to cut off her words. "I'm not still angry, Tasha." Far from it. Everything about her called to him. He'd dated since the demise of his marriage and had no problems saying goodbye at the end of the evening. But Natasha was different. With her, the control he normally had crumbled like an old building each and every time they were together. And he was tired of fighting.

Tilting her chin, he locked his eyes on hers. Just like the last time they were this close, while sitting on the bench outside, Antonio felt the chemistry pulling them. This time there would be no interruptions. He lowered his head and touched his lips to hers. "I don't hate you." When their lips met again, sparks turned into a flame, and he devoured her mouth with an intensity that stunned him. Every stroke of his tongue against hers took him closer to the brink of losing complete control, but he couldn't stop. An onslaught of memories bombarded him, from their first kiss behind the school gym and the day he asked her to be his girlfriend at her sweet sixteen party right outside of this shed to the first time they made love after their high school graduation. Usually, he forced the thoughts away. This time he let them come, flooding his heart and mind.

"Tonio," Natasha whispered against his lips as her hands burned a path across his chest and wound around his neck, holding him in place.

Hearing her call him by the special name she'd given him snapped the last shred of his restraint. Antonio lifted her in his arms, bringing her closer to the fit of his body so she could feel just what she did to him. How much he *didn't* hate her. At length, he eased back, but he held her firmly in his arms and rested his forehead against hers. Now that he'd crossed the line, he didn't know if he could go back. But he still needed answers.

CHAPTER 10

Natasha had no idea how long she stood there in Antonio's arms, but she didn't complain. For the first time in years, she was exactly where she wanted to be—with him. She tightened her hold on him and relished the closeness she'd never experienced with any other man.

"Do you know how long I've waited to kiss you and hold you this way?" Antonio murmured, trailing kisses along the column of her neck.

He didn't give her a chance to answer. His tongue slipped between her parted lips and curled around hers in a long, drugging kiss. Natasha had always loved the way he kissed her, but those they shared years ago were as two kids who really didn't have a clue. Clearly, he'd learned a thing or two because he'd mastered the art and kissed her with a finesse that broke down every barrier and reason why this shouldn't happen.

As much as she enjoyed it, they still had a major hurdle. He'd said he didn't hate her, but she didn't believe all his hostility and resentment had been swept away in an instant. Natasha broke off the kiss and rested her head against his shoulder, her breathing harsh and uneven. "We need to talk, Tonio." The nickname slipped out again.

He lowered her to her feet. "I know."

He sounded as reluctant as she felt, but it was time. She had to tell him why she ended their relationship.

Antonio removed the dust-covered plastic covering from the love seat and gestured for her to sit before lowering himself next to her. He rested his forearms on his knees with his hands clasped and head bowed. "Why, Tasha? Why did you leave me?" he asked quietly.

The pain in his voice magnified the one in her heart. She grasped his hand. "I didn't want to, and I truly never meant to hurt you."

"But it did hurt because I loved you. You were my world. When I got your letter, it nearly killed me."

Tears burned the back of Natasha's eyes. "And it killed me to send it. Remember how we made a promise to call each other twice a week?" Back then cell phones only had limited minute plans, and they'd had to be careful about using their minutes and not incurring overage and roaming costs. Most of the time, they tried to make their calls after nine in the evening or on weekends, when it was free. "It was fine for a while, but then you started missing our scheduled calls. I wasn't worried at first because I knew basketball season was in full swing." A nostalgic smile curved her lips. "I used to love watching you play and was so excited you'd attended a school that televised your games. Until the one where you scored thirty-three points and hit the buzzer-beating basket to win the game."

"I remember that game. I couldn't wait to call you. When

I finally made it back to my dorm, I tried several times that night and the next two nights and you never answered."

"Because I saw *her*."

Antonio sat up straight and frowned. "Her, who?"

Natasha averted her gaze. "The cheerleader who practically jumped into your arms at the end of the game. It made me wonder why she would feel so comfortable doing that if she didn't know you." She lifted her eyes to his. "If there was nothing going on between you."

He sat for a moment, seemingly contemplating her words. "I remember now." Shifting in his seat, he took both her hands and brought them to his lips. "Tasha, baby, there was *nothing* going on with that girl. I didn't know her, not even her name. I'm not going to lie and tell you she didn't make her interest in me known, but I told her I already had a girl, *you*. Every guy in my dorm knew how much I loved you and teased me mercilessly. But I didn't care. You were all that mattered." He got up and paced.

"And then... when I called that night, a girl answered your phone." Natasha had been crushed, and that's when she decided to end things.

Antonio froze, then spun around. "*What?* No girl should've answered my phone. I didn't even have it. Because of the game, I'd left it in my room, and I *never* had a girl in my room." He scrubbed a hand down his face and sighed. "But my roommate did. It had to be her who answered the phone. She was there when I got back, and she never said anything about taking a call." He shook his head.

"But I didn't know that because you never answered my second call that night. We hadn't talked for a good three weeks, and I didn't know what to think." Relief flooded her knowing he hadn't been involved with the cheerleader or some other girl, and she finally understood why he'd ignored her attempt to apologize after she'd sent the letter. It had only taken a few days to realize that she still loved him and wanted to try again. But by the time she returned home after visiting her grandparents during the first part of the Christmas break, he'd already left, and her call to apologize was never returned.

"And you didn't answer mine, either," he said and dropped back down on the sofa. "How could you think I'd cheat on you? We were together for *two* years." Antonio threw up his hands. "Hell, even longer than that if we count the year and a half we dated secretly behind our parents' backs." Her parents had explicitly forbidden her to date until she turned sixteen, but they'd used studying and hanging out with other friends as covers. "There had to be some other reason you didn't trust me."

Trust. No one could've told Natasha she didn't trust Antonio. She did. Until she started listening to her so-called friends telling her she was a fool for believing he'd remain faithful with all those beautiful girls willing to engage in no-strings-attached sexual relationships with athletes. Serenity had been the only one who tried to talk some sense into Natasha. And she hated herself for not listening to her one true friend. "It wasn't you at first, not really. I'd seen several of the football and basketball players at school claim to have 'a girl back home,' yet they slept around. And a lot of the girls kept telling me you were probably doing the same, even though those girls didn't mean anything to you."

"So, basically, I'd screw around to keep myself busy until I finished school, then come home and marry the hometown girl."

When he put it that way, it sounded crass, and she felt like even a bigger fool. "Something like that, I guess." Natasha buried her head in her hands as the tears she'd tried to hold back came in waves. "I messed up," she cried. "I'm so sorry I messed us up."

"Tasha, look at me, sweetheart."

Her head popped up at the endearment.

"You're right. I wanted to lay all the blame at your door, but these past few weeks I've done some thinking, and I was wrong, too. I missed a few of our calls because I was studying. Seriously. Trying to do the dual business and engineering program while playing ball was kicking my butt, not to mention finals. But I figured since it had been only two or three weeks since our last conversation, we'd catch up when I got back." Antonio quieted. "You'll never know how much it broke my heart getting that letter from you three days before coming home and then arriving and finding you gone." He closed his eyes briefly. "But you're right. I *should* have called you to tell you I was studying, and I should've listened when you called and tried to apologize, but I was too angry. So yeah, I messed us up, too, and I'm sorry. So sorry."

The softness in his eyes and the sincerity in his voice as he moved closer and wrapped his arm around her shoulder were her undoing, and the tears fell faster. How could she have believed he'd cheat on her? They'd lost so much. He didn't speak, just held her as she cried out years of guilt and pain.

Antonio lifted her head and wiped her tears with the pad of his thumb. "Grandma Nora said something to me when I first got back that I ignored initially, but I get it now. She said we have our youth to make mistakes, but sometimes we get a second chance to make it right."

Natasha's heart pounded. "What are you saying?" Surely he didn't mean...

"I'm saying we have a second chance to get it right, and I want to take it. Tell me you'll take this chance with me."

She sat in stunned disbelief. "I...um...yes, but we can't go back, Antonio."

He caressed her face. "I don't want us to go back. I want to start from here, today. We can take things slowly and get to know each other again, if that's okay."

"Yes, *yes*." Their lips met in a passionate kiss, one of healing and new beginnings, and Natasha vowed to do everything she could not to make the same mistake again.

* * *

It had been a little over a week since he and Natasha had agreed to try again, and Antonio experienced a peace he hadn't felt in a long while. His productivity soared, and he looked forward to the time they would spend together on the phone in the evenings, talking about any and everything. He'd suggested they not go public with the relationship yet, and she'd wholeheartedly concurred. After the previous fiasco, she wanted to keep the town out of their business for as long as possible. Only her friends and his brother knew of their decision. His desire for her had climbed to an all-time high, but he didn't want to rush the physical aspects of their relationship. However, his body didn't quite approve, and he had the cold showers to prove it.

Turning back to his computer, he finished the payroll and finalizing everything for his meeting with the mayor the following week, then locked up for the evening. His sister-in-law had invited him to dinner, and he was looking forward to spending time with his niece. As usual, he was the last to leave.

Antonio made the short drive to his brother's house, thinking about all the gas he was saving by everything being so close.

"Uncle Tony!" Noelle barreled out the door and ran to him.

He picked her up, swung her around, and planted a kiss on her cheek. "How's my girl?"

"Good. I made a picture for you at school today because Mama said you were coming over. You wanna see it?"

"Absolutely." He carried her up the steps and hugged his sister-in-law. "Hey, April."

"Come on in. I heard your good news, and I'm excited for you two."

"Thanks." Noelle wiggled to get down, and he set her on her feet. She took off down the hall, and he chuckled.

"Noelle, *walk*," April said, shaking her head. "I swear that girl has two speeds—sleep and full throttle."

Antonio threw his head back and laughed. He followed April to the kitchen, where Nate stood at the stove, removing steaks from the stovetop grill. "What's up, big bro?"

"Hey. You're just in time."

It wasn't unusual for his brother to share the cooking duties with his wife. Both Antonio and Nate were competent in the kitchen thanks to their mother. She'd told them they needed to learn to fend for themselves instead of waiting on some woman to do it. His father had also prepared the meals in their home growing up, especially during parent conference week, when his mother wouldn't get in until late. "Let me go wash my hands. I'll be right back." He used the half bath off the kitchen, and when he returned, Noelle handed him a drawing.

"It's a picture of me and you playing on the swings in my backyard, and you're pushing me high."

He was glad she'd explained because the only thing he could make out were the two different sized stick figures. He'd had no clue about the other various shaped objects. "Thank you. I love it, and I'm going to hang it up in my house."

"Yay! Daddy, Uncle Tony's gonna hang up my picture at his house." Noelle turned back to Antonio. "Can I come to your house and see it?"

"You sure can."

"Then I can spend a night with you? Mama said you live by yourself."

April plucked her out of Antonio's arms. "Little girl, you can't just invite yourself over to people's houses. You have to wait until they ask."

Her little lip drooped, and she stared up at her mother with sad eyes. "But he was going to ask," she said in a small voice.

"She's right. I was going to ask her." Those big brown eyes got to him every time, and he caved like a sandcastle hit by a wave.

April rolled her eyes, then leaned down and whispered, "Just wait until you get your own. You're going to become immune to sad eyes, tears, and everything in between."

Antonio had been waiting a long time. He wanted children but had given up hope that he'd have them. *Maybe I'll be given a second chance for that, as well.* Antonio dismissed the thought, cautioning himself to slow down. He and Natasha had just reconciled and were nowhere near that kind of discussion. They'd both changed and still had a lot to learn about each other.

Over dinner, he caught up with April and Nate, and Noelle kept up a running dialogue, so as not to be left out of the conversation. Afterward, he and Nate went to sit on the back deck.

"I'm glad you and Tasha are going to try again," Nate said. "I know it's going to sound cliché, but I truly believe you two were made for each other. I hope it works out this time."

More than one of his family members had told him that, and Antonio started to believe they might be right. "So do I." He didn't think he'd be able to handle a different outcome.

"So when do you plan to tell Mom? I know Grandma is going to be beside herself, and you'd better believe she's going to take credit for bringing you two back together," he added with a laugh.

"I don't know. Soon. Tasha and I are taking it slow for

now—spending time together and figuring out if this will work—and neither of us want to be the subject of town gossip."

"Only it won't be gossip this time, Tony. It's a fact. You're back together, and the sooner folks know, the less trouble you'll have with women like Claudia thinking they have a chance."

Antonio hadn't thought of that, but it had merit. He had to concede that point to his brother. *Yeah, maybe it is time to let the town know I have my girl back.*

CHAPTER 11

Saturday, Natasha set the table while Serenity and Gabriel prepared the meal for their meetup. Today they'd decided on brunch, and she couldn't wait for the homemade waffles and vanilla maple syrup. She kept saying she would try to make the syrup on her own—Serenity said it was easy—but so far the only thing she'd done was devour it when her friend added it to the menu or shared a bottle.

The off-and-on rain finally stopped two days ago, and the temperatures had climbed to a sunny seventy-four degrees, making the weather perfect for outdoor dining. Since they kept things casual, Natasha had gone with a simple blue and white theme.

Serenity and Gabriel carried out platters of fluffy waffles, Gabriel's fried chicken wings, bacon, and scrambled eggs. Terri and Dana followed with a fruit salad and pineapple mimosas, respectively. After plates were filled, music and conversation flowed around the table.

Serenity poured syrup on her waffles. "Tasha, how's it going with you and Antonio being back together?"

"Is that the guy you were kissing in Ms. Ida's?" Gabriel asked with a smile.

Natasha pointed her fork toward Gabriel. "Don't start. I'm still mad about that foolishness."

"What? Nana mentioned him and wanted to know if we'd met yet."

"Mm-hmm. But to answer your question, it's going okay. We're trying to take it one day at a time. We're still not ready to go public yet, though." They'd been very careful to remain somewhat distant while in public, but she didn't know how much longer she'd be able to keep up the facade. She'd experienced a few bouts of jealousy seeing other couples strolling hand in hand and wanted them to be able to do the same.

"Girl, you know I understand. Ms. Adele's nosy behind was enough to keep me incognito forever," Serenity said.

Terri laughed. "I am so glad I was already married when I moved here. Even after being here for three years, I still have a hard time getting used to the way people are all in other folks' business. In LA, you could go days without someone even speaking to you, much less taking time to be knee-deep in your private life."

"Well, I for one can't wait," Dana said. "These crazy women are going to lose their minds knowing Antonio chose you, not once but twice."

Natasha smiled. It would be interesting to see how everything played out.

"I'm surprised you didn't invite him," Gabriel said around a bite of food.

"He's working today. With all the rain, they've gotten behind."

"You should take him and his crew some food. There's plenty. How many are working with him?"

Serenity's offer mirrored Natasha's earlier thoughts of stopping by Ms. Ida's to pick up something and dropping it off before heading home. "I think he told me three, but I can text and ask."

"Working with tools, they can't have mimosas, but I can do a little mocktail using lemon-lime soda, instead," Dana offered.

This was why Natasha loved her friends. "That's a great idea. Y'all are so sweet. I'll take it over after I finish eating."

Serenity never did anything by half and decided to do individual brunch boxes that included generous portions of everything.

"Oh, wait, I forgot to text him." She dug out her phone and sent the message.

A moment later, he responded: *Hey, baby. It's only me, Todd, and Gerald. Why?*

Natasha: *Just wondering. How long are you guys working today?*

Antonio: *I can leave right now if it means spending time with you, but we'd planned to knock off around 4.*

She smiled and wished he could leave now. It had been so long since she'd dated someone, she'd almost forgotten how it felt to be in a relationship.

"Stop all that smiling," Dana said, sidling up to Natasha and bumping her shoulder playfully. "You used to do the same thing back in the day, only then you two were sending those sappy notes."

Natasha laughed. "Oh, hush. Serenity, it's only three of them."

She helped put the boxes together, and Gabriel loaded everything into her car.

Serenity hugged Natasha. "Let me know how it goes."

"I'll call you later. Thanks again."

"You helped me get my forever love, and I want you to have the same."

Natasha had encouraged Serenity to take a chance on Gabriel and had even plotted with Gabriel for the marriage proposal. She got into her car and drove off. Still thinking about Serenity's last statement, she didn't realize Gabriel was behind her for a moment. Initially she thought he might have been taking some food to Ms. Della, but he matched her turn for turn until she pulled into the Wards' driveway.

"What are you doing here, Gabriel?"

"You need help carrying that heavy box."

She shook her head. "I could've had Antonio or one of the other guys help me."

"Natasha?"

She turned at the sound of Antonio's voice, and just the sight of him made her heart race. "Hey. I want you to meet Gabriel Cunningham, Serenity's husband. Gabe, this is Antonio Hayes."

"It's nice to finally put a face to the name," Gabriel said. "Nana's told me a lot about you." The two men shook hands.

Antonio chuckled. "Nice to meet you, too. Between Ms. Della and my grandmother, I don't know who's worse. What brings you out?"

"I don't know if Natasha has mentioned the supper club she, Serenity, and two of their other friends have."

"She mentioned they got together a couple of times a month, but I can't say I've heard the term 'supper club.'"

Gabriel grinned. "Natasha will have to tell you the story."

"Anyway," Natasha said as Gabriel removed the box from her car, "we brought food for all of you."

A smile kicked up at the corner of Antonio's mouth. "Thanks. That saves me from having to leave and go pick something up." He took the box Gabriel handed him and looked inside. "Waffles?"

Natasha wiggled her eyebrows. "Yep. Homemade."

"You guys enjoy," Gabriel said. "I'm heading back." He started to his car, then paused. "Oh, Natasha, you should invite Antonio to the next supper club." He winked.

Natasha's mouth fell open, and then she burst out laughing, recalling how she'd done the same thing when Serenity was still mad at Gabriel.

"Just returning the favor. Antonio, the box on the bottom is yours. It has an extra piece of chicken for Natasha. I figured she might want to stay around while you eat."

This time Antonio laughed. "Thanks, man. And yeah, I definitely want to check out this supper club." After Gabriel left, Antonio placed a soft kiss on Natasha's lips. "You are going to stay, right?"

Like she wanted to be anywhere else. "Yeah, I'll stay."

"Come on. Let me give the guys their food, and we can sit on the bench out back."

The bench had quickly become their favorite place, not only because it had been the spot where their official relationship began, but it also offered privacy. Todd and George

111

thanked her profusely and asked her to relay their gratitude to Serenity as well.

After they were seated, Antonio opened the box and turned his shocked gaze her way. "I know you said she cooks, but I didn't know you meant like this." He offered her one of the wings before starting in on the meal. He groaned after the first bite.

"Good, huh? And that syrup is homemade, too."

"I see why you said you don't ever miss the supper clubs. Serenity can *cook*. And this chicken is better than Ms. Ida's." He pulled all the meat off the drumstick part in two bites.

Nibbling on her own piece of chicken, she said, "Gabriel makes the chicken."

Antonio nodded. "Yep, I'm all in for the next supper club. Oh, and how did you all decide on the name?"

Natasha smiled. "Gabriel's sister, Andrea, used to be the fifth member of our group until she got a job promotion and moved last year. She gave our little gatherings the name 'Serenity's Supper Club' because she said they reminded her of the old underground places where people spent hours eating, drinking, listening to music, and generally having a good time."

He nodded and sipped his juice. "I like that. Do you cook like this? I remember you not liking to cook."

"That has not changed. I can cook the basics, bake from a box, but the only thing homemade is that it's made *in* my home."

He laughed so hard, he almost choked.

"What? I don't mind cooking and helping out, but every woman can't be Suzie Homemaker, with all the fancy stuff. Can you cook?"

"Yes. I like getting into the kitchen. Would you cook with me?"

"I'd love to cook with you." She'd often watched Serenity and Gabriel when they prepared a meal together. It had been more than just about food, and Natasha found herself wanting the same thing.

"By the way, Grandma's party is three weeks from today. What do you think about letting everyone know we're back together then?"

"Funny you should mention it. I've been thinking about the same thing. I want to be able to hold your hand and walk near the lake with you or go to Splendid Scoops for ice cream. So, yes, I think it would be a great day to make the announcement."

He leaned over and kissed her until she melted against the seat. Natasha just hoped she could last that long.

* * *

Antonio didn't know what to expect when he and Natasha arrived for the supper club dinner, but he hoped they were nothing like the dinners his ex-wife had insisted they attend. Those affairs might have been billed as casual, but they were anything but. Instead, they most often turned out to be filled with stuffed shirts who spent the entire evening lauding their accomplishments and debating who had the biggest bank account.

"If it isn't Antonio 'Lights Out' Hayes." He'd been given the nickname in high school because they claimed it was lights out for the other team once he hit the court.

"What's up, Dana 'Pit Stop' Stephens?" He laughed and pulled her into a hug. "It's been a long time, girl. You still messing around with cars?" She used to spend summers working at her father's garage and got the nickname after a guy in auto class challenged her to see who could change a tire the fastest. Not only did she change two tires in the time it took him to do one, but she also had time to wipe down the windows. Everyone thought she should be on some racing team's pit crew.

"More like running the shop these days."

"Good for you." He greeted Gabriel with a fist bump. "What's up, man? Thanks for the invite."

"Anytime."

"You must be Serenity," Antonio said to the woman curled into Gabriel's side. "It's a pleasure to finally meet you in person."

"Same here." Serenity reached out and gave him a hug. "Come on in and get comfortable. We have a couple more people who should be here in a few minutes. In the meantime, help yourself to appetizers and wine."

"Thanks, and thank you for the brunch last week. Everything was delicious."

She waved him off. "Oh, it was nothing. I'm just glad you enjoyed it."

Enjoyed was an understatement. Natasha looped her arm in his and steered him over to the bar where Serenity had lain out a charcuterie board, bacon-wrapped scallops, and spinach dip. "She did all this, *and* she's cooking an entire meal, too?"

Natasha smiled. "I told you she loves to cook." She got two plates and handed him one.

114

Antonio added a little of everything, then poured them both glasses of wine. The group laughed and talked with a relaxed camaraderie that he'd longed for while living in New York. This was the complete opposite of the pretentious gatherings he'd endured. Most of his childhood friends had moved away, and aside from his brother, he didn't really have any other friends here. But he and Gabriel had bonded immediately and had already made plans to get together. Being here convinced him even more that he'd made the right decision in returning.

"Oh, yeah, this is my jam!" Natasha hopped down from the stool, threw her hands in the air, and shook her hips to Silk Sonic's "Fly As Me."

He sat mesmerized by her movements in her body-hugging jeans and sweater, and his hands itched to trace every one of her luscious curves. She danced over and pulled him to his feet.

"You still know how to dance, don't you?" she asked teasingly.

"I might be able to do a little sumthin' sumthin'." Antonio wrapped an arm around her waist and moved to her beat. They used to love dancing together and had often made up choreographed routines to songs and showed them off at school dances. When the song ended, she came up on tiptoe and kissed him.

"Yep, you still got it." She did a little hip sway and sashayed over to refill her wine.

One more minute of her dancing like that and *she* was going to get it...all of it. He tossed back the remainder of his wine and met Gabriel's knowing gaze.

The doorbell rang, and Gabriel let in another couple, whom he introduced as Jonathan and Terri Rhodes.

"Okay, everybody, dinner is served," Serenity announced. "Tonight we decided on a little surf 'n' turf—beef tenderloin, lobster medallions in a butter cream sauce, twice-baked potatoes, roasted Brussels sprouts, and rolls."

Over dinner, the women argued good-naturedly about the latest R&B singers, while the men discussed their predictions for which NBA teams would make it to the finals.

Brussels sprouts had never been high on Antonio's list of foods, but whatever Serenity had done to them made him go back for seconds. And he wasn't the only one.

Gabriel came over for more food. "I heard you and Natasha are trying to keep a low profile, but you look like you're having some trouble with that."

"Maybe." But being here, he didn't have to worry about it. He could touch, caress, and kiss her as much as he liked. His biggest problem lay with his decision not to make love to her until they were on solid footing. Being around her kept him in a state of arousal. "But I don't plan to wait much longer."

"No, I don't suspect you will," he said with a smile and went back to the table.

Antonio doubted he'd last the three weeks until Grandma Nora's party.

CHAPTER 12

I think Mayor Brewer is going to give you a key to the town and name a street and his next grandchild after you the way he acted in there," Natasha said as she and Antonio left their meeting. The mayor couldn't stop talking about how proud he was that one of their own would be building the first major complex in two decades.

Antonio smiled. "Don't hate. I can't help it if the town loves me."

"Ugh. You know what? I can't stand you right now." She rolled her eyes, and he laughed.

"You sure about that? Because your kisses say something entirely different," he added for her ears only.

She did a quick scan of the area to make sure no one was in earshot. "How would you know what my kisses are saying? You haven't indulged since Saturday, and it's Wednesday." They'd spent a couple of hours together after leaving Serenity and Gabe's house.

Desire lit in his eyes. "Say the word and I'll *indulge* right here. Right now."

Her pulse skipped. Natasha bit her lip and seriously

considered throwing caution to the wind and letting him find out exactly what her kiss said. The more time they spent together, the harder it became to hold on to the we-should-take-it-slow thing they'd agreed upon. And Dana, with her crazy self, had told Natasha, "Y'all are grown, and it's nobody's business what you do. Go on and give those nosy folks something to really talk about."

"Are you on your way back to the office?"

She shook her head. "I have to go pick up some fabric samples and drop them off at home first. Why?"

"As you said, it's been four days since I tasted your lips, and I need to satisfy my craving for you. Any other questions?"

"Yeah, just one. Can you meet me at the inlet in fifteen minutes?"

"I'll be there in ten." Without another word, he loped down the steps and strode purposefully down the street to his car.

Have mercy! Natasha almost melted with the heat of his words. Not wasting any time, she nearly sprinted to her car.

They arrived at the same time. Antonio took her hand and guided her through the dense trees to her spot. He didn't say anything, just stared at her for what seemed like hours.

His hands came up to frame her face. "I've missed having you in my life, Tasha."

The kiss that followed was soft, sweet, and infused with so much emotion, it brought tears to Natasha's eyes. She gripped the front of his shirt, deepened the kiss, and tried to convey just how much she'd missed him, too. How much he was coming to mean to her again. His hands trailed a path down her spine, caressed her hips, and came around the front to her breasts. She moaned, his touch sending pleasure flowing through her. "Tonio."

"Every time you call me that, I lose control," Antonio murmured against her mouth before plunging in again, their tongues tasting, teasing.

Natasha's body trembled as she felt the solid ridge of his erection pressed against her belly. She reached out and stroked him, wanting him to know he wasn't the only one losing control.

He gasped sharply and grabbed her hand to halt its movement. "Don't, baby. I'm barely hanging on."

"That makes two of us," she muttered, still trying to calm her breathing. Running a hand over her hair, she backed out of his hold. Antonio aroused her in ways no man ever had and made her forget her vow to proceed with caution. He braced his back against a tree and closed his eyes, his breathing as harsh and uneven as hers. When he finally opened them again, the longing radiating in their depths nearly took her breath away. "Are you going out to a job site today?"

"No. I promised my grandmother I'd take her to see Grandpa. She's been a little worried about him, and I'm going to try to get her out there at least every week, if not more."

"It would be nice if we had a place here, instead of folks having to drive all the way to Napa."

"That's the same thing Grandma said." He pushed away from the tree and grasped her hand. "Come on." They strolled hand in hand back the way they came. Antonio held her car door open. "I'll call you tonight."

"Okay. Drive safe." Natasha almost asked him to tell

Mama Nora hello until she remembered their agreement. She watched him get into his car and back out of the space. Giving him a little wave, she started up her car and cranked up the air-conditioning to its highest setting, despite the mild temperatures, to cool herself off. The chemistry drawing them together was far stronger than last time, and if things didn't work out this time, it would destroy her.

* * *

Antonio parked in his parents' driveway and shut off the engine. He sat there for a moment recalling every sensual moment of kissing and touching Natasha. Obviously, she had no idea how much she affected him because he'd been a heartbeat away from carrying her back to his car and making love to her the way they'd done once before. Thankfully, his sanity returned. The first time they reconnected, he wanted it to be in a bed, not somewhere in the woods like two kids sneaking around.

He didn't see his father's car and his mother was still at the school, so he went around back and knocked on the screen door. "Grandma, it's me."

"Come on in, Antonio," she called from somewhere inside.

When he entered, she came from the back with her purse and jacket.

She offered her cheek for a kiss. "What's the weather like outside?"

"It's a little windy but not too cold. I checked the temperatures in Napa, and they're close to the same as here—seventy, seventy-one."

"Then I'd better take this jacket."

Antonio escorted her to his car, helped her in, and got them under way. He knew she enjoyed jazz, so he selected a playlist from Spotify and turned the volume down some.

"This is nice." She leaned forward to read the track information. "I'm going to have to download some of this music."

He looked over at her briefly. "Download?"

"Yes. Your father bought me one of these fancy phones, so I figured I should learn how to use it. I have all my music on it, so when I want to sit outside while relaxing, I don't have to worry about lugging out that big old boom box from thirty years ago."

Evidently, he'd been more out of the loop than he thought.

"What? Just because I'm pushing eighty doesn't mean I have to act like I've got one foot in the grave. I plan to live every day to the fullest until it's my time."

He chuckled. "I didn't say anything." Antonio couldn't imagine a time when he wouldn't have his grandmother in his life. She'd always been in his corner, even with her gentle discipline when he'd gotten out of line as a kid. He didn't think she'd missed one of his high school basketball games and had often cheered the loudest. Back then his grandfather had been there as well. "Are you ready for your party in two weeks?"

"Just about. I hope you didn't forget you're supposed to be bringing Natasha."

"You haven't let me forget, Grandma." Not that he had. In fact, he was looking forward to having her by his side almost as much as the party itself. Once again his body heated recalling what took place earlier, particularly when she'd boldly stroked him. Antonio thought it best to get his mind off Natasha and what he wanted to do to her and focus on the conversation at hand. "I'll be over sometime that Friday before to help Dad and Nate set up the backyard." At last count, at least eighty people had RSVP'd in the affirmative. Fortunately, their yard could hold that number easily.

"How are the renovations coming at Velda's? You and Natasha working okay?"

"Everything's going fine."

"Good. There haven't been any more incidents like that first day, with her running off upset, have there?" She peered over her glasses at him.

Damn, how many people know about that? "No. We've worked out our differences."

She patted his thigh. "I knew you'd come to your senses."

Antonio opened his mouth to ask what she meant but decided he didn't want to know. Besides, she'd know everything soon. They passed the remaining miles catching up on all he'd missed over the years, from new babies to marriages and deaths. As they came closer to the facility, he noticed his grandmother had gotten quiet, her features lined with concern.

"You can just park over there near the door on the left."

He followed her directions.

"I sure hope he's having a good day today," she said, seemingly more to herself, as they walked toward the entrance.

His heart clenched, and he searched for the right words to say. "I believe that no matter what kind of day he's having, his soul will know you even if his mind doesn't."

"Thank you for saying that, sweetheart." She gave him a sad smile.

As they walked through the automatic doors and to the receptionist, he took in the modern yet rustic feel of the place, mentally cataloging everything.

"Good afternoon, Mrs. Hayes."

"Hello, Portia. This is my grandson Antonio."

Antonio greeted the young woman.

"I believe Mr. Hayes is in the garden. It's his favorite place."

"Thank you, dear." She led Antonio through the lobby and another set of doors to a secluded and gated outdoor area. Her face lit up when she saw his grandfather, and she swiftly crossed the space to his side.

A middle-aged man sat near his grandfather but stood at their approach and hugged his grandmother. "How are you, Mrs. Hayes? He's been asking about his Nora today."

She answered his question, introduced him to Antonio as Tyson, his grandfather's aide, then took the chair next to her husband. "If it isn't the most handsome man in the world."

His grandfather's expression went from confusion to recognition, and his lips curved into a wide smile. "My beautiful Nora." He leaned over and pressed a kiss to her lips. "I've been waiting for you."

"I'm here, baby. I'm here," she said, curving a loving hand along his cheek.

Emotion clogged Antonio's throat, and he had to turn away for a moment to regain control. The tall, strong man who'd taught him how to ride a bicycle at age three now looked like a shell of his former self. Through his conversations with

Nate, Antonio learned that their grandfather had wandered off in the middle of the night three times despite the safety precautions they'd put in place and had injured himself in a fall the final time. Neither his grandmother nor his parents had wanted to place Grandpa in a facility, but the concern that something more serious might occur, coupled with the difficulty they'd had in getting Grandpa to take his medication, had left them no choice.

"Look who's here, honey." Grandma Nora reached for Antonio's hand.

"Hey, Grandpa."

His eyes widened. "An . . . tonio?"

Antonio crouched down in front of the chair. "Yeah, it's me, Gramps."

The older man threw his thin arms around Antonio and broke down crying. "My boy is home," he repeated over and over.

The emotional outburst caught him off guard, and Antonio almost lost it. Struggling to keep his composure, he held on until his grandfather calmed. Claiming the chair on the other side, he took the tissue Tyson offered and gently wiped his grandfather's tears, then discreetly swiped at the moisture pooled in his own. He stared into the eyes that mirrored his. "Hey, what're all the tears for?" he asked, trying to lighten the moment. "And yes, I'm back home for good."

"Good. Missed you."

"Same here, Grandpa. I'll be bringing Grandma to see you as often as I can."

The older couple shared a smile, then drifted off into their own world.

Not wanting to intrude on their private time, he struck up a conversation with Tyson, inquiring about his grandfather's health.

"It's up and down, and like I said earlier, today has been a better day. But don't be surprised if he doesn't remember you by the time you leave."

Never having been around someone with dementia, Antonio didn't know what to expect. "It can change that fast?"

"Sometimes. He tends to be more alert in the mornings, so you might want to take that into account when you plan your visits."

"We'll do that. Thanks." He asked a few more questions about the types of programs they offered and about the building itself. "You mind if I take a little walk around?"

"Not at all. You'll have to go back through the lobby because we keep this area locked for patient safety."

"Okay." Antonio touched his grandmother's shoulder. "I'll be back in a minute."

She nodded and tuned back in to whatever his grandfather was saying.

As he strolled around the area, he made note of the building's design. This particular facility had three separate buildings for the different levels of care they offered— independent living, assisted living, and memory care, where his grandfather resided. On the way back to the garden, he snagged a brochure.

Grandma Nora sat with tears glistening in her eyes. Tyson shook his head, letting Antonio know that his grandfather had slipped back. Frederick Hayes Sr. and Nora Hayes had sixty years of marriage under their belts and until now had never slept a night apart. He couldn't begin to imagine how difficult it was to navigate this new reality and to have to settle for seeing him five or six times a month.

She'd asked Antonio if he could build something in Firefly Lake. With his current schedule, he didn't think he'd be able to pull it off, but he vowed to get it done . . . one way or another. And soon.

CHAPTER 13

Saturday, Antonio stepped onto the basketball court at his high school, and a flood of memories engulfed him. He'd spent nearly every day here practicing, sometimes for three or more hours at a time, to be the best he could be at the game. It had paid off when he earned a full scholarship to Syracuse University. But it had also come with a cost—he and Natasha had planned to attend college in LA—her at Long Beach State and him at UCLA. Even though she told him she understood and he couldn't pass up the opportunity, that had been the first fracture in their relationship. Antonio had honestly, and naively, believed that it would be easy for them to maintain their connection because they loved each other.

He bounced the ball, then sank a jumper. So many times over the years, he'd asked himself if, given the chance, he would do things differently, and he could never say definitively one way or another. The only thing he'd change for sure was not giving up on him and Tasha so easily. He'd even stopped coming home in the summers because he couldn't handle being around her and seeing all the pitying stares from the townsfolk. Antonio sank another shot.

"Showing off already?"

Antonio chuckled at Gabriel. "Nah. I'm saving all that for showing you up on the court." During their conversation at dinner, he'd found out they had a mutual love of basketball and had made plans to shoot around sometimes.

Gabriel spread his arms. "Bring it on, my brother."

"Since you're a guest on *my* court, I'll let you go first." He tossed the ball to Gabriel. "First one to eleven?"

"Bet." He dribbled, stepped back, and tried to go around Antonio, but Antonio anticipated the move, stole the ball, and dunked it. "Oh, so that's how it's gonna be, huh?"

"That's exactly how it is," Antonio said, sending the ball back with a bounce pass. This time Gabriel dribbled once and shot. The ball went around the rim a couple of times before falling through. The trash talk continued throughout the game, and Gabriel pulled ahead by two.

"Looks like you're about to lose on your home court." Gabriel cupped a hand near his ear, grinning. "You hear that? Do you hear Vince Carter?"

Antonio snatched the ball. "Ain't nothing over." He proceeded to show Gabriel why he'd earned his nickname. When they were both tied at ten, he asked, "Anybody ever tell you my name on the court?" He did a fake left, spun right, and launched the ball. *Swish!* "Lights. Out."

Gabriel doubled over in laughter, trying to catch his breath. "All right, I'll give you this one."

Winded, Antonio lowered himself to the ground. "I haven't played ball since I left New York. That felt good." He and a couple of college buddies used to get together almost weekly for a game or to just shoot around and it had helped to keep his skills sharp.

Gabriel dropped down across from him. "Speak for yourself. I haven't been on a court since I don't know when."

Antonio laughed tiredly. "How long have you lived here?"

"Less than a year. Came last summer because my sister got a promotion that forced her to move away. We wanted one of us here to keep an eye on Nana, and my sister had given up several years of her life to do it after our parents passed away, so it was my turn." He told Antonio about never staying more than a day or two whenever he visited over the years because he couldn't stand being in such a small town. "I figured I'd hang around for the summer, convince Nana to move back to Atlanta, and be good."

"Obviously, that didn't work out as planned."

"*Nothing* worked out like I planned. Nana shut me down cold, and I ended up having a thing for my sexy neighbor, who couldn't stand me in the beginning. Man . . ."

Antonio laughed so hard at the stories Gabriel told him about his and Serenity's run-ins, he could barely catch his breath. "She *threw* something at you? Nice, sweet Serenity?"

"My baby is nice and sweet, but she also has a throwing arm that would do a major league baseball team proud." Gabriel smiled and shook his head as if remembering. After a minute, he asked, "How are things going with you and Natasha? Still trying to keep a low profile?"

Antonio released a deep breath. "It's better than I had ever imagined, and yeah." He was counting down the days and minutes until his grandmother's birthday bash next Saturday.

"Why? You're both adults."

He had asked himself the same question several times over the past few days and came to one conclusion. "The last time we were together, everybody in town expected us to get married after college, and you know how that turned out. This time, I want—no *need*—to make sure what we've got is going to last. I don't think I could take a repeat."

Gabriel nodded. "I get it. I had some of the same hang-ups with Serenity, but I had to decide whether I was going to be all in or not. Anything less isn't going to work. Trust me, I know. I almost lost her because of my fears and insecurities. Besides, I'm sure you don't want any of these other brothers around town kicking it with your girl."

Oh, hell no! The thought of any other man with Natasha, touching and kissing her, spiked his anger.

"That's what I thought," Gabriel said with a grin, slowly getting to his feet. He did a couple of stretches. "I'm definitely going to have to get out here a little more often. I'll be ready for you next time."

"Only in your dreams," Antonio shot back, jumping to his feet. They trudged to their cars, scheduled another time, and said their goodbyes.

On the way home, he stopped by the grocery store to purchase what he needed for his dinner with Natasha. After putting away everything and showering, he prepped the crab for the crab cakes.

An hour later, he left to pick up Natasha. Up to this point, they hadn't had what he would call a formal date but more like hanging out. He knew it was a risk, but no way would he allow her to drive over for their date, especially a first date, even if they were staying in. His heart pounded when she opened the door to him. Antonio felt more nervous tonight than he had the first time they went out, at age sixteen. "Hey, baby."

"Hi, yourself. Come on in." Natasha moved aside so he could enter.

He closed the door, drew her into his arms, and slanted his mouth over hers in an intoxicating kiss. Her tongue dueled with his as he angled his head and tasted every corner of her mouth. Feeling his restraint slipping, he eased back. Each time they kissed drew them closer together.

"I think I'm going to enjoy us dating again. I always thought you were the best kisser, but now...*whew*!" She fanned herself.

"Quit tempting me. Are you ready?"

"Depends on how much of this cooking you're expecting me to do."

He kissed the tip of her nose. "It'll be fun, so come on."

Waving a hand, she said, "I'm not worried about the fun. That's a given. Will it be edible is my concern."

Antonio laughed. "Tasha, you're the most fearless woman I know, and I'll be there right with you."

"Okay, but if it turns out bad, don't say I didn't warn you."

He pointed toward the door. "Let's go, woman."

They were both laughing as they got into the car, and Natasha said, "Is it crazy that I'm nervous? These butterflies have been dancing in my belly all day. I mean, it's not like we don't know each other and used to be best friends...and more."

"No, it's not crazy because I'm feeling the same way. We might have known each other then, but we've grown into different people." He brought her hand to his lips and kissed it. "And I'm looking forward to learning all about the new Natasha Leigh Baldwin."

Natasha laughed softly. "Dang, why you gotta use my entire name?"

"You used mine." They shared a smile, then spent the rest of the short drive in companionable silence. His godfather owned all the property surrounding the house where Antonio stayed, and it happened to be the farthest from the main home, so chances were no one would see them. He unlocked the door and gestured for her to enter first.

She surveyed the living room. "You know, this is the first time I've ever been in one of the guest houses Mr. Davenport built. This is nice. How many bedrooms?"

"Just two. Make yourself comfortable. And don't start trying to get ideas about how you can redecorate this place."

A giggle escaped. "How did you know I was doing that?"

"I saw that little gleam in your eyes, and I know you. I'm only staying here until I decide whether to buy something or build it."

"Uh-huh, and because I know *you*, it's probably the latter."

Grinning, he mumbled a "no comment" and headed for the kitchen.

Natasha followed, still laughing. "This is a nice-size kitchen."

She'd been in his home only a few minutes, but already Antonio could see her there going forward. He'd said some things had changed over the years, but the easy rapport they shared from day one hadn't. When he washed his hands at the sink, Natasha squeezed her body in front of his and stuck her hands under the running water with his. "Saving water."

"Yeah, right." He grabbed a couple of paper towels and handed her one. After drying his hands, he went about retrieving everything he needed from the refrigerator and cabinets.

She rubbed her hands together. "Okay, let's do this. What's on the menu?"

"Crab cakes, lemon pasta, and a green salad."

"I'll take care of the salad."

"And the crab cakes and pasta." Antonio pulled her over to the counter. "We'll start with the crab cakes because they'll need to sit in the fridge for a few minutes before cooking. I don't put a lot of fillers like crackers and eggs in mine."

"That means it's *all* crab, just the way I like it. Music?"

"Of course. I don't cook without it." He chose an R&B playlist, and they got busy. She mixed the wet ingredients while he finely diced the bell peppers and added them to the mixture.

"Done." She plucked a piece of the crab out of the bowl he placed on the counter. "Mmm, it's so sweet."

Antonio poured the seafood into her bowl. "Fold it in gently to keep the pieces from breaking up too much." While she finished that, he lined a baking sheet with parchment paper, and they formed six medium-size balls. Then he placed the pan in the refrigerator and preheated the oven. "Next up, pasta." On his way past, he kissed her briefly. The peace and contentment he'd been searching for filled his soul. *This is what I want, but only with Tasha.*

CHAPTER 14

While the pasta and crab cakes cooked, Antonio wrapped an arm around Natasha's waist and swayed to the mid-tempo groove pouring through the speakers, and she melted against him. She'd never cooked with any of the guys she'd dated, had never even thought about it, but it felt natural with Antonio. And she was enjoying every minute. He danced her over to the fridge for the salad fixings. "Now, this I can handle," she said, giving him a bright smile.

"And while you handle that, I'll handle you." Trapping her between the counter and his body, he braced his hands on either side of her and rained kisses along her jaw, neck, and shoulder.

Her head dropped back against his chest. "Mmm, Tonio, I...can't...*ohhh.*"

"You can't what, baby?" Antonio asked as his warm hands slipped beneath her top and caressed her bare skin.

She dropped the knife on the counter, turned in his arms, and pulled his head down for a smoldering kiss. Natasha wanted to touch him the same way and pushed his shirt up. Her hands made a path across his muscled chest and down to his sculpted abs. The man's body was a work of art. Some-where in the back of her mind, an insistent beeping sounded. Finally, through the sensual fog, she realized it was the oven timer.

Antonio kissed her one last time, grabbed an oven mitt, and removed the crab cakes from the oven. He checked the pasta. "It'll be done in about three minutes. I'll make the sauce while you finish the salad."

Though his voice was steady, the slight trembling in his hands let her know he'd been just as affected as she was. It took Natasha a few seconds to collect herself. They managed to keep their hands off each other long enough to finish pre-paring the rest of the meal.

"I'll take the pasta and crab. Can you grab the salad?"

She picked up the bowl and trailed him to the dining room, where he'd set the table using a crisp white tablecloth, pale-blue fine china, with coordinating blue-patterned cloth napkins. A small bouquet of pink roses sat in the center, sur-rounded by taper candles. "It's beautiful."

"Thanks. I wanted this night to be special for us. I learned a thing or two watching you."

That he'd gone out of his way to set a beautiful table using her favorite color and flower tilted the scales of her heart a little more toward him. He seated her, then took the chair across from her.

After pouring glasses of wine, Antonio gestured for her to fix her plate. "Ladies first."

Natasha added portions of everything to her plate. "It smells so good." She waited for him to fix his before sam-pling the crab cake. The tender, flavorful seafood nearly melted in her mouth. She tried the pasta next and savored the creamy lemon taste. She eyed Antonio. "Did you take professional cooking classes or something?"

"No," he answered with a chuckle. "I just followed recipes and played around with different combinations until I found what I liked. And cooking wasn't that bad, was it?"

"It was the best time I've ever had cooking in the kitchen." She'd helped Serenity a few times, but it was different with Antonio. "Can we do this again?"

"We can do it any time you'd like." Something like a shadow crossed his face, and he lowered his head.

"Hey, everything okay?"

Antonio waved her off. "Fine. Just a memory."

She nodded. "We haven't really discussed our pasts. Maybe it's time we do."

"You want to know about my marriage." He placed his fork on the plate. "I met Lori at a business conference, and we hit it off. We dated for a while, wanted the same things, and I thought she was the one. After we married and she got a promotion, I realized that climbing the career ladder was more important to her than our relationship. I have no problem with moving up in the workplace but not to the exclusion of everything and everyone else," he said in between bites of food. "And I wanted children...but it wasn't in her plans anymore."

Her heart went out to him. "I'm so sorry. How could she think it would work if you two wanted different things, and why lie at the beginning? She could've saved you both some heartache."

"She said she wanted children initially, but it was never

the right time. We grew farther and farther apart. I wanted us to do things like this, but she preferred hosting parties almost every week. We rarely went out just the two of us. Every outing turned into a networking opportunity. At the end we were nothing more than polite strangers and barely lasted two years."

"It's her loss." Natasha continued eating and tried to process what he'd gone through. He'd had his heart broken twice, and she'd caused one of them. She wouldn't make the same mistake again. Silence rose between them, and for the next few minutes the only sound came from the music playing.

"I was surprised to find out you moved back home. I thought you planned to stay in LA and open your own interior design business."

She gave him a wistful smile. "So did I. I guess we have picking the wrong partner in common. Julian and I met during my senior year of college through a mutual friend. He talked about us going into business together after graduation with another friend in our class, but I wouldn't commit to it because I had my own plans. What I didn't know at the time is that *friend*—and I use the term loosely—hadn't been doing as well in our classes. In fact, she was close to failing." Natasha felt the old anger surfacing again. "And that Julian had only come on to me to steal my designs for her so she could pass. She was the woman he really wanted to date."

"That son of a—" Antonio cut off the expletive.

"My thoughts exactly. I wanted to strangle both of them. Can you imagine working for weeks on a senior project only to receive a failing grade and a threat of expulsion? The saving grace is that I had sketched some of it by hand first and discussed it with my counselor at least three months prior. Serenity and I threw a party when they got kicked out of school."

Chuckling, he said, "That sounds like something you'd do."

"After that I stayed in LA and got an entry-level job at a design firm. But I missed home so much, I couldn't take it." Natasha shrugged. "I guess I wasn't as ready to be away as I first believed, so I came back home after a year." And when she returned, she'd endured more snickering behind her back from those same girls—Antonio had made it as a big-time investment manager in New York, but Natasha hadn't, confirming in their minds that she would never be good enough for him. *They were wrong*, she told herself and pushed the wayward thought away. "Anyway, a job at the real estate office opened up, and I took it. I started out doing some marketing and administrative work, and then studied my butt off, took and passed the exam to become an agent. But I have done a few small design projects here and there, and eventually I plan to do it full time. I'm excited because I've gotten a few more clients. The condo project will be my largest and, hopefully, will be the thing that allows me to leave real estate behind."

Antonio lifted her hand and placed a kiss on the back. "I have no doubt you'll be opening your own interior design business in the near future. What about marriage?"

That was another thing that hadn't worked out. "I've dated a few of the guys here, but nothing came of it."

He covered her hand with his. "I guess neither one of us

got it right the first time, and we both know what we don't want."

"True. What *do* you want?" she asked tentatively, hoping they wanted the same things.

"I want to do what we did tonight, to spend time at the inlet talking, to take walks at sunset and share kisses under the moon, to dance in the kitchen even if it's to music only we can hear. I want to have candlelight dinners and take trips just for pleasure. But what I want most of all is you, Tasha."

Natasha didn't realize she was holding her breath until she felt the pressure in her chest. His deep voice poured over her like warm honey, and each word of his impassioned confession hit her squarely in the heart. "I want to do all those things, too, Tonio, but only with you."

Without releasing her hand, he rounded the table and gently pulled her to her feet. "I'm going to enjoy doing all those things with you."

"Me too. Thank you for giving us another chance." This time she was determined to make it work.

* * *

Sunday afternoon, Natasha, Serenity, Dana, and Terri sat around a picnic table at Seaside Meadows Park, eating ice cream. Natasha had called her besties, in need of some advice and bursting at the seams with her good news. "Antonio and I had dinner together last night."

"Really? It must have been somewhere other than here, because I haven't heard one peep," Dana said.

"No, we were here. At his place. We cooked together."

There was stunned silence for a few seconds. Then they bombarded her with questions.

"Can he actually cook?"

"Does this mean you two are ready for the town to know?"

"And what kind of cooking did you do *after* the meal? Oh, and can you or Serenity send one of them to my house for lessons because Jon can barely boil water."

Natasha held up a hand and laughed at the last two questions, which had come from Terri. "Yes, he can actually cook. Yes, we're going to take the wraps off at Mama Nora's party next weekend, as planned. Though it's going to be hard pretending we're nothing more than friends every time I see him. Terri, we'll see about the cooking lessons, and we didn't do any *cooking* after the meal," she said with a grin. "But not because I didn't want to. *Bay-bee*, the man's kisses are beyond amazing." She pretended to swoon, then fanned herself.

The women broke out into a fit of giggles.

Serenity bumped her shoulder playfully. "Girl, I am so happy for you two."

"So am I," Dana said. "But there are going to be quite a few women who aren't, and I can't wait to see their faces when they find out."

"Dana, you are so bad." In the back of Natasha's mind, she'd wondered what would happen as well. While in high school, several of the girls who had fancied themselves in love with Antonio had done everything they could to break them up, from "accidentally" leaving notes he'd supposedly written to them for Natasha to see to outright telling Natasha to her face that he could do better and to watch her back. Most of them still lived in town, and a few were divorced or single and on the hunt. She just hoped that those women acted like the thirtysomething-year-olds they were, rather than the catty teenagers they used to be in school.

"What? You know it's true."

Terri laughed. "I guess that kind of foolishness wasn't limited to the big city."

"Right," Serenity said, shaking her head.

"I'm still a little scared we'll end up the same way as before," Natasha confessed. She pushed the ice cream around in her cup. "What if we find out we're too different now?" Last night she'd been caught up in the moment, but this morning every *what-if* scenario ran through her mind.

Serenity laid a comforting hand on Natasha's arm. "Sis, you know you can't go into this expecting it to fail, just like you told me when I was going through the same thing with Gabriel last year."

"I know, and I'm trying. But this time what I'm starting to feel for Antonio is so much stronger than when we were kids."

Dana brought a spoonful of ice cream to her mouth. "I know I'm the only single one at the table, but it should feel that way. You both have grown and matured, and this new relationship should reflect that change."

"See, this is why I called y'all. I needed somebody to talk me off the ledge." She had gotten so worked up earlier, she'd been tempted to call Antonio and tell him she needed more time before letting the town into their lives.

"That's what sister-friends do," Terri said. "Just take it one day at a time like you've been doing and don't let all the *what-if*s consume you. Everything will work out."

Natasha smiled. "Thanks, Terri." She finished the last of her ice cream. "Okay, subject change. You all are going to the party, right?"

The women nodded, and Terri said, "I was honored to be invited since we've only lived here a few years. I met Antonio's grandparents when they brought his grandfather to the emergency room. Mrs. Hayes told me I would always hold a special place in her heart because of the way I took care of the man who was her heart. You know, I started crying right there in the hallway."

"She's an amazing lady," Natasha said. "I'm just sad Mr. Hayes won't be there."

"So am I. They've been married forever and are still so much in love. Those are *goals*." The women all agreed. Then Serenity said with a sly grin, "Now, you know we have to go shopping this week. We've got to find a dress that will make Antonio's eyeballs fall out." This brought on more laughter and chatter about the kind of dress Natasha should wear.

"We'll coordinate our schedules." A smile curved Natasha's lips. She knew exactly the type of dress she needed.

CHAPTER 15

Friday afternoon, Natasha could barely contain herself as she waited for Serenity at Brenda's Bake Box. Only one more day.

"Hey, girl. Sorry I'm late." Serenity slid into the chair across from Natasha. "Are you getting something?"

"Just a couple of apple-cinnamon muffins to go. I'm ready to shop." She wiggled her eyebrows.

"Mm-hmm. I bet you are. Get your muffins and come on."

It didn't take long to make her purchase, and the two women strolled up the street to the Back Porch Boutique.

"If we don't find something in here or the other boutique, we still have time to make a quick drive over to Napa," Serenity said, looking through a rack of dresses.

"Sounds good." Natasha held up one dress, turned it one way, then another, then put it back. She had an idea of what she wanted and hoped they wouldn't have to make that drive. The boutique had gone through major renovations and its space had been enlarged over the winter, and it now carried a larger selection. She tried on and discarded at least six dresses before finding a sky-blue off-the-shoulder one that skimmed her curves, stopped just at the knee, and had a modest slit that exposed a few inches of her thigh. She smiled and exited the fitting room.

"Oh my goodness. That's it!" Serenity rushed over. "Turn around and let me see." She smiled and nodded. "Antonio is not going to know what hit him when he sees you in this dress. I'll try to be on standby to pick up his eyeballs."

Natasha laughed. "You do that. And I have the perfect sandals already." She went back to change, then paid for the dress. "Now, this is my kind of shopping."

Serenity checked her watch as they walked out of the shop. "And since it didn't take too long, I think I'll go home and surprise my sexy husband. Are you going back to work?"

"No. The baseboards came in for Ms. Velda's house, and I'm going to stop by to make sure they're the correct ones before they start installing it."

"And no doubt to take a peek at that fine man of yours."

"*Nooo* doubt at all." They fell out laughing. After sharing a hug, Natasha continued up the street to her car, and Serenity headed back to the doctor's office, where she'd left hers.

A few minutes later she parked in front of the house. Today there were two guys in the yard cutting the flooring to size, one adding the last touches to the porch, and the man who had always held a spot in her heart on the roof. Her heart started pounding, and she couldn't stop the smile that spread across her face when he spotted her. It took everything inside her not to climb that ladder and run her hands all over his body while kissing him senseless. It had been the same thing she'd thought back when he worked summers with Mr. Davenport. With his good looks, muscular body, and charm, every girl in town found one reason or another to walk by whichever site he was at that day. And she was no exception. Just the sight of him still made her heart race, her pulse skip, and her palms damp. Antonio must have interpreted her thoughts because he grinned and mouthed, *No*, while shaking his head.

She shrugged, climbed the steps, and went inside. "Hi, Todd. You called about the baseboards?"

"Hey, Natasha. Yeah." Todd led her back outside to the yard, where a large stack of boxes sat. He took one out of the box and held it up.

"Yes, this is the right one." Instead of the three-inch ones that had originally been installed, she'd opted for some that were eight inches. With the twelve-foot ceilings, the taller boards would give a more contemporary and elegant feel to the rooms. "Thanks. You're good to go. I'll stop by one day next week to see how it looks."

"All right. See you later."

Natasha loved how the house was coming together and hoped Chase and Mike would be pleased. She took a step back and ran into a solid mass. She gasped softly.

"Hey, sweetheart," Antonio whispered.

She rotated slowly to face him. "Hey."

"Everything okay with the baseboards?"

"Yes, and I can't wait to see them installed. The house is coming together nicely. You guys are doing a fabulous job." She knew she was rambling, but she had to do whatever she could to keep herself in check.

"Thanks." Antonio stood there staring at her.

"What?"

"I need you to stop looking at me like that."

"Like what?" Natasha asked innocently. "Like I want you to kiss me or something?"

He remained silent.

"Or . . . like *I* want to kiss *you*?"

"You're playing with fire, Tasha." His voice dipped lower, his breathing increased, and his hands clenched at his sides.

"I'm not afraid of a little fire. Are you?" Natasha had never been as bold with any other man, but this was Antonio. *Her Tonio.*

"You need to take your sassy self back to your office before you get us both in trouble."

She burst out laughing and pointed to herself. "Who, me?" She batted her eyelashes at him.

Antonio leaned closer and whispered heatedly, "Wait until tomorrow. I'm going to give you all the trouble you can stand."

Her hand came up to touch him, and she quickly snatched it down, remembering they weren't supposed to be doing that yet. She took a furtive glance around, relieved not to see anyone. "And I can't wait." She gave him a sensual smile, then strutted off, adding a little extra sway in her hips. Natasha paused and called over her shoulder, "Oh, I hope you'll like the dress I picked out. I want to look extra nice for Mama Nora." *Tomorrow can't come soon enough.*

* * *

Saturday morning, Antonio helped his father and brother with the last of the party setup. Yesterday he'd been there to pull out and clean up the outdoor furniture and drop off some of the rented chairs. He glanced at his watch.

Nate chuckled. "That's like the tenth time you've done that in the last five minutes. You have somewhere else to be, or should I say some*one* you're anxious to see?"

Was he really that obvious? "I'm just checking to see how much time we had to finish," he lied with a straight face, which turned out to be useless when it came to his older brother.

"We don't have much left, so if you want to take off to go pick up Natasha, feel free. And if you don't want anyone to know about you two, you're going to have to do a better job at keeping those smoldering looks to a minimum, especially around Mom and Grandma. And the legion of women who still think they have a shot at being the next Mrs. Antonio Hayes."

Antonio shot his brother a dark glare. "Whatever." They positioned another table and added the rented folded chairs. When he looked up, Nate stood there with his arms folded, staring at Antonio in that know-it-all way. Sighing and making sure their mother wasn't nearby, he said quietly, "We'll let everyone know today that we're back together."

Nate clapped him on the shoulder. "About time."

"You boys done over there?" their father called.

"You need something?" Antonio started in his direction, with Nate following.

"Can one of you go by the bake shop and pick up the cake? Your mother just gave me another task." He shook his head.

Antonio really didn't want to make any other stops aside from picking up Natasha.

147

"I'll get it, Dad," Nate answered, then threw Antonio a look that said, *You owe me*.

He scanned the yard. "If you don't need anything else, I'm heading home to shower. I'll be back before one in case something comes up." They didn't, so he took that as his cue and waved at his mother on the way out.

His grandmother had decided to have the party earlier in the day, saying she was too old to be hanging out all night and needed her beauty rest. At the time, Antonio hadn't cared one way or another about the start time. Now he was grateful because it meant he'd see Tasha sooner.

He'd tossed and turned all night with one erotic dream after another behind that little display she'd put on yesterday. He couldn't help wondering what her dress would look like. She'd had no idea how close he had been to throwing her over his shoulder and finding the nearest bed. Even now a low hum of arousal remained in his body.

When he got home, he sent Tasha a text letting her know he'd pick her up at twelve thirty. After grabbing a quick bite to eat and showering, he was back out the door.

The closer Antonio came to Tasha's house, the more anxious he became. Beads of perspiration popped out on his forehead despite the midseventies temperatures and the fact that he had the car's air-conditioning cranked up to its highest setting.

He parked in her driveway and released a long breath as he got out. "Get a grip, man," he muttered. This was worse than when he'd had to endure her father's inquisition at sixteen.

The moment she opened the door, he forgot to breathe.

"Hey, handsome. Are you going to stand there staring all day, or are we going to a party?"

His gaze made a lazy tour over her body in the blue dress that lovingly caressed every one of her magnificent curves, then down to her feet, with their red-painted toenails and encased in a pair of thin-strapped sandals, which sent a jolt of lust straight to his groin.

"Antonio?"

"Huh? What?" Antonio shook his head to clear it. "Did you say something?"

Natasha chuckled. "I said hi...and a couple of other things."

He moved closer until their bodies touched. "You look *amazing*, sweetheart, and I have to tell you, I'm seriously tempted to skip Grandma's party in favor of a private one for two." He brushed his lips across hers. "We should get out of here now, because you are trouble, beautiful."

"Probably." She locked the door behind her. Once in the car, she added with a wink, "There's always later, though."

Antonio lifted an eyebrow. "I don't recall you being this bold back in the day. But I like it." Gone was the shy girl he'd fallen in love with, and in her place stood a gorgeous, confident woman he couldn't wait to know better.

"Are there a lot of people coming?" Natasha asked as he drove.

"At last count, it was close to a hundred."

"Wow. That's a lot of people, but everyone loves Mama Nora, so I'm not surprised."

Antonio was thankful he arrived early, because ten minutes into the party, there wasn't a place to park within two blocks. The consummate hostess, his grandmother was in her element. "We should probably go say hello."

Natasha looked up at him. "Before we do, I want to call my mother. If she hears about us before I call, she'll be fussing from now until Christmas."

He laughed softly. "We definitely don't want that, so by all means go ahead. Maybe it'll even score me a few points because she'll know first."

She dug her phone out of her purse and made the call. "I didn't think about that, but you're probably right." A few seconds later, she said, "Hi, Mom. Yes, I'm at Mama Nora's party. Mm-hmm, I just got here and I'll tell her you said happy birthday. Mom . . . mom . . ."

Antonio stifled a laugh at Natasha's exasperated expression. "May I?" He extended his hand for the phone. She slapped it in his palm. "Hi, Mrs. Baldwin. It's Antonio."

"Antonio? Hey, baby. How're you doing? I'd heard you were back. Of course, not from my daughter." She went on and on about being kept out of the loop.

Natasha mouthed, *I told you*, and rolled her eyes.

"Ah, Mrs. Baldwin?" he cut in.

"What is it, honey?"

"We wanted you to be the first to know that Natasha and I are back together."

"*Whaaat?*" she screamed into the phone.

He jerked the phone away from his ear for a moment.

"I'm just so happy," she cried. "Oh, this is so wonderful."

Natasha took the phone back. "Mom, we have to go. I know . . . yes . . . yes, Mom. I'll call you next week. Okay, love you. I'm hanging up now, Mom." She disconnected. "She is so dramatic sometimes. Let's go say hi to Mama Nora." She walked off.

Antonio just shook his head and followed, knowing this was just the beginning. Mama Nora was talking to three women when he and Natasha approached, but she immediately excused herself and opened her arms.

"Oh, here they are," his grandmother said, grabbing Natasha up in a crushing hug. She held her away from her. "You look absolutely stunning, my dear. Doesn't she, Antonio?"

Her tone dared him to do anything other than agree. "Yes, she does. But you're the prettiest girl here."

Grandma Nora blushed and giggled like a schoolgirl. "Go on with you, boy." Gabriel, Serenity, and Ms. Della joined them a moment later. The group continued to chat and, eventually, the four of them stepped away to join Dana, Terri, and Jon when they arrived, leaving the two older women to continue their conversation.

"I just want you to know there are a group of women standing over there with daggers in their eyes," Serenity said to Antonio. "I'm expecting you to protect my girl."

Antonio didn't bother to look. He'd seen them earlier trying to get his attention. "You know I've got her."

His brother's sharp whistle sounded across the yard. He waited a moment until it quieted.

"Do you know what's going on?" Natasha whispered.

Antonio leaned down close to her ear. "We have a special surprise for Grandma. Be back in a minute."

"We're going to do things a little out of order today because we have a special guest," Nate continued. "Grandma, if you would join me here, please."

"What in the world is going on?" his grandmother said as she made her way across the yard. "What are you up to?"

Nate nodded and Etta James's "At Last" came through the speakers. At the same time, Antonio escorted his grandfather out of the house.

Grandma Nora gasped and brought her hands to her chest. "Oh, my word. You're here. My love, you're here." Tears ran freely down her cheeks. She rushed over before Antonio got three steps into the yard.

His grandfather wrapped his arms around her, and she rested her head against his chest. "I can't miss your birthday. And this is our song." They started a slow sway.

Antonio moved back to Natasha, who was crying, too. In fact, there wasn't a dry eye among the hundred or so guests there. He wiped her tears.

"Did you do this?"

"Yeah. She misses him, and because he's been doing so well, the doctor gave us permission for this short visit. I picked him up this morning, and Nate will take him back in a little while."

"You are . . . You are so wonderful, Tonio." She started crying again.

Without giving any thought to who might be watching, he pulled her into his arms and kissed her.

"Guess the cat's out of the bag now," Jon said dryly. "Man, you sure know how to make a scene. First with your grandmother, and now this."

"Hey, if you're gonna do it, go all the way," Gabriel said, giving Antonio a fist bump.

That's exactly where Antonio wanted to go. All the way.

CHAPTER 16

"Now, *that's* what love looks like," Natasha said about Grandma Nora and Papa Fred as everyone sat around eating. Every time she thought about what Antonio had done, her emotions surged. She spotted him not far away, laughing with Gabriel, Jon, and Nate. Something so simple but as priceless as a rare gem.

Serenity nodded. "Girl, those are relationship goals! I hope Gabriel and I will still be like them at that age."

"How long have they been married?" Terri asked.

Natasha wiped barbecue sauce off her fingers. "Sixty years. They need to write a book to show us how to maintain that kind of love." Or how to not mess it up in the first place.

"What they need to include is how to avoid the losers," Dana chimed in, then angled her head thoughtfully. "On second thought, maybe I should go ahead and write that one." The women laughed.

Yep, Natasha could probably pen the one on how *not* to throw away a good man. Some days, especially since she and Antonio had rekindled their relationship, she found herself wallowing in every *what-if* scenario. Would they be married with two or three children by now? Would they have followed through on their joint business dreams? Instead of selling real estate, would she be designing the interiors of spaces here, as well in as neighboring towns and cities? Granted, with him taking over the town's construction company, Antonio had begun to live his dream. However, Natasha had barely scratched the surface of seeing hers blossom. *I lost so much time.*

"Hey, you okay?"

Antonio's voice cut into her mini pity party. "Hey. Yes, just thinking about some things." She scooted her chair over to make it easier for him to get his long legs under the table. "I still can't get over what you did for Mama Nora. What made you think of it?"

"I drove her to Napa to see him, and it broke my heart knowing they had to be separated this way. She'd told me that up until now, the two of them had never spent a night apart. While Grandpa still has some good moments, there's no way any of us can take care of him without medical assistance. I don't know how much time—" His jaw tightened with emotion.

Natasha grasped his hand. "I get it."

"I just want to give them as many good moments as I can."

"And I can tell she appreciates it. Just look at how her face is glowing with joy." Even though Mama Nora had to help her husband with his food, the patience and love with which she'd done it was visible to everyone in attendance.

"I know. Nate's going to have to take him back soon." Antonio shifted his gaze to his grandparents. "He tends to have a harder time the later it gets."

"Then we should crank up the music and let them have one more dance." She stood. "Do they have another special song, or will anything slow work?"

"I'm sure whatever you request will be fine."

"Good. Because while she's dancing with her man, I'll be back so I can dance with mine." His mouth fell open, and she laughed. Nosy neighbors or not, Natasha didn't want to waste another moment in hiding. Life was too short.

She spoke to the DJ for a moment, then asked to borrow his microphone. "May I have everyone's attention, please." After waiting until the chatter died down, she continued. "It's time for the birthday girl to share another dance with the love of her life. I have it on good authority that she's a huge Kenny G fan, and I think "Forever in Love" describes Mama Nora and Papa Fred's story perfectly. And if anyone else is inclined, feel free to join them." Natasha handed the mic back.

Mama Nora was up on her feet before the first notes of the song started. Antonio's father moved quickly to help Papa Fred stand. Natasha could tell by his slow steps that he was tired, and it broke her heart. But the song's slow tempo made it easier for him to follow. She headed back to the table as a few more couples joined them, including Serenity and Gabriel and Terri and Jon.

Antonio stood and met her halfway, claiming a spot on the concrete patio that had been set up as a makeshift dance floor. He pulled her into his embrace and swayed in time with the rhythm. Natasha rested her cheek against his chest, closed her eyes, and inhaled the citrus and woodsy fragrance that always smelled so good on him. The last time they'd danced together this way had been prom night, and she relished being in his arms again.

"I've missed having you in my arms," Antonio said softly near her ear. "My beautiful Tasha, I'm glad you're back in my life." He pulled her closer and placed a kiss on her forehead.

She stared up at him. "I missed you, too, Tonio. More than you know." After the breakup, she'd cried for months, and it had taken her over three years before she'd given another guy the time of day. And that turned out to be disastrous.

"You know, we haven't been out on a real date yet, and I don't mean us cooking in. I want to take you out."

"I'm ready anytime you want to go. But can we go somewhere else? I'd like to eat in peace."

"We'll go wherever you like. Is there anywhere in particular you had in mind?"

"No." As long as she didn't have to worry about people staring at her, he could take her to a fast food joint for all she cared.

"I'll think of some places and let you know."

"It's about time you two got yourselves together. Don't mess it up this time," Ms. Della said as she passed, not breaking stride.

Natasha and Antonio startled slightly, then laughed. He said, "And now it begins."

Natasha did a quick scan of their surroundings and, indeed, saw several pairs of eyes trained on them. But none of it mattered. Not when she had her Tonio back.

* * *

Antonio expertly tied his tie and adjusted it. He surveyed his reflection. This was the man he'd left behind in New York. Six out of seven days a week, he'd had to be impeccably dressed at the firm where he worked or for some other function. He'd been home for more than a month, and tonight would be the first time he donned a suit. It would also be the first time he had gone on an actual date—not counting the dinner in with Natasha—in almost six months, shortly before Thanksgiving.

They had been dating only a couple of months, but the woman had spent the entire evening hinting at her hope of not being alone for the holidays. She'd also had the audacity to suggest that he let her move into his house, so neither of them would have to suffer the loneliness that often accompanied that time of year. Antonio had wasted no time letting her know it wasn't going to happen and had dropped her off at home that night and never looked back. Shaking off the irritating remembrance, he grabbed his suit coat and keys, then left for the florist.

As soon as he walked through the doors of Beautiful Blooms & Blossoms, he saw the owner, Mrs. Dunbar. The petite woman had a line or two bracketing her dark-brown face and a few strands of gray in her hair, but her bright smile hadn't changed.

"Antonio Hayes, it sure has been a long time. How are you?"

"Doing well. I'm here to pick up an order."

"No doubt for Natasha," she said with a little giggle. "So, how long have you two been back together?"

"Mama, can you please give the man his order and not get into his business? How's it going, Antonio?"

"Hey, Casey." He mouthed a thank-you for the save. After being away for so long and not having to worry so much about people asking questions about his personal life, it was taking some time to get used to it again. Her mother came back with the half dozen pink roses arranged in a vase he'd selected, and he said his goodbyes.

In the car, Antonio carefully placed the flowers on the passenger seat. Casey had graciously provided a transportation box to keep them from spilling out of the vase. Two minutes into the drive, his brother called. He engaged the Bluetooth and said, "What's up, Nate?"

"Hey. Noelle wanted to talk to you."

He smiled. "Put my beautiful niece on."

A few seconds passed, then Noelle's sweet voice came through his speakers. "Hi, Uncle Tony."

"Hey, baby girl. How are you?"

"Good. When am I gonna come to your house? You said I could come."

The following Saturday evening, Antonio had completely forgotten about his promise. "I'm not at home right now, but how about I pick you up next Saturday, and you can spend the night with me?"

"*Yay!* Daddy, Uncle Tony said I can spend the night on Saturday," she yelled.

Her delightful squeals filled his heart. He longed to hear that sound from a child of his own.

"Uncle Tony?"

"Yes?" He turned onto Natasha's street.

"How long is it before Saturday?"

"Seven days." She didn't quite have a sense of time, and Antonio knew she would be bugging her parents about it every day.

"But that's a long time," Noelle said sadly.

"It'll go by fast, sweetheart. I promise." He parked and shut off the engine. "How about I come by in the middle of the week? That way you'll get to see me two times."

"Okay," she said, her voice brightening. "I love you, Uncle."

"Love you, too, Noelle." He leaned his head back as his emotions surged. Antonio loved that little girl as if she were his own. He'd flown down for her birth, and she'd stolen his heart from the moment April placed her in his arms and Noelle stared up at him with her big brown eyes.

Antonio's thoughts shifted to his date with Natasha. He could admit the thought of them having children had crossed his mind more than once. Back then he'd had his life all mapped out: graduate, work with his uncle for a while, marry Natasha and have two or three children, and open his own construction company. Until he moved back to Firefly Lake, his only big achievement had been graduating with his dual degrees. He could add owning the company to his list, but the jury was still out on whether he'd get that third one.

He got out and slipped into his suit coat before reaching back inside for the flowers. On his way to the door, he studied Natasha's house. Her two-bedroom home was located in one of the newer developments and had a small porch just wide enough for the chair and bistro table she had there. Antonio rang her doorbell as his gaze took in the manicured lawn. Did she have a lawn care service, or did she take care of it herself? The thought of her doing her own yard didn't sit well with him.

Antonio turned at the sound of the door opening. Once again, she'd left him speechless. She had on another dress that outlined her curves, this one a burnt-orange color that complemented her rich, dark-brown skin. "Hey, beautiful."

"Hi." Natasha held the door open for him. "Wow, you look good."

Chuckling, he handed her the flowers. "Thanks. These are for you." He bent and placed a sweet kiss on her lips.

"Thank you. They're gorgeous, and I can't believe you remembered that I love pink roses."

"I remember a lot of things," he said, holding her gaze. Like the way she slowly licked the strawberry ice cream all around the cone or how she always used to climb onto his lap so they could read together.

"And I remember everything." She placed the vase in the center of her coffee table, then picked up her purse and jacket. "Ready?"

Still trying to decipher what she meant, he said, "I am. I just hope there isn't a lot of traffic." He led her out to his car. The drive to San Francisco would take about an hour. He'd googled it, and so far the roads weren't too congested. He had made reservations for seven but opted to leave two hours earlier, just in case.

"There's always traffic these days, unless you leave before five in the morning or eight or nine at night."

"I guess things have changed since I left." As he drove, Antonio noticed far more commercial buildings and housing developments along the way, which definitely accounted for the increase in cars on the road.

"Ooh, I love this song." Natasha did a little dance in her seat as she sang along with India Arie's "Brown Skin."

A smile tipped the corner of his mouth. She loved music, and no matter where she happened to be, she would often sing or dance along. As he listened to the words, he couldn't help but think about Natasha's brown skin and how much he wanted to touch and caress every inch of it. Antonio jerked his head in Natasha's direction when he felt her hand on his thigh. "What are you doing?"

"Telling you how much I love *your* brown skin." Natasha walked her fingers up his thigh.

Antonio clamped down on her hand with his to halt her progress. "Unless you're ready for me to pull over and show you just how much I love yours, I'm going to need you to keep your hands to yourself." She had him so aroused, it wouldn't take much for him to make good on his promise.

Her eyes sparkled with mischief. "Well, since I really want this dinner, I'll keep my hands to myself. For now."

He didn't even want to know what that last part meant. All his efforts to take things at a slower pace crumbled each time she made a bold statement like this one. To take his mind off all the ways he wanted to seduce her, he asked about her favorite music artists. They passed the remainder of the drive discussing music, artists, and concerts they wanted to attend.

"Is the restaurant far from Pier 39?" she asked as he exited the freeway.

"Not too far, why?"

"I was thinking that since we're about thirty minutes early, can we stop at the Chocolate Store? Serenity asked me to bring her more chocolate for the desserts she makes. It's only a block or two away from the pier."

"Sure." Antonio followed all the turns to Embarcadero and her directions to the store. "I don't see any parking." The streets were crowded with cars and people.

"Don't worry about parking. Just drop me off near the store and circle the block. It won't take long to get what I need. I'll be in and out."

He wasn't too keen on the idea, seeing all the men out and about, but had no other choice if they planned to make their reservation. After he pulled into a no-parking zone near the store, Natasha hopped out and strutted up the street. For a second, Antonio toyed with just waiting there, but he didn't want to risk a ticket, so he merged onto the street.

By the time he made it back around, he spotted her coming out of the store with a large bag. He frowned when he saw a man walk up and try to engage Natasha in conversation. She seemed to be politely trying to step around him, but the man placed a hand on her arm. Antonio never considered himself a jealous person, but at that moment it swept through him like wildfire. He eased to the curb and almost jumped out of the car until he saw Natasha point his way.

The man had the decency to back off, and called out, "My bad, brother."

"Yeah, yo' bad," Antonio muttered.

"Perfect timing," Natasha said, sliding into the seat.

"So, what was he saying?"

She waved a dismissive hand. "He wanted to know if I was free for dinner."

Antonio grunted and eased into the traffic. "Next time I'll just park and come inside with you."

Shifting in her seat, she said, "Do I hear a bit of jealousy in your voice?"

"Maybe?" More like a *lot* of jealousy. She was a beautiful woman, though, so it was probably unreasonable for him to never want another man to hit on her. He slanted her a quick glance and saw her smiling. "What?"

"I haven't had anyone to be jealous about another man talking to me in a long while." She laid a hand on his thigh. "But you don't have to worry, Tonio. I don't want anyone but you."

"Same goes for you. So, did you get what you needed?"

"Yep. Now Serenity will have plenty of chocolate for those strawberries and truffles she makes. The truffles are second on my list of weaknesses behind the dipped strawberries."

He wanted to tell her she was quickly rising to the top of *his* list of weaknesses. It had taken him only a few short weeks to fall for her again, despite trying to convince himself of the risks.

CHAPTER 17

Natasha studied Antonio after the server took the food orders and left their drinks. The man looked breathtakingly handsome in the navy suit, and she knew by the fit it had been expressly tailored for him. And with his height and sexy stroll, he could grace the runway of any fashion show. She imagined this was how he'd dressed every day while working at the firm in New York, and she couldn't decide which she preferred—the laid-back, jeans-wearing version or this polished businessman one. *It's a good thing I can have both.*

"I meant to ask you if everything's okay. I noticed you sitting in your car for a moment at my house," she said.

Antonio seemingly thought for a moment. "Oh, yeah. Fine. I was talking to Noelle. She called to remind me that I still hadn't let her know when she could spend the night with me. Since I live alone, apparently, I need the company."

She smiled. "Aw, aren't you a cool uncle. Are you going to do it?"

"Absolutely. Next Saturday. We're going to have a ball— movies, popcorn, ice cream, staying up late. All the things a parent would most likely veto." He sipped his wine.

Natasha giggled. "You are so wrong. I bet you won't do that when you have your own. I'm sorry. I didn't mean—" The words slipped out before she could stop them. They'd talked about having children and both had wanted them— she still did. She just didn't want him to think she was try- ing to push him in any direction so soon.

Antonio reached for her hand. "Whatever you're thinking, don't. This is us, Tasha. You can say or ask anything and not have to worry about me taking it a certain way. We've always been able to talk to each other about everything, I don't want that to change. And I know what you meant." He gave her hand a little squeeze. "You're right, I probably won't let my child do that . . . well, not all the time," he added with a wink. "You know how much I want kids, so if I'm blessed enough to ever have them, I'm going to spoil them a little."

This man made it extremely difficult not to jump all the way in emotionally. She'd already admitted to herself that a part of her never stopped loving him, but that part appeared to be spreading like a brushfire across her heart, and she had no idea how to slow it down. Natasha already knew Antonio would be an incredible father. She'd watched him with his niece that night at the town meeting, and the way he had interacted with the little girl melted Natasha's heart. "You're really good with her, and it's great that she remembers you."

"While I was living in New York, we'd FaceTime every week. She stole my heart the day she was born, and even though I knew I couldn't be here, I wanted to be part of her life. Being here to watch her grow up was one of the reasons I wanted to come home."

"What's the other reason?"

He smiled faintly. "I was tired of working sixty or more hours every week and missed the slower pace of home. I wanted a career change, and I missed my family. With Grandpa not doing that great, it just seemed like the right time to come back."

"That's a lot of hours." She'd be burned out, too, if she had to work that many hours every week. When did he have time to relax? He had mentioned that he and his ex-wife had wanted different things, but did those long work hours also contribute to the demise of his marriage? They'd talked about it briefly, and she wanted to ask but figured it might be best to wait until he brought it up again. Natasha decided to change the subject. "Did you decide to take over the construction company before you moved back?"

Antonio shook his head. "Nope. I had planned to take a month or so off, then decide what to do. He sprang the offer on me that first day I saw you." He quieted for a few seconds. "Didn't think we'd be here this way."

"That makes two of us, but I'm so glad we are."

"So am I."

The server returned with their food, and they continued to converse over the meal. Although they both had grown and changed, in all the ways that counted, they were still the same. Natasha could spend hours with him and never run out of things to talk about. By the time they left, she wasn't ready to head back home.

As if reading her mind, he asked, "It's not too late. Do you want to head over to Pier 39 for a while?"

"I'd love to." This time they were lucky enough to find

parking across the street from the pier. He entwined their fingers, and she marveled at how perfectly their hands fit.

"I haven't been here since we graduated from high school," Antonio said as they strolled past the many shops and eateries toward the back of the pier.

It had been their last date right before they both left for college. It was then that he'd given her the promise ring. Natasha leaned against the railing and stared out at the water and the Golden Gate Bridge in the distance. The breeze kicked up, and she shivered.

"Cold?" He stood behind her and wrapped his arms around her middle. "We can head back if you want."

"Not yet. It's peaceful out here." His body heat surrounded her and warmed her from the inside out. "You know, I still have the necklace you gave me for my sweet sixteen and the promise ring." She twisted around and gazed up at him to gauge his reaction.

"Really? What made you keep them? Especially after..."

Natasha faced the water. "For a long time I didn't know, then I realized it was because I wanted to hold on to a part of you."

Antonio turned her in his arms. "Baby," he whispered as his head descended, and he slanted his mouth over hers.

She moaned as their tongues danced slowly, sensually. He pressed closer, deepening the kiss. They stood under the moonlight, kissing, as the water lapped against the rocks. She wrapped her arms around his waist and urged him closer still, wanting to feel every inch of his hard body against hers.

Antonio eased back, still gifting her with fleeting kisses along her jaw. "We should probably head back."

"Mm-hmm." And she planned for them to pick up where they left off once they got back to her place.

Natasha's nerves were stretched tight by the time she and Antonio made it home later that evening. The kisses and intimate touches had her on fire and forced her to recall just what she'd been missing. "Can I get you anything? I have water, tea, wine, coffee."

He slowly shook his head as he closed the distance between them. "The only thing I want right now is you."

The kisses began again, and she didn't know how much more she could take. Her arms slid up the hard wall of his chest and circled his neck. She moved closer to him and heard his deep groan. Every stroke of his tongue pushed her closer to the point of no return until nothing remained except thoughts of him and the pleasure he was giving her. "Make love to me, Tonio," she whispered against his lips.

Antonio's head came up sharply, his breathing ragged. "Tasha, are you—"

Natasha placed a finger to his lips. "Don't talk. Just love me."

Without a word, he swept her into his arms. "Bedroom?"

"Down the hall, second door on the left." She clung to him as he hurried in that direction. Once there, he placed her on her feet, and she turned on the nightstand lamp. It provided just enough light to give the room a romantic atmosphere. Without taking his eyes off her, he removed his jacket and tie and tossed them on the chair in the corner. Her pulse skipped as he unbuttoned his shirt and added it to the growing pile of clothes. She waited for him to continue, but he didn't. Instead, he slowly and sensually removed her dress, kissing her until she lay flat on the bed.

Antonio stepped back and finished undressing, then donned a condom.

Natasha smiled. "I see a few things that are different." His body was a pure work of art, from his muscular chest and abs to his strong thighs. He also had an intricately designed tattoo that spanned the right side of his chest and shoulder. He came back to the bed and slowly finished undressing Natasha, kissing and licking his way up her body. Desire raced through her body, and she trembled as his tongue made sweeping, swirling motions inside her mouth. He brought his hands up to frame her face and deepened the kiss, devouring her with an intensity that left her breathless.

He lifted his head. "Are you sure about this, Tasha?"

"Very sure. Have I told you how much I love your eyes?" She'd been mesmerized by them from the first, and nothing had changed.

Chuckling, his hand swept down her body. "You might have mentioned it once or twice. Have I told you how beautiful you are, how beautiful you've always been to me?"

A smile curved her lips. "You might have mentioned it a time or two." She gasped softly as his hands skated across her torso and up to the curve of her breasts, gently caressing each one and teasing the sensitive peaks. Shifting slightly, he replaced his hands with his tongue—sucking and nibbling the hardened buds—and she cried out.

"I love touching you, kissing you," Antonio murmured.

"Tonio." Natasha needed him inside her.

"I know, baby. I feel it, too. But I want to take my time."

His hands roamed over her body, singeing her in every spot he touched. She squirmed and moaned beneath his caress as liquid fire spread through her. Without breaking the seal of their mouths, Antonio shifted their bodies and guided himself slowly, inch by incredible inch, inside her. They both groaned. Their eyes held as he started a slow rhythm. The way he moved inside her was unlike anything Natasha had ever experienced. She wrapped her legs around his back and gripped his shoulders.

"Tasha." He called her name almost reverently. Antonio slowed his movements, bent, and kissed her softly, thoroughly.

This went way beyond sex. He used a finger to trace her lips and gazed at her with such tenderness, tears pooled in her eyes. He increased the tempo again, and her desire spiraled. The sensation started deep in her belly and flared out to every part of her body. He plunged faster, each stroke coming harder, and she arched up to meet them. She exploded with white-hot pleasure, shaking uncontrollably and screaming out his name again.

He went rigid, then bucked inside her. Throwing back his head, he groaned out her name. "My sweet Tasha," he murmured. His head fell limply forward, and he shuddered before collapsing on top of her. He rolled to his side and cradled her in his arms, both breathing heavily.

As Natasha lay there with her eyes closed, waiting for her heart rate to slow, she realized she was in danger of losing her heart to him all over again.

CHAPTER 18

Antonio woke up and stared down at the woman in his arms. He'd dreamed about making love to Natasha again, and his fantasies didn't come close to the real thing. Though things were progressing faster than he'd anticipated, he didn't have one regret about tonight. And even after all these years, she still had the ability to affect him like no other woman. He was enjoying getting to know her all over again, and it had been the first date in a long while where he didn't have to worry about putting up a front, like with his ex and the few others he'd dated afterward. Antonio could be the down-to-earth man he'd always been without the criticism. Natasha had shocked him, though, when she confessed to still having the gifts he'd given her. There was nothing she could have said that would've meant more to him, and he'd fallen a little harder.

He carefully pushed back the hair covering her eyes. She'd cut the long style she used to wear, and now the strands fell just below her ear. It gave her a more sophisticated appearance and enhanced her beauty, and he loved the change. Antonio glanced over his shoulder at the nightstand clock and sighed. *It's almost two.* He wanted nothing more than to wake up next to her. But this was Firefly Lake, not New York, and all hell would break loose if folks found out he'd spent the night. He and Natasha were adults, but neither of them needed to deal with a lecture from the nosy townsfolk who acted as if they were the morality police. She slept so peacefully, he didn't want to wake her, but he didn't have a choice.

"Tasha," Antonio called softly, placing fleeting kisses on her lips and cheek. "Wake up, baby."

Natasha groaned and snuggled deeper in his arms. "Five more minutes."

He laughed softly. "You can have all the minutes you need once I leave."

Her head popped up. "Antonio? What time is it?"

He idly ran his hand up and down her spine. "Relax, sweetheart. It's just after two. I need to go."

She flipped over onto her back. "I know."

Antonio left the bed and got dressed. He shoved his tie into his pocket, then leaned down and kissed her slowly and thoroughly. "Come lock the door." She flipped the covers back and padded naked across the room to the closet. Just the sight of her tempted him to stay for just one more round.

Yawning, she slipped her arms into a short robe and tied the belt. "Are you going to be busy tomorrow?" Natasha shook her head. "I mean later today."

"Mowing the lawn and dinner at my parents. What about you?"

"Sleeping in."

He laughed, took her hand, and led her to the front. "I'll

call you tomorrow night." Unable to resist, he kissed her once more. "Sleep well."

"You too. Drive carefully." She ran her hand down his chest and abs and gave him a sleepy smile.

Antonio's body reacted with lightning speed. *Time to go.* He quickly closed the door behind him and loped down the driveway to his car, knowing he had a cold shower waiting for him at home.

* * *

Antonio woke up the next morning to the insistent chime of his phone. He blindly reached for it, knocking it to the floor. He muttered a curse and leaned over the bed to find it. Sitting up, he squinted at the display and read the text from his brother: *FYI, Mom found out about your date last night, so get ready . . . lol!*

He flopped back against the pillow and groaned. *Here we go again.* He typed back: *Thanks for the warning. I expect you to do your big-brother duty and run interference.* Tossing the phone aside, Antonio lay there a while longer, thinking about Natasha. As exhausted as he'd been last night, it had taken him almost two hours after showering to fall asleep because of all the emotional turmoil in his mind. They had decided to go slow, but after last night, he wasn't sure if he wanted *slow* anymore. His phone buzzed again. He sat up and went still when he saw a message from Lori: *Antonio, I know it's been a while. You didn't respond to my voicemail a few weeks ago, but I really need to talk to you. I miss you. I miss us. Please call me.*

Antonio couldn't believe her audacity. If she'd been this

interested in talking, maybe they could've salvaged their marriage. He started to ignore it, like he'd done the first time, but then sent back a short reply: *There's nothing to talk about. We've both moved on, so let's just leave it.*

Going back to sleep was out of the question now, so Antonio decided to go for a run before doing his yard. He used to start his day with at least two cups of coffee but realized that he hadn't drunk more than two cups in the past week, opting for smoothies instead. His body felt better because of it.

He headed back to his favorite park, did two miles, and came back home to tackle the lawn. Afterward, he showered and powered up his laptop to work on a design for a house. He still hadn't made a decision on whether to buy or build, but he wanted to have the option available whenever he was ready. Unlike other bigger cities, Firefly Lake still had a lot of open land for purchase, and his first choice would be something that backed one of the lakes. Once again his thoughts strayed to Natasha. He knew she loved being near the water, and he could see them enjoying sitting there in the evenings to unwind. Antonio brought his thoughts to a screeching halt. *I'm getting way ahead of myself.*

Seeing that it was just about time to leave for his parents' house, he saved the file and shut down everything.

He made the short drive over, and before he could get in the door good, his mother started in.

"Why didn't you tell me you and Natasha were dating? I had to find out from someone else."

"Mom, you found out the day of Grandma's party, just like everybody else. I brought Natasha, remember? No, I didn't make a grand announcement, but I'm sure you saw us together."

"And I have to say they make such a cute couple," April said, placing two platters on the dining room table. "You need me to get anything else, Mom?"

His mother surveyed the table laden with serving dishes. "No, baby. I think that's it. I think we're ready."

"I'll go let everyone know," Antonio said, nearly sprinting out of the room. His mother acted like he'd never dated before. He stuck his head in the family room, where his father and brother were watching a basketball playoff game. "Dinner." Noelle, who had been asleep when he arrived, sat up on the sofa next to Nate, somewhat disoriented. Her eyes cleared and she noticed Antonio in the doorway.

"Uncle Tony, is it time to go to your house yet?" Noelle asked around a yawn.

He scooped her up in his arms. "Not yet. It's only been one day. We have six more to go. But how about you sit next to me at dinner today, and we can talk about what we're going to do. What do you think?"

Her eyes lit up, and she nodded vigorously. "Okay." She threw her arms around him and kissed his cheek.

Antonio would give anything to have this every day. He put her on his shoulders as they went back to the dining room, and her squeals of delight made him smile. His grandmother was at the table when he returned. Noelle giggled when he dipped his head to kiss the family's matriarch. He placed his niece in her booster seat and took the chair next to her. Everyone filled plates and started in on the meal.

"So, I heard you and Natasha went out last night," his mother said casually.

"We went out to dinner."

"And you spent the night at her house."

He choked on the lemonade he'd just swallowed. "What?" he croaked, trying to clear his throat. "I don't know who told you that, but I did not spend the night. I brought her home and stayed for a while talking, then *went home*." Okay, so he just didn't say what kind of talking they did. He'd heard everything her body said.

He tried to engage Noelle in conversation, but his mother was not going to let up.

Nate's low chuckle floated across the table. "What time is the groundbreaking ceremony for the condos next Saturday?"

Antonio sent his brother a grateful look. His grandmother smiled knowingly. "It's at eleven. Are you all going to be there?"

"Definitely," his father answered. "It's going to be nice having a place for some of the younger folks."

"And a few of the older folks who mentioned wanting to downsize."

His mother opened her mouth, no doubt to return to her favorite subject, but his brother and sister-in-law kept steering the conversation to other topics. Antonio owed them dinner or something.

Finally, his mother cut in, "You should invite her over for Sunday next week."

Antonio paused. "I'll check and see what her schedule is like and let you know." The last time he'd had a woman at his family's dinner table was his ex-wife, during her one and only visit to Firefly Lake shortly after their marriage.

After they'd left, she'd complained about everything from the color scheme to the fact that everyone had come casual except her. She felt Sunday dinners should mean dressing up. He wouldn't have to worry about that with Natasha. She fit in well with his family . . . and with him.

* * *

"Do you know how long this thing is supposed to last?" Natasha whispered to Antonio Saturday morning as the town gathered for the groundbreaking ceremony for the new building project. The mayor had been talking for a good fifteen minutes already.

Antonio shrugged. "I figured it would be a welcome, toss some dirt with a shovel, a cheer, and done. Not sure why he needed an entire agenda of activities."

She bit her lip to stifle a giggle. "I see you still don't have patience for long, drawn-out stuff."

He took a peek at his watch again. "Yeah, no. I really wanted to skip the whole thing. I don't need to be up there, front and center."

"Of course you do," she said, placing a comforting hand on his back. "This is big news for this little town. One of their own is making dreams come true and pumping money into the economy. The mayor didn't mention it at the town meeting last month, but I heard that in addition to the other development company wanting to go big, they'd also planned to bring in their own folks, instead of using Davenport employees first, then supplementing, as agreed. Just shady all around."

"Well, at least we don't have to worry about that."

"Antonio, where are you?" The mayor shielded his eyes from the sunlight as he searched the crowd.

"That's your cue, handsome."

Chuckling, Antonio shook his head, then weaved his way through the throngs of people to reach the front.

Natasha couldn't have been any prouder to see him up there, living out his dreams. She saw Serenity and Dana a few feet away and made her way over to them.

"I need the mayor to wrap it up," Serenity said. "I have to get home and start the prep for our dinner tonight."

"Girl, you know Mayor Brewer has always been long-winded. Somebody needs to go up there and tell him to hush." Dana waved a hand. "We don't need to know the history of how this project came about and all the pitfalls and delays that happened along the way. Get. To. The. Point."

"Amen," Natasha said. She almost laughed at the look of irritation Antonio kept throwing at the mayor. Most people wouldn't notice the subtle change in his expression, but because she'd known Antonio most of his life, she could tell. The man wrapped up his comments a few minutes later. *Finally.* Along with the mayor and Antonio, Mr. Davenport and two other town officials joined them. Each held a shovel with a yellow ribbon. After a count of three, they all dug in and flipped the dirt. A loud round of applause went up, and people rushed over to congratulate them.

Dana leaned close to Natasha. "You might as well either make yourself comfortable and wait or catch up with Antonio later, because those folks are going to keep him hemmed up for hours."

"Looks that way." Natasha caught Antonio's gaze and held her hand up to her ear, intimating that she'd call him later. He gave her an imperceptible nod and went back to greeting the long line of people. She faced Serenity. "What color scheme are you thinking for tonight?" She often brought the table linens and centerpieces.

"I have no idea. Something spring-ish sounds good. I'm thinking of using my plain white china, so whatever colors you come up with will be fine."

"Okay, I'll see what I have at the house." She spoke to her two friends a moment longer, then made her way to her car. As she settled in the seat, her cell rang. She frowned, not recognizing the number, but answered.

"Hello, is this Natasha Baldwin?'

"May I ask who's calling?"

"My name is Jenny McBride. I got your name from Daphne Lockett. I saw the redesigned bedroom you did for her, and I wanted to hire you to do mine."

She almost let out an excited shout but reined herself in. "Ms. McBride, I'd be happy to set up a meeting to discuss your needs. What's your availability for next week?" Natasha put the phone on speaker, then accessed her calendar. She had something just about every day. "I can meet with you on Tuesday or Wednesday after four, if either of those days works."

"I have to leave town on Tuesday morning, and I won't be back until late Thursday. Perhaps we can meet the following week."

She debated with herself for a minute about offering to drive over today. The supper club wouldn't start for another four hours, and it wouldn't take long for Natasha to select what she wanted for the table. "We can do that, but I have a couple of hours today, if you like. I can stop by and get some preliminary information from you, and then we can schedule another appointment for when you get back."

"Oh, that would be wonderful."

"This is my cell, so you can text me your address. I can be there around one."

"Yes, I'll do that. Thank you so much."

"You're welcome, and thank you." As soon as she disconnected, she let out a shout. *"Yes!"*

"What are you so happy about?"

Natasha gasped sharply and jumped, hitting her knee on the steering wheel. Pain shot through her leg, and she moaned. She clutched her chest and jerked around. "Oh my goodness, Antonio. You scared me to death." She sucked in a couple of deep breaths and let them out slowly, trying to slow her heart rate.

"Sorry." Antonio squatted down beside the open door and brought her hand to his lips. "You okay?"

She nodded. The way he turned those mesmerizing eyes on her made her heartbeat ramp right back up. "How did you get out here so fast? I thought you'd be over there smiling and taking pictures forever."

"You know I've never liked being in front of the cameras, so I did what I do best . . . sneak away."

Laughter bubbled up in her. "For somebody who spent years in front of one camera or another while playing ball, I can't believe you're not used to it."

"I never liked it then, either. So, what's going on?"

"I just got another interior design job," she sang. Natasha practically danced in her seat.

A smile lit his face. "Congrats, baby. I'm so proud of you. You're getting closer to being able to quit your day job."

"Yes, I am. It's really starting to build from word of mouth, and I plan to do whatever it takes to make it happen this time."

"If there's anything I can do to help, let me know." Antonio leaned in and kissed her.

What started as a simple touching of lips turned into a scorching, red-hot explosion of passion in a nanosecond. His hand cupped the back of her neck, drawing her closer. Natasha lost all thoughts of place and time. The only thing that mattered was him and the way he made her feel. At length, he eased back. She rested her forehead against his. "Tonio." Her body trembled and struggled for calm.

"I know. I'm right there with you. I should probably let you get going before you get us into trouble."

Her mouth fell open, and he laughed. "*Me?* I'm not the one nearly pulling somebody out of the car and on top of you. You're the one who's trouble. Got me out here engaging in all this PDA. If I see a picture in the local paper, I'm coming after you."

Still laughing, he asked, "And once you catch me, what are you going to do with me?"

The deep timbre of his voice poured over her like warm honey. "Okay, go. Don't you need to pick up Noelle or something?"

"You trying to get rid of me?" Antonio placed a hand over his heart. "I'm hurt."

She playfully shoved him in the chest, unable to hide her smile. "You ain't hurt. Bye, trouble."

"What are you doing for the rest of the day?"

"I'm going to meet with this new client, then supper club."

He rose to his full height. "Have fun, and tell the ladies I said hello."

"I will, and you and Noelle have a great time. Try not to spoil her too much."

"No promises on that front." Leaning down, he kissed her once more, then closed the door and stepped back.

Natasha threw up a wave as she drove off, her body still humming with desire. *That man is going to get me in so much trouble.*

CHAPTER 19

"Girl, we thought you got lost or something." Serenity hugged Natasha and pulled her inside the house.

"I know. I got another design referral after I left today," Natasha said, following her friend to the kitchen. "Hey, y'all. Sorry I'm late." She hugged Terri and Dana. "I was telling Serenity I got another design referral and went over to get some preliminary information." She unearthed a pale-blue tablecloth, candles with holders, a small bouquet of flowers, and a vase from a large reusable grocery bag.

Dana helped her cover the table. "Which translates to you getting caught up in color schemes, paint swabs, and a whole host of things."

"I don't know what you're talking about," Natasha lied with a straight face. That's exactly what had happened. The short visit she'd planned turned into more than three hours, especially when the woman decided she also wanted to update her living and family rooms in anticipation of an upcoming visit from her in-laws. It never took long for her to lose herself. She added the place settings, navy napkins, navy candles in crystal holders, and the mixed bouquet of blue, purple, and white flowers.

Terri handed Natasha a glass of wine. "Forget the whole interior design thing. I want an update on you and Antonio. A few of the nurses were talking about how good he looked today at the ceremony. They also noticed he only had eyes for you. So, just sit yourself down and spill *all* the tea."

The women broke out in a fit of laughter, and Natasha said, "I can't even take a sip of wine or eat before you start?"

"No!" they all chorused, which brought on more amusement.

"Fine." She plopped down in the nearest chair and rolled her eyes in mock disdain. "We went to San Francisco last weekend for dinner, walked along Pier 39, then went back to my house." She took a long sip of her wine and saw the moment her friends realized what she meant.

"Well, damn, you two aren't wasting any time," Dana said. "Normally I'd be asking you if you're moving too fast, but it's not like you and Tony don't know each other. So I can see how things heated up quickly."

"Girl, whew." Terri fanned herself. "By the look on your face, I'm assuming the brother can bring it in the bedroom."

Natasha fell back against the seat and released a satisfied sigh. "Oh my goodness, *yessss*."

Serenity placed a large platter filled with hearty appetizers in the center of the table. "Sounds like you've fallen in love with him all over again."

She sobered. "He makes it hard not to fall for him." On some level, she'd always known it would be easy to fall back in love with Antonio. It didn't help that he was the same sweet, sensitive guy who stole her heart the first time.

She'd already admitted to herself that a small part of her never stopped loving him, but she hadn't confessed it out loud for fear of it ruining everything. Irrational? Maybe. But Natasha didn't want to risk it because she was already in too deep.

Serenity gave Natasha's shoulders a squeeze. "Take it one day at a time, just like you told me. I have a feeling things will straighten themselves out."

"I hope so. I don't want—" She cut herself off. "Enough about Antonio and me. What're all these fabulous creations that smell so heavenly?"

Thankfully, her friends took the hint and let the subject drop.

"I kind of liked the appetizer theme we did last year and wanted to do it again." Serenity pointed as she spoke. "We have two kinds of bruschetta—chicken, bacon, and ranch, and beef tenderloin with caramelized onions and mushrooms—pastry-wrapped asparagus with Parmesan, spinach dip with sliced baguette, and shrimp cocktail. Of course, dessert will include those strawberries and chocolate cups."

Natasha rubbed her hands together. "My kind of meal." She grabbed a plate and added some of everything, and the other ladies did the same. Conversation flowed around the table about the week's escapades, while music played in the background. "Okay, am I the only one who thinks these chicken and beef bruschetta are amazing? These things are so good."

"Girl, no. Didn't you see me add two more of each to my plate?" Terri said, biting into a chicken one. "I need to find a gym soon because I overeat every time we get together."

Serenity chuckled. "Terri, all that running around the ER is exercise enough."

She made a show of thinking. "You know what, you've got a point." She scooped up more spinach dip and shrimp cocktail.

Dana topped off everyone's wine. "Serenity, you're not drinking wine tonight?"

A smile played around the corner of her mouth, and she shook her head. "I won't be drinking wine for the next several months."

They all froze with their glasses halfway to their mouths. Natasha asked, "Are you saying what I think you are?"

"Yes!" she said excitedly. "Gabriel and I are having a baby. And baby Cunningham is going to need all three of you as godmothers."

"I am so happy for you guys. That wedding night must have been all that and more," Natasha added, wiggling her eyebrows.

"So much more, my sister. *So* much more."

After a round of congratulations and hugs, they finished the meal. Serenity and Dana went to the kitchen for the dessert, and Natasha noticed Terri had gotten a little quiet. "Hey, you okay?"

"Yeah, fine." Terri hastily dabbed at the moisture in her eyes. "Just happy for them."

She sensed it was more than that. "You and Jon okay?"

"Some days I think yes, but others..." Terri shrugged. "And before you ask, no, I don't think he's cheating or anything like that. It's mostly him being preoccupied with work. Moving here was supposed to allow us to slow down some and start a family, but that hasn't happened."

She could see how Serenity's news could put a damper on things because Terri wanted the same. "Maybe you two need to get away for a little while, so you can talk without the stress of your jobs."

"Maybe. Please don't say anything to Serenity. You know she'll worry, and that's the last think I want. Jon and I will be okay. His caseload has increased. Hopefully, once they bring in the new attorney, it'll drop back down." She tried to smile.

"I won't, but if you need to talk, call me anytime. Promise me. That's what sister-friends do."

"I will. Now, no more of this. We have some celebrating to do."

"Natasha, you cannot eat all the strawberries. Dana and Terri, I suggest you get yours first," Serenity added as she and Dana returned, placing the berries in front of Terri. Dana placed another small plate with the molded chocolate cups filled with chopped raspberries and strawberries next to the first one.

"I need extra strawberries after what happened to my other ones," Natasha muttered, her anger rising all over again, thinking about what Kathleen had done.

Dana picked up a berry. "What are you talking about?"

She told them what Kathleen had done and how she'd replaced the eaten ones with hers. "The next day, she had the nerve to ask me if my clients enjoyed their treat. I was so mad, I wanted to knock that smug smile off her face."

Serenity frowned. "Why didn't you tell me? I would've made you more. That woman is truly out of her mind. You really need to talk to George about this mess."

"I did," she said, snagging a strawberry and a chocolate cup. "He said he's going to be watching her because it isn't the first time she's done something like this." Natasha groaned. "These are the best things ever. Strawberries, chocolate . . . there's nothing better."

"Since we're sharing news," Dana started, "I've been asked to fill in for a small symphony orchestra for a couple of weeks in Southern California. Their piano player is recovering from a surgical procedure. I went to school with one of the members, and she recommended me. Thank goodness I still practice every day."

"I am so happy for you, girl. I know you've been wanting to get back out there," Natasha said. They toasted Dana's good news. "When are you leaving?"

"The end of next week. I've been studying and practicing the music ever since I found out, but I need to get down there so I can practice with the orchestra before the performances."

"Which means you'll be gone for close to a month?" Terri asked.

"Pretty much. And y'all better not be having all these supper clubs without me." She popped the rest of a chocolate cup into her mouth. After chewing, she added, "Or at least send me a care package."

"We got you, sis," Serenity said. They chatted a little longer about Dana's itinerary. Then Serenity said, "Tasha, I know you said no more Antonio talk, but are you two hooking up after you leave here?"

"No. He's got another date tonight with his niece. Apparently, she invited herself to spend the night."

"He's keeping her overnight?" Dana asked with surprise.

"Yes, and he sounded so excited."

"Maybe he's practicing for when he has his own," she mumbled.

Natasha skewered Dana with a look. "Don't try to act all innocent. I heard that comment." She'd be lying if she didn't say the thought had crossed her mind as well. She could imagine him holding their child. *Whoa, girl! You are getting way ahead of yourself,* her inner voice chimed. This time she agreed with the annoying voice. They hadn't even made it to the two-month mark yet. Dating. That's all she needed to concentrate on right now. No babies, no nothing. Just. Dating.

* * *

Antonio had barely gotten out of his car when he heard Noelle's voice. The screen door opened, and she greeted him with a grin stretching across her face.

"Uncle Tony, I'm ready to go with you." Noelle came out onto the porch, dragging a bag that was almost as big as her. She staggered a little, and Nate steadied her. He tried to take the bag. "No, Daddy. I can do it."

Antonio chuckled as he stepped up onto the porch. He and Nate shared a brotherly hug. "You and April ready for your night alone?"

"You'd better believe it. And this one here," Nate said, pointing at Noelle, "has been sitting in front of the door for the past ten minutes."

"That's because she knows we're going to have fun tonight. Let me go say hi to your mama, and then we can go, okay?" Antonio picked her and the bag up in one arm.

April met them near the door. "I thought I heard your voice." She hugged Antonio. "You sure you're ready to keep her all night? She can be a handful."

He tickled Noelle, and her little giggles filled the room. "We'll be fine, right, Noelle?"

"Yes," she said, clapping her hands. "Let's *gooo*."

"Hold on a minute. I know we talked about what she likes, but I forgot to ask if she's allergic to anything."

"Sleep," April said with a snort. "But seriously, nothing so far." She leaned up and kissed her daughter. "You be good and listen to Uncle Tony, okay? Love you, baby."

"Okay. Love you."

"You two have fun and try not to make another one of these while we're gone." He gestured to Noelle.

Nate slid his arm around April and nuzzled her neck. "No promises."

She blushed and playfully swatted him. "Cut it out."

Laughing, Antonio retraced his steps to the car. Nate followed with Noelle's car seat. Antonio watched his brother strap it in and couldn't believe all that went into it. With an engineering degree, it should be a piece of cake to install it, but gone were the days of sliding the seat belt through, snapping it into place, and leaving. Now it was an entire process.

Once Nate finished, he kissed Noelle, strapped her in, and reiterated April's instructions. "Love you, angel girl."

"Love you, Daddy."

Nate closed her door. "If you need us to pick her up, call."

Antonio slapped his brother on the back. "Man, relax. She'll be back tomorrow. We'll be fine. I've got pizza, ice cream, and Disney Plus." The only time he'd seen his normally unflappable brother nervous was when it came to his wife and daughter. Antonio suspected he'd be the same way. "Later." He slid in behind the wheel, backed down the driveway, and headed home. Noelle kept up a running dialogue about all the shows she wanted to watch.

"Did you hang my picture up, Uncle Tony?"

"I sure did." He'd forgotten about it until yesterday. After leaving work, he'd stopped by the store, picked up a frame, and placed the drawing on the fireplace mantel.

As soon as they got to his house, she asked to see it. Her pleased smile lit up his world. He carried her bag to the second bedroom, which had two twin beds. "Let's go start dinner. We're making pizza."

"I like pizza."

Pizza topped the list of her favorite foods, along with chicken quesadillas, string cheese, strawberry ice cream, and raw broccoli and cucumbers with ranch dip. It amazed him that she enjoyed broccoli. He hadn't liked the vegetable until well into adulthood.

Antonio washed his hands, then went to the refrigerator and got the ball of dough, sauce, cheese, and pepperoni and for his pizza, bell peppers and mushrooms. "Let's wash your hands so you can help make the pizza."

"Yay!"

After he helped her wash her hands, he sat her in the booster chair he'd purchased and brought all the ingredients to the table. She had fun pressing out the dough, but he quickly found out she wasn't too keen on letting someone assist.

"I can do it," Noelle insisted when Antonio caught her just before she dumped half a jar of sauce on her dough.

"I know, but I'm going to help you a little bit. Use the spoon." He guided her as much as she allowed. When it came time for the cheese, he placed a measured amount in a small bowl and let her add it to her heart's content. Same with the pepperoni.

"Look, Uncle Tony, I did it all by myself."

Grinning, he placed a kiss on her temple. "You sure did. We have to take a picture to show your mom and dad." He whipped out his cell and snapped one of her smiling in front of her pizza. He added toppings to his pizza and put both in the oven. While the food baked, he set Noelle up with one of the Disney animated shows, and he cleaned up the kitchen.

The show lasted long enough for the pizzas to be done and cool enough to eat. He added veggies and dip, and they enjoyed the meal seated on a blanket while watching *Encanto*. It was obvious that she'd seen the movie because she danced and sang along with many of the songs.

"Dance, Uncle Tony."

Antonio got up and held her hands while they danced to the song about Bruno. He found himself enjoying the catchy Latin rhythm. He twirled her around and laughed as she shook her hips like she'd been dancing for a lifetime. And she kept the beat perfectly. Once the food settled, he dished up the ice cream.

Noelle's eyes widened, and she jumped up and down. "Ice cream, ice cream."

April was right. Noelle had more energy than three people put together. When the movie ended, she asked him to play the songs again. He obliged and danced with her again. After the last song, he said, "All right, it's time for bath and bed."

"Aww, but I'm not sleepy," she protested, yawning.

"Mm-hmm, I know." Antonio got her bathed and into her pajamas.

"Mommy always sings before I go to sleep."

Antonio went still. "Ah, what does she sing?"

"'Twinkle, Twinkle, Little Star'" and 'This Little Light of Mine.'"

The first one he could handle, but he needed to go way back in his Vacation Bible School memory banks for the second one. "Okay." He cradled her in his lap and sang the first song. She was out before he finished. Antonio placed a soft kiss on her forehead and watched her sleep. He held her closer. This was what he'd always wanted, and he hoped this time would turn out in his favor.

CHAPTER 20

Monday, Natasha hit send on an email and leaned back in her chair. It was the first break she'd had all day. If nothing else popped up, she might be able to leave a little early and start putting some things together for her meeting with Jenny. She toyed with walking down to the bakery for a sandwich now or waiting until she got back from checking on the Ward house status. She had talked with Chase earlier and told him she'd send photos this afternoon.

Her cell rang, and she smiled when she saw Antonio's name on display. They'd only talked briefly yesterday after playing telephone tag all day, and she didn't get a chance to find out all the details of the sleepover. "Hey, love. How was your sleepover?" she asked. She slapped a hand over her mouth and groaned inwardly. She hadn't meant to call him that.

Antonio's low chuckle floated through the line. "Hey, yourself, beautiful. It was great. We ate pizza and ice cream and danced to the music on *Encanto*."

"Aw, sounds like a lot of fun." She could imagine him dancing with Noelle, and the thought set off a longing she'd kept buried.

"Yeah. She's a ball of energy, but I can't wait to do it again. Speaking of sleepovers, what do you say about us having one?"

"Mmm, sounds interesting. Does this sleepover come with food and dancing?"

"Food, dancing, and anything else you want. Kissing, touching..."

"All right, stop." She squeezed her eyes shut to block out the images of all the ways he'd kissed and caressed her.

Antonio laughed. "You asked. Are you still stopping by the Ward house today? We're just about done, and I wanted to make sure we didn't miss anything."

"I'll be there so I can take pictures to send Chase. And I want to show you something, too." She'd been working on a brochure with the different furnished designs and wanted to get his opinion.

"What is it?"

"It's a surprise. You'll see when I get there. Now, Mr. Hayes, I need to finish up a few things before we meet."

"Does this surprise include a couple of kisses?"

Natasha smiled. "No, but I might be willing to throw a little one in for you."

"I'll go with that, then. See you in a bit, sweetheart."

Every time the endearment rolled off his tongue, it melted her heart. She held the phone against her for a minute, then rotated in her chair to face her laptop. After reviewing everything and making a few minor changes, she printed it.

Natasha folded the brochure and left to show it to George. As she passed the break room, she met Lydia coming toward her, struggling beneath a stack of boxes. "Let me help you with these." She quickly set the brochure on the table nearest to the door and took half the boxes.

"Thanks. This is what happens when you only want to make one trip to the supply room," Lydia added with a little laugh.

"I do the same thing sometimes." She unloaded the boxes. "Do you need help putting this stuff away?"

Lydia waved her off. "No, I'm fine. Thanks for the help."

"Okay. I'll see you later." Natasha retraced her steps to the break room. The brochure was gone. "I just set it down." Pulling the chair out, she checked to see if it had fallen there or under the table but didn't see it.

"You lose something?" Brett asked, passing.

"I just set something down for a minute to help Lydia, and now it's gone." A thought came to her. "You don't think . . . ?" She rushed down the hall to Kathleen's office in time to see the woman feeding her brochure into a shredder. "What the hell do you think you're doing?" Natasha slapped the OFF button.

"Nothing that concerns you. Get out of my office."

"I don't think so. You had no business taking my stuff and shredding it." Her voice rose with each word, and she was a heartbeat away from snapping.

"I don't know what you're talking about."

George and Brett appeared at the door. George asked, "What's going on in here?" He divided a questioning gaze between Natasha and Kathleen.

"I left a brochure on the table for *two* minutes and came back to find it gone and in her damn shredder."

"Kathleen?"

"She's lying."

Natasha was across the space in a flash. She pointed a finger in Kathleen's face. "Then I shouldn't find half my paper still in your shredder if I'm lying." She yanked out the bottom half that hadn't gone through yet and waved it in the woman's face. "So, who's lying now?"

"That's mine," Kathleen insisted.

"Prove it. Pull up the file." She folded her arms and waited. Kathleen started fumbling with the keys. "That's what I thought." Natasha stormed out of the office and came back moments later with her own laptop, which had the open file on it. "Unlike you, I can prove it's mine. Besides, the last time I checked, you didn't have a degree in interior design." She clamped her jaw shut and swept out before she was tempted to do or say something that would guarantee her losing her job.

On her way out, she heard George say, "You've done some dumb things, Kathleen, but this time you went too far. My office. *Now!*"

Back in her quiet space, Natasha paced the floor, trying to calm down. Her head pounded, and her hands shook. She usually didn't advocate for someone to lose their job, but this time she could care less if that crazy woman got fired. Stopping, she braced one hand on the desk and the other across her middle. The deep breathing didn't help, and it took every ounce of her control not to walk back down the hall and curse Kathleen out. She thought it best that she leave. She hit the keys on her laptop with more force than necessary. The last thing she needed on top of everything else was to break her computer, so she eased up. After printing another copy, she stuck it into her tote, locked her desk, and walked out.

"You okay?" Brett asked with concern.

Not trusting herself to speak, she simply nodded and kept going. She would apologize to him later. Before she realized it, her steps took her up the block to the construction company. She took a chance that Antonio hadn't left yet.

"Hey, Leah. Is Antonio still here?"

"Hey, Tasha. Yep. Let me see if he's available." She picked up the phone and spoke for a few seconds. "He'll be right out."

Antonio appeared on the heel of Leah's words. Natasha's expression must have given her away because he didn't say anything, just led her back to his office, closed the door, and wrapped his strong arms around her. He always knew what she needed.

Some of Natasha's anger dissolved as his hand made a lazy path up and down her back. She didn't think she'd ever been this upset with a co-worker. What she felt now rivaled her emotions when she found out about Julian's shenanigans. Closing her eyes, she listened to the rhythmic sound of Antonio's heart beating beneath her ear. It was steady and even, much like the man, and a semblance of calm worked its way through her body.

"What's going on, Tasha?"

"Kathleen." She explained the situation and how close she'd come to losing her control. "I really wanted to hurt her, and that scares me."

Still holding her, Antonio said, "That's understandable. She's been tap-dancing on your nerves for a while. This just happened to be the last straw. Don't beat yourself up, sweetheart. You're human just like the rest of us, and sometimes our emotions get the best of us. Hopefully George will put a stop to it."

"She needs to be fired or at least *encouraged* to take an early retirement." Natasha sort of felt bad for wanting the woman to be fired. Sort of. "I don't know what her problem is, other than everyone is selling better than her these days. She's always had an air about her because she's the oldest and been there the longest, but it's gotten worse over the past year."

He leaned back and tilted her chin. "I know it's hard, but try not to let her get to you." He kissed her softly. "You're good at what you do, so just concentrate on that. And on getting your interior design business off the ground. Then you won't have to see her at all."

Natasha released a deep sigh. "I know, and I've been trying. But today . . . today was too much." She backed out of his arms and smoothed her hair down. "I'm sorry for interrupting you. I just started up the street and ended up here."

Antonio leaned against the desk and pulled her to stand between his legs. He stared intently at her. "No need to apologize. I'm glad you came to me. You can always, *always* come to me."

When their lips connected, she forgot all about Kathleen, being angry . . . everything. This man had eased his way back into her life and reclaimed a big chunk of her heart.

* * *

Antonio's heart finally returned to a normal pace. As he continued to hold Natasha, myriad emotions swirled in his gut. When he'd first seen her, fear unlike anything he had ever experienced gripped him. Not knowing what was going on, he did the one thing that had always come naturally—wrapping her in his arms and holding her close. Even now, the slight tremor in her body let him know her anger hadn't fully dissipated. He hated that she had to deal with this kind of mess.

"Do you need to get back right away?"

"No. I was thinking about going to the bakery for a sandwich before I left to meet you. Why?"

"Come take a ride with me."

Natasha angled her head and frowned. "Where? You can't just leave, and I didn't mean to interrupt your work. I'll be okay."

"One, I'm the boss. Two, you are more important to me than any job." Okay, *that* wasn't what he'd planned to say. "And three, you're not okay. We'll only be gone a short time. Actually, to make it easier, we can stop by the house on the way back. No need to take both cars." He straightened and rounded the desk to save and close the file he'd been working on. "Come on."

Antonio stopped to let Leah know that he'd be gone for about an hour before escorting Natasha out to his truck. "Are you okay with riding in the truck?"

"Of course. Why wouldn't I be?" Natasha climbed into the cab, and he closed the door behind her.

When he got in on the driver's side, she shifted in her seat to face him. "What?" he asked, starting the engine.

"You didn't answer my question."

He hesitated briefly. "Let's just say not all women are okay riding in a work truck and prefer something a little flashier." His ex topped the list and had told him on more than one occasion that she wouldn't be caught dead riding in a dusty old truck, regardless of whether it had been washed and buffed to a shine.

She rolled her eyes. "Some women are so ridiculous," she muttered.

On that he agreed. Looking back, there were probably subtle signs that Lori wasn't all that compatible with him, but he'd been in love. Antonio glanced over at Natasha. She sat with her head back and eyes closed. No, she definitely wasn't okay. Normally, she would have asked where they were going, but she didn't say another word. Only when he pulled into the back lot of Summerhill Creek, closest to the inlet, did she perk up. He got out and went around to help her.

"I wish I had known we were coming here so I could have gotten my blanket out of the car. There's nowhere to sit. That's okay, though. I appreciate you bringing me here."

He reached behind her seat, grabbed the blanket he'd been carrying around since the last time they'd met there, and held it up. He had another one in his sedan. "I've got you covered."

She smiled, the first one he'd seen since she arrived today. "Thank you for this." She came up on tiptoe and pressed her lips to his.

Antonio took her hand, and they strolled to their spot. He spread the blanket out near a tree with a clear view of the water, and she immediately dropped down onto it. He lowered himself next to her, braced his back against the tree, and scooped her up and onto his lap. Because of their height differences—at six four, he stood almost a foot taller than her—her head rested comfortably on his chest.

"How did you know this is what I needed?"

"You've been coming here since we were kids, whenever you're upset or want to think things through. And when I found you here the day I acted like a butthead, as you said, I realized nothing had changed."

"No, it hasn't," she said softly. "I'm glad you're not acting like a butthead anymore."

Chuckling, he tightened his arms around her. "Me too. This is much better."

Natasha smiled up at him. "Much better."

He'd brought her here to help her relax, but the way she stared at him, her gaze going to his mouth, relaxing was the farthest thing from his mind. Unable to resist, he tilted her chin and touched his mouth to hers. Her lips parted, and he slid his tongue inside, kissing her with an urgency that stunned him and would have knocked him to his knees had he been standing. Antonio didn't remember moving, but she ended up on her back with his body stretched over hers. His hands charted a path down the front of her body, stopping first to caress her breasts, then moving lower and around to her hip. He slid his hand beneath her shirt to touch her silky bare skin. Leaving her mouth, he kissed his way across her belly.

Natasha moaned and arched her back, her hands gripping his shoulders. "Yes, Tonio."

With a flick of his wrist, he undid the front clasp of her bra. He circled his tongue around her breast until he reached the nipple. Taking the hardened bud into his mouth, he sucked gently, then lavished the same sweet torment on its twin. Her sounds of pleasure ramped up his desire tenfold. The sound of birds taking flight filtered through his sensual fog. Antonio rested his head on her belly and willed his body to calm. They still had work to do. After a minute or two, he lifted his head. "Girl, you make me lose myself." He rolled over onto his back and threw an arm over his face.

"That makes two of us," Natasha mumbled. She sat up and redid her bra. "But one thing's for sure."

He eyed her. "What?"

"I completely forgot about Kathleen's crazy behind." They both laughed.

Sitting up, he stroked a finger down her cheek. "Then mission accomplished." Antonio reluctantly stood and extended his hand. "We'd better go." *While I still can*, he wanted to add. The next time he brought her, he'd be prepared.

CHAPTER 21

Natasha managed to do the walk-through of the house and photograph the repairs and upgrades, but her insides were still simmering with desire. She could feel Antonio's stare as she went about the task, and whenever their eyes locked, she saw the banked fire waiting to be unleashed. "You guys did a fabulous job. I know Chase and Mike are going to be pleased."

"Thanks. Your suggestions for the taller baseboards, paint colors, and crown molding were spot on, but then, I knew they would be. You outdid yourself, baby."

"That means a lot, coming from you." He knew better than anyone how much she wanted to succeed in this business. She glanced around and had to agree. Ms. Velda was special, and she wanted to make her proud. A wave of sadness hit her. Once the house sold, she most likely wouldn't be able to visit and sit out back facing the lake or spend time in the "ladies' room," as Ms. Velda called the shed she'd turned into her personal space.

"Hey, everything all right?" Antonio touched her hand.

"Yeah. Don't mind me. Just having a sentimental moment. I have so many memories here, it's hard to imagine that

I won't be able to stop by whenever, that's all. If I had the money, I'd buy it myself," she added with a wistful smile. She made a good living and had a decent amount of savings in her account, but this was a little out of her budget. Clearing her throat, Natasha asked, "Do you know how much longer before you'll be done?"

Still scrutinizing her, he said, "We should be done by the end of the week. There are only a few things we have to touch up."

"Okay. That means I can most likely get a selling price from Chase and get it listed by the end of next week. I'll probably do an open house the following week, most likely a Saturday to get the largest number of people." She got so lost in her planning, she completely forgot about Antonio standing there until she heard his phone.

Antonio checked the display and frowned. "Hey, Grandma Nora. Are you okay?"

Natasha could only hear his side of the conversation, but he seemed concerned. She hoped nothing was wrong with her or Papa Fred. She searched his face when he ended the call. "Is she all right?"

"Yeah, she's good. I promised to take her to visit Grandpa tomorrow morning because my dad and Uncle Charles are gone fishing and won't be back until Wednesday. She hasn't seen him since Saturday and doesn't want to wait that long."

"I can't say I blame her. They've been together more years than not, so I can imagine how difficult this must be for her. I wish we had something here. Maybe Ms. Velda wouldn't have to leave the only place she's known, either," she added, gently running her hand over the fireplace mantel.

"It would, and Grandma has already mentioned it to me."

She whipped her head around. "Wait. Are you planning to build one here?"

Antonio dragged a hand down his face. "I wish I could, but we've already started on the condos, and there's no way I can do both. But I also don't want to have to wait two or three years to get it done. I don't even know if he'll—"

Natasha hugged him tight. "I get it. You want them to have as much time together as possible. But, baby, there's only one of you, and you can't do it all. Right now you're doing the best thing, and that's making yourself available to drive her to Napa."

"I know, but I plan to make calls to a couple of buddies who work in the field."

She nodded. "Hopefully they can help or know someone who can." Surveying the room one last time, she said, "I'm done, so we can head back." They closed up the house and got in the truck.

"By the way, Grandma also reminded me that I'm supposed to invite you to my family's Sunday dinner," he said after several minutes. "And before you say anything, my mom was the one who extended the invitation. She's as bad as your mother, so be warned."

"Nobody can be that bad," she said with a shake of her head. "And I'd love to come to dinner. What time?"

"Usually, they're around three or four, but I'll confirm with her and let you know."

"Sounds good."

"When we talked earlier, you said you wanted to show me something."

"Oh, shoot. I completely forgot. I'll show it to you when we get back." Between the mess with Kathleen and the side trip to the inlet, the brochure had completely slipped her mind. Three minutes later, he turned onto the street and parked in front of her office. She retrieved the brochure from her tote. "I started working on the designs for the condos and wanted to get your opinion. I've only done six so far." She bit her lip nervously as she waited while he flipped through the pages.

"These are amazing, Tasha. I know you enjoy being a Realtor, but you have a gift and really should be doing interior design full time."

She released the breath she'd been holding. "You think so?"

Antonio flipped back a couple of pages. "I really like this one. I may have to hire you to design my home."

"Whenever you decide to buy or build, I'll be happy to work my magic," she said brightly. But inside she wondered whether she'd be the one living there with him or decorating it for some other woman. The thought didn't sit well with her, and she didn't want to analyze the reasons for that. Her stomach growled, and she placed a hand on her midsection to muffle the sound.

"Maybe I'd better drive you over to the bake shop to get your sandwich," Antonio said, a grin tugging at his lips.

"You heard that?"

"Hard not to when it was loud enough to rattle windows."

She burst out laughing and punched him in the arm. "Shut up."

"Dang, girl." He rubbed the spot on his arm.

"That little tap didn't hurt you. I'm lucky I didn't break my hand on those big mus—"

"Don't stop now. Go ahead and finish." Antonio flexed his biceps. "I should've known you only wanted me for my body."

"I'm not talking to you. I am getting out and going to get my sandwich." Yeah, she wanted him for his body, his mind, his heart. And she wanted him because of the way he made her feel. Because she loved him.

* * *

"Why are you so nervous?" Antonio asked Natasha as they arrived at his parents' house on Sunday afternoon. He parked in the driveway behind his brother's SUV. "It's not like you don't know them, and you talked to my mom at the party."

"I know, but this is different. There were a hundred people at the party, and she couldn't focus on me. Today I'll be sitting at the table right in front of her. And she knows that I was the one who messed up our relationship."

He covered her hand with his. "Baby, my parents don't blame you for that. Trust me when I tell you my mother is happy we're back together. And you know Grandma is with all her matchmaking." His entire family understood that everyone made mistakes when they were young and didn't hold the past against her.

Natasha flopped back against her seat. "I guess. But what about your brother?"

"Actually, Nate is firmly in your corner." And the first one who recognized Antonio still had feelings for her. "We'd better go in before my mother comes out. She's peeked out the window twice."

"Oh my goodness. Why didn't you say something?" Natasha reached for the door handle.

Laughing, Antonio said, "Let go of the handle. I've got it."

She glared at him as he helped her out of the car. "I can't believe you didn't tell me your mother was waiting for us."

He pressed a kiss to her forehead. "Relax, baby." The front door opened before their feet hit the steps.

His mother stepped out with her arms wide. "Natasha. I'm so glad you could join us today."

"Told you," Antonio whispered. Natasha gave him a look, then smiled at his mother. He chuckled inwardly.

"Thank you so much for inviting me, Mrs. Hayes. These are for your table." The two women embraced. Natasha handed his mother a bouquet of flowers in a square crystal vase.

"Oh, honey, you didn't have to bring anything, but these are gorgeous and will fit perfectly. Hi, son."

He bent and kissed her cheek. "Hey, Mom. Glad you remembered I was standing here."

"Hush, boy, and come on in here. Dinner is ready. We're just waiting for your grandmother."

Antonio urged Natasha forward and watched as the family surrounded her, showered her with hugs, and expressed how happy they were that she and Antonio were together.

Noelle sprinted over and wrapped her arms around his legs. "Hi, Uncle Tony." She raised her arms for him to pick her up.

He swung her around, then planted a kiss on her cheek. "Natasha, this is my beautiful, energetic niece, Noelle. Noelle, say hello to Ms. Baldwin."

Natasha reached up to shake Noelle's hand. "Hi, Noelle. It's nice to meet you."

"Hi. Are you going to be my auntie?" Noelle asked with a big grin. "My mommy said—"

April rushed over and plucked Noelle out of Antonio's arms with a nervous chuckle. "Natasha, you'll have to forgive my daughter."

"She's a lot like her mother," Nate said.

She whispered something to Noelle that made the little girl cover her mouth and say, "Oops."

Antonio and Natasha shared a look, and she tried to hide her smile. He shook his head and draped his arm around her shoulders. "Come on, baby." As they gathered around the table, his grandmother entered from the side door that connected her cottage to the house.

"Mama Nora." Natasha hurried over and hugged her.

"Here's my girl," Grandma Nora said. "It's about time Antonio brought you over."

Nate moved closer to Antonio and said quietly, "Looks like everybody's happy about the two of you. I hate to say it, but I told you so."

"Obviously not, since you said it anyway." But he was glad to see his family embrace her just like they'd done years ago. His grandmother had made it no secret that she believed they belonged together.

Once everyone had their seat, his father blessed the food. Plates were filled, and lively conversation ensued.

"Natasha, I didn't get a chance to congratulate you on being the Realtor for the new building project," his father said.

"Thanks, Mr. Hayes. I'm pretty excited about it. It gives me a chance to finally put my degree to use."

"I wish I had remembered that when we did Mama's cottage."

Grandma Nora nodded. "The place can always use a little sprucing up."

"And I'd love to see what you can do with Noelle's room, Natasha," April said. "She's moving out of the toddler stage, and I've been trying to find something that's not babyish but not too grown."

"I'd love to talk to you. Let me know when you want to get started."

"These services do come with a family discount, since you're . . . practically . . . family?" Nate asked with a wave of his fork.

Antonio recognized what his brother was doing and wanted to knock him out. He didn't want Natasha to be put on the spot or be made to feel uncomfortable in any way.

"Since we haven't graduated to the whole family discount level, I'll be more than happy to give you the we're-not-quite-family-but-you-could-be-a-friend discount." Natasha winked at Antonio.

He should've known she could handle herself with his family, and her statement proved it when everyone erupted in laughter.

His father wiped tears of mirth from his eyes. "Nate, I bet you'll think twice before you try that again."

Nate chuckled. "I'll let you have that one, Tasha."

"So when will she become family?" his mother asked innocently, not looking up from her plate.

Antonio groaned and sent Natasha an apologetic look. He hadn't expected her to go there. "Mom, we're not at that stage yet."

"Mommy, what's a stage?" Noelle asked.

April stammered and stuttered, then finally said, "It's grown-up talk, so you don't need to worry about it."

This brought on another round of laughter and comments about watching what's said around kids. The conversation shifted to stories about Noelle and some of the things she'd said. Antonio couldn't have been happier to have the spotlight off him and Natasha. She must have sensed his turmoil because she reached under the table and gave his thigh a gentle rub, letting him know she was okay. They were still laughing and eating when the doorbell rang.

"I wonder who that could be," his mother said, wiping her mouth and pushing back from the table. "I'll be right back."

A moment later Antonio thought he heard his brother mutter something that sounded like, "Oh shit." He opened his mouth to ask him what happened but froze when he heard a familiar voice.

"Hello, my love."

No, no, no. It can't be. Yet when he turned, he came face-to-face with his ex-wife. She smiled at him as if she had every right to be there and hadn't ripped his damn heart out. He had to hand it to her, though. She came dressed to kill in an ensemble he knew cost at least a grand, but he didn't care. He wanted her gone.

"Aren't you going to greet me, Antonio? I've missed you, baby." Lori held her arms open as if she expected him to walk into them.

One could hear a pin drop as his family sat stunned. His mother wrung her hands as if she didn't know what to do. He shifted his gaze to Natasha's stricken expression and wanted to fly his ex to another planet on the first rocket leaving. He'd finally gotten over her and was now moving forward with the beautiful woman at his side. *I do not need this kind of drama in my life.* Antonio jumped to his feet. "What the hell are you doing here, Lori?" he gritted out, completely forgetting about his young niece. April must have sensed something because out of his periphery, he saw her hustling Noelle out of the room.

Lori gave him the smile that used to make his heart skip a beat, but the only thing it turned now was his stomach. She came toward him, and when she reached up to touch him, he took two steps back.

"Yes, what are you doing here?" Grandma Nora said. "The last time you were here, you couldn't wait to leave this little hillbilly town, as you called it. Now you come waltzing in here like you own the place, interrupting the family dinner you wanted no part of, so answer it and go on. My dinner's getting cold." She waved a dismissive hand.

Leave it to his grandmother to say what everyone around the table wanted to say. His family had no love for her after she'd acted as though small-town living equated to *lesser than*. "You have two minutes, and I'm being generous." Antonio wanted no part in whatever game she came to play, and he'd bet his life savings she had an ulterior motive.

Natasha stood. "I'm going to just go."

"No, baby. The only person leaving is her. Just give me a minute, okay?" His heart beat double time as he waited for her to say something. She finally nodded, but the sparkle in her deep-brown eyes had gone out. Antonio glared at Lori. "Let's go." He latched on to her arm and escorted her to the living room. "What are you doing here?"

"I miss having you in my life," Lori said with a sad expression he wasn't sure was real "I . . . I'm hoping we can try again. I realize I do want the things you want—quiet date nights with just the two of us. I want us to have children. Don't you still want those things? I know there are some things we need to work out, and I'm willing to give you the time and space to do that." She reached for him. "Just say you'll come back home."

He stared at her incredulously. "You're kidding me, right? I am *home!*" She sounded sincere, but after everything, it was hard for him to believe her. "Do you remember what you said to me? You said I wasn't ambitious enough, that you needed a man who was willing to climb as high as you. Not someone who just settled for middle ground. You wanted someone who didn't spend his time fixing and building things, that we should be people who *hired* workers, not *do* the work. And the worst thing . . . you started taking the pill behind my back so you wouldn't get pregnant, then acted like you were devastated each month it didn't happen." Antonio pinched the bridge of his nose. He hated her for making him relive one of the worst times in his life. "Nothing has changed, Lori. *I haven't changed!* So, no. Make that *hell no.* You need to go back to wherever you came from because you and me, it's not happening. Ever."

"Baby, I know you don't mean that. I said a lot of stupid

things, but I was angry and we were fighting and...where am I supposed to stay?"

She took another step toward him with tears in her eyes, and he held up a hand. "You're welcome to try the Firefly Lake Inn. I'm sorry you came all this way, but I've moved on just like I told you in the last text message I sent. It's time you do the same."

Lori stared at him for a long moment, seeming to measure his words. Her expression registered a mixture of guilt and disappointment. "Antonio, I'm really sorry about the things I said and not putting our marriage first, and I promise things will be different this time."

"I accept your apology, and I understand that you wanted to do some things for yourself, but it doesn't change how I feel now." As hard as it was, Antonio had to let go and forgive Lori, so he could be free to move forward with the beautiful woman waiting at the dinner table. He walked to the door and held it open. "Have a safe flight home, Lori," he said softly.

"So, it's going to be you and the hometown girl now?" When he didn't answer, Lori said, "I'm sorry, too." She crossed the room, gave him one last look of regret, and walked out.

Antonio closed the door softly and leaned his head against the cool wood. He recalled Natasha's stricken expression and didn't know what he'd do if this messed up things between them.

CHAPTER 22

Are you okay, dear?"

Natasha didn't realize Mama Nora had taken Antonio's seat next to her until she felt the touch on her arm. She tried to smile. "Um...I'm fine." Not exactly the truth. In actuality, her emotions vacillated between shock, anger, and embarrassment, and she wasn't sure of anything at the moment. A part of her couldn't believe the audacity of the woman showing up like she'd been invited and still had a place in the family. In Antonio's life.

Antonio. She hadn't seen him this angry since one of the guys on his high school basketball team tried coming on to her, wouldn't take no for an answer, and tried to get rough. That guy never said another word to her after Antonio threatened to do him bodily harm if he laid a hand on Natasha again. Her easygoing and even-tempered boyfriend was usually unflappable, but not that time. Natasha knew for a fact he wouldn't lay a hand on his ex, but from the yelling, she could tell he'd reached his limit.

"I'm so sorry for all this, Natasha," his mother said, drawing her out of her thoughts. "I don't understand why she decided to come all this way when she never wanted to while they were married."

Interesting. "It's not your fault, Mrs. Hayes." The only reason for a woman to fly clear across the country out of the blue and show up at her ex's *parents'* house was for some kind of reconciliation. And that's what concerned Natasha. Wearing an outfit that screamed haute couture and hearing the woman use the phrase *hometown girl* as if it were something bad brought back all the emotions she'd experienced the day she saw the cheerleader all over Antonio. That this small-town girl was no match for a big-city, sophisticated woman. She dropped her head.

"Tasha, can I talk to you for a minute?"

Her head snapped up when she heard Antonio's voice. They probably did need to talk, but right now she couldn't do it. Not with everything swirling around inside her. She didn't want to risk saying something she regretted or letting the anger she felt toward the other woman spill over into their relationship. Natasha followed him to the living room without a word.

Antonio took her hands. "I'm sorry she ruined your day."

"It's not your fault. I'm not angry at you, but I can't do this right now. I think it would be best if you took me home."

"What are you saying?" His voice held a slight tremble. "Are you having second thoughts about us?"

"I'm saying I need some time to think things through. For me." She placed a hand on his chest, wanting him to understand it wasn't about him. It was her. "Please, take me home."

"Baby, how about you finish your food first, and then I'll take you home? Okay?"

His eyes pleaded with her, and she finally nodded. Natasha went back to the dining room and forced herself to eat the delicious meal his mother had prepared. Although his family tried to keep the conversation going, the rest of the time was awkward, to say the least. In the end, she thanked Mrs. Hayes and said goodbye to his family.

"Don't be a stranger, Natasha," Mrs. Hayes said. "You'll have to come back to dinner soon."

She just smiled but didn't commit to anything.

April embraced Natasha. She whispered, "Trust me, you don't have to worry about Lori. Let me know if you need to talk. I got you, girl."

That made Natasha smile. "I'll let you know." She slung her purse on her shoulder and trudged back to the living room, where Antonio stood waiting at the door. They didn't exchange words from the time she walked out until he parked in her driveway. Despite the tension between them, he still helped her out of the car and walked her to the door. "Antonio, I—"

"You said you needed time," he said, cutting her off. "And I'm going to give it to you. But I won't wait another fifteen years, Tasha."

"You won't have to, Tonio. I promise." She came up on tiptoe and placed a tender kiss on his lips. She watched him lope back to his car, his hands shoved in his pockets. He didn't look back.

Tears filled her eyes again. She closed the door and leaned against it, her arms wrapped around her middle.

Natasha made her way to the bedroom and dropped down on the side of the bed. She tossed her purse aside and massaged her temples. Maybe she should've just talked to him, but she didn't want him to know how humiliated she'd been. She dug her cell out of her purse, scrolled through her top contacts, and hit the button for Serenity's number.

"Hey, Tasha," Serenity answered, giggling.

"Hey. Did I catch you at a bad time?"

"Yes!" Gabriel yelled into the phone.

"*No*," Serenity countered. "Hush, Gabriel, and go make sure those brownies don't burn. Sorry, girl."

Natasha smiled, wishing she didn't have any worries. "No problem. I can call you another time if you two are busy."

"We're not busy. Gabriel is just being Gabriel." Serenity paused. "What's going on? I thought you were having dinner with Antonio's family today. Did it get canceled or something?"

"No. I went, but his ex-wife showed up."

"*Whaaat?* What do you mean she showed up? Doesn't she live in New York?"

"Yep." She gave Serenity a play-by-play of the disaster.

"I can't even imagine Antonio's reaction."

"He was beyond angry, and they went into another room to talk. It actually sounded more like an argument, and then he asked her to leave."

"Wow. I can't believe she'd just show up like that. Who does that kind of crap anyway?"

"I think she was hoping for a reconciliation, but Antonio shut her down." Even now the memory of the woman conjured up all the insecurities she'd worked so hard to leave behind. She shifted on the bed and leaned against the pillows. "Part of me was so embarrassed, and it dredged up all the self-doubt I thought I'd left behind." Dana had been there to support her during her high school years and Serenity during college.

"Oh, sis. I'm so sorry. Sweetie, don't let her get inside your head. You can hold your own against any woman."

"You didn't see this one," she muttered. "The woman came dressed to impress. I've seen a similar outfit, and I know it cost upward of a thousand dollars, not to mention her shoes."

"Whatever. *Any* woman. What did Antonio say when you told him?"

"Well," she hedged. "I didn't actually talk to him. I asked him to bring me home because I needed to think some things through. I was afraid I'd sound like a lunatic between being mad and hurt."

"Girl, do I need to come over there and knock some sense into you?"

Natasha laughed. "No."

"Apparently I do if you let that man leave without talking to him. I seem to recall a certain someone telling me the same when my fears got the best of me last year when Gabriel and I started dating."

"That was different." The lie even seemed hollow to her.

Serenity snorted. "Bull. It's exactly the same. Actually, you and Antonio would have an easier time getting through this snag because you've known each other so long and were friends. You used to tell me that was one of the things you loved about your relationship—that you two could talk about anything even if it was uncomfortable."

"Why are you always bringing up old stuff?" Natasha

slouched against the headboard. She and Antonio did have that special bond, and she hoped she hadn't messed it up.

Her friend's sparkling laughter came through the line. "Because you need to hear it. Now stop acting up and get yourself together. You have a man you need to call . . . *tonight*. And miss me with the whole I'll-call-him-tomorrow spiel. You can thank me later."

"You're lucky I love you. Otherwise I'd find myself another best friend," she grumbled, knowing she could never replace the sister of her heart.

"Ha ha, I love you, too. Oh, and if you don't straighten things out with him, I'm cutting off your chocolate-dipped-strawberry supply."

Her mouth gaped. "That's a low blow, sis. I can't believe you. You owe me one of those brownies for this abuse." They dissolved into a fit of laughter. Natasha wiped tears of mirth from her eyes, feeling much better. "Thanks, Serenity," she said sincerely.

"Anytime. You've done the same for me. Maybe I'll save you a brownie, after all. Let me know how it goes."

"I will." They chatted a moment longer, then ended the call.

She was angry at herself for letting a complete stranger rattle her. Serenity was right about Natasha and Antonio having history, but he also had a history with his ex. She could finally admit that deep down some of her fears stemmed from the knowledge that he might decide he wanted a second chance with Lori. After all, they'd been married before. With the way Antonio discussed his marriage, coupled with what occurred earlier, she didn't think so, but she never thought they'd reconcile, either.

Natasha picked up her phone again to call Antonio. Her heart pounded as she waited for him to answer. She was disappointed when it went to voicemail, but did she really expect him to pick up after she'd basically shut him out? "Hey, Tonio. Give me a call when you get a chance. I...I'm sorry, and I want to explain." She disconnected, leaned back, and closed her eyes. She had to make this right. *I cannot lose him again.*

* * *

Monday morning, Antonio was up at six and out running thirty minutes later. He'd tossed and turned all night with thoughts of his ex and Natasha. He still couldn't believe Lori had flown here thinking that he would simply fall into her arms as if nothing had happened. But his biggest concern lay with Tasha. He had no idea what was going through her mind. Did she honestly believe he'd walk away from her to reunite with Lori? She knew him better than that, or at least he thought she did.

He sprinted up the hill, his running shoes hitting the trail in a steady rhythm, his mind bombarded with scenarios of *what if.* It had been why he'd let her call go to voicemail. The day had been emotionally draining enough, and he couldn't take it if she was calling to end their relationship. But they had to talk soon because being in limbo wasn't his style.

Antonio reversed his course and completed the three-mile run. When he got home, he spent another forty-five minutes lifting weights. Afterward, he showered, made a smoothie, picked up his cell, and headed out.

When Antonio arrived at the office half an hour later, he didn't see Leah at her desk and figured he'd finally made it there first. They had an ongoing friendly battle. No matter how early he came in, she was always there and greeted him with a smile.

He heard voices in the back and started in that direction. His steps slowed when he saw Leah talking to Natasha in his office.

"Ha! I bet you thought you beat me today, huh?" Leah teased. "Morning, boss. See you later, Natasha." She made a hasty exit.

"Hi," Natasha said.

"Hey. What are you doing here?" He resisted the urge to cross the space, haul her into his arms, and kiss her until she couldn't think of anything but him . . . and them. But her pensive expression kept him rooted to the spot.

"We need to talk, and I wanted to catch you before you left for a job site." Natasha ran her hands up and down her sides and bit her lip. A sure sign she was nervous.

He reached back and closed the door. "Have a seat." She perched on the edge of the chair, and he braced a hip on the desk. For a long moment she didn't say anything, and his heart rate ramped up. Had he set himself up for another heartbreak? "Tasha?"

"I'm sorry. I should've talked to you yesterday. It's just her showing up out of the blue, looking as if she'd just stepped off the cover of a fashion magazine, and wanting you back even though she saw me at the table made me feel some kind of way."

Obviously the argument had been louder than he'd thought. "What she said doesn't matter. She and I are done."

"I know that, but all I saw was a déjà vu of high school and college."

Antonio's brows knitted in confusion. "I don't understand."

"I heard so many times that I would never be able to keep a star player like you that I started to believe it. Then I saw the game on TV . . . and the girl answered your phone that night." She released a deep sigh. "I thought they'd been right."

He sat in the chair next to her. "Baby, you never told me that. Why?"

Natasha shrugged. "I didn't think I needed to because while we were together, you never glanced at another girl. I wasn't worried until you left. Then yesterday, seeing Lori with her expensive clothes and jewelry and hearing her call me the hometown girl just took me back to that place. I felt insulted, humiliated, and self-conscious," she added softly, her voice cracking.

"Baby, you should have told me what you were feeling. We're friends first, and we promised to talk about everything." She averted her eyes, and he gently turned her face toward his. "Listen to me. You are intelligent, beautiful inside and outside, talented, and one of the sweetest women I have ever met. Her words don't matter. *She* doesn't matter. You are the only one who matters to me." Antonio had no plans to let Lori come between him and Natasha.

"I guess I was the one acting like a butthead this time," Natasha said, swiping at her tears.

He smiled. "Maybe, but I understand. Not sure I would've handled it any better if the shoe was on the other foot." The pressure in his chest eased. "I don't want to lose you, Tasha."

She caressed his face and placed a lingering kiss on his lips. "I don't want to lose you, either, Tonio."

There was something about the way she said the name—a mixture of sensuality and sweetness—that fired his blood. It wouldn't take much for him to lose control. After kissing her again, he said, "You need to take your beautiful self to your office before you get us in trouble. You know what it does to me when you call me that."

Natasha boldly ran her hand over the solid ridge of his erection. "Yeah, I do."

Antonio stilled her hand. "I'm going to have to ban you from my office if you keep this up." She laughed, and it sounded like music to his ears. "How about I treat you to dinner at Ms. Ida's tonight?"

She rubbed her hands together and wiggled her eyebrows. "I'm down with that."

He stood and pulled her to her feet. "What time are you off today?"

"I should be done around five thirty if my meeting doesn't run over. I'll text you if I'll be later."

Antonio nodded. "I'll come to your office and pick you up."

Natasha rolled her eyes. "You have to pass the restaurant to get to my office. I can just meet you there."

He folded his arms and glared at her. "I have never *met* you anywhere for a date, and I won't be starting now. So let me know when you're at your office, and I'll come down."

She held up her hands in mock surrender. "Okay, you win. See you later, baby."

His heart flipped at the endearment, and his smile was still in place minutes after she left. Now that things were straightened out between them, he turned his full concentration to his to-do list. First up: reaching out to a friend about the memory care center.

Antonio took a seat behind his desk and found the number he wanted.

"Well, if it isn't Mr. Finance. It's been a while. How's life in the Big Apple?"

He chuckled. "Hey, Zo. I wouldn't know, since I'm no longer there. How's Sactown treating you and Ced?" Antonio had met Lorenzo and Cedric Hunter at an engineering conference several years ago and had developed a friendship with the cousins, who now owned their family's construction company in the Sacramento area.

"Wait. You left New York?" Lorenzo asked with surprise. "The last time we talked, you'd just been promoted to senior investment manager. I thought you liked it there and would for sure be a partner or something by now."

"Yeah, same. But things changed. I've been divorced for two years and moved back home."

"Oh, man. Sorry to hear that. Hey, Ced, you won't believe who's on the phone. Let me put you on speaker." There was a pause, then Lorenzo said, "Okay, you're on."

"What's up, Ced?"

"Antonio Hayes?" Cedric asked after a brief hesitation.

"The one and only. How's life treating you two?"

Cedric laughed. "Good. Married with a baby girl who's

my heart. Zo's got a little boy who's going to be running the company in the near future."

Lorenzo took up the tale. "My little man is barely three but is already trying to draw and help me build whatever project I'm doing. My wife is amazing and doing well with her bath and body shop."

Both men spoke with such passion about their families that a pang of envy hit Antonio. "Sounds like you two are pretty busy. Congrats on the wives and babies."

"Tony's back in Cali now, Ced," Lorenzo said.

"Really. You should come up for a visit. We can show you around, and you can hang out for the weekend. Are you still in finance?"

"Actually, no. On my second day home, I went to visit my godfather—the one I mentioned who owned the town's construction company."

"Yeah, I recall you saying you worked with him in the summers," Cedric said.

"Well, he decided he wanted to retire, asked me if I wanted to run the business, and turned it over to me when I said yes. My head is still spinning." He told them about the upcoming condo project. "So I'm finally using that engineering degree."

Lorenzo laughed. "About time. That baptism by fire sounds a little familiar. I don't know if we told you, but our fathers did the same thing. They called us into the office and said they were retiring."

"Effective *immediately*," Cedric finished.

"Glad to know I'm not the only one. What's up with this older generation with their 'I'm out' mentality? No transition, nothing." The three men howled with laughter. "With that said, I know you guys have your hands full, but I wanted to talk to you about something. You know Firefly Lake is a small town. We have a hospital with a small rehab center, but nothing for the older folks who are suffering from dementia or need round-the-clock care. My grandfather has Alzheimer's, and we have to drive a good thirty minutes to get to the facility, and my grandmother is having a hard time because she can only see him once or twice a week, when one of us can drive her out there."

"I'm really sorry to hear that, Tony," Lorenzo said. "I completely understand because my mother-in-law has the same thing. It was hard on my wife because she lived in Chicago, and her sisters are the siblings from hell. We were finally able to move her out here to a really good place near our house."

"What do you need, Tony?"

"We need to build a small facility in town, but the condos are going to take up most of my time for the next year to year and a half, not to mention the other smaller projects. I don't have a big crew, and there's no way we can do both. I have no idea how long Grandpa has. I know you guys are busy, but I wanted to see if you knew any other companies I can check with who might be available to do something within the next month or two." Antonio hadn't talked to the mayor or city council yet because he wanted to have as much information as he could and make it hard for them to say no.

"Nah, my brother. We got this," Cedric said. "If you're not busy the weekend after next, come on up, and we can figure out what you need."

"Ced is right. And after we meet, he and I will take a trip down there to check out the land."

Antonio felt as if a boulder were lifted off his chest. "Thanks, Zo. You too, Ced. I appreciate this. Do you mind if I bring someone with me?" He thought it might be a good opportunity for him and Tasha to get away.

"Ah . . . someone, as in a woman? Your wife?" Ced asked.

He cringed at the mention of his ex. It also made him wonder if she'd left town. "No," he said with a little more force than necessary. "I've been divorced for two years. The woman I'm seeing now was my high school sweetheart."

"Definitely bring her. She can meet my wife, Randi. Zo, you think Desiree can get away from the shop for a day?"

"Since we have a couple of weeks' notice, probably."

"Thanks. I'll check with Tasha tonight and let you know."

"Looking forward to catching up," Lorenzo said.

"Same here. Later."

Antonio leaned back in his chair and smiled, grateful for his two friends. He'd start working on a sketch of what he thought would work. He knew he would have to talk to a couple of the doctors to find out what type of equipment they'd need. He still had his notes from the facility in Napa and was confident he would be able to come up with something to help his grandmother and the other families in the same predicament. Then there was the financing, but he'd figure it out.

He also hoped Natasha would be free to accompany him because he couldn't wait to have her to himself for two days with no interruptions.

CHAPTER 23

Natasha's day went smoothly thanks to Kathleen not being in the office. George had convinced her to take some time off to deal with whatever problems she was having, and Natasha hoped that when the woman returned, things would be better.

She sent a quick text to Antonio to let him know she'd be ready at five thirty, then uploaded the photos to email to Chase. Her meeting with a couple who were looking for a larger house to accommodate their growing family had gone well, and she'd already found three listings that fit and emailed those, as well. She shut down her computer and went to the bathroom to freshen up and add a fresh coating of lipstick.

When Natasha returned to her office, Antonio was there. He stood looking out the window, and she took the opportunity to study his tall frame, from his wide shoulders and well-defined arms to his narrow waist and long legs encased in a pair of jeans, showing off a toned butt and thick thighs.

"If you're done checking me out, we can leave." Antonio slowly turned to face her.

She smothered a giggle. "How did you know I was standing here? You couldn't even see me."

"Maybe not, but your fragrance gave you away. It's sweet and sexy, just like you, and my favorite." He closed the distance between them and dipped his head to kiss her. "Ready?"

Natasha just stared at him. Any lingering apprehensions and uncertainties she had about them dissipated like a puff of smoke. He always knew the right thing to say when she needed it. "Yes." They met Brett as they left. "Are you done for the day, Brett?"

"Yes, ma'am. Heading home before the streetlights come on for the first time in a week."

She chuckled. "I hear you."

"How's it going, Antonio? Are you getting used to being back in gossip city yet?" he teased.

Antonio shook his head, and the two men did a fist bump. "Not sure I'll ever get used to that."

"Same, man. You two have a good evening."

"We will," Natasha and Antonio chorused, sharing a private smile. He held the door open for her, then held her hand as they strolled up the block. More than a few people commented on how good they looked together.

"Gotta love small-town living," Antonio said with a chuckle.

She glanced up to respond, and his smile faded. His steps slowed, and she shifted her gaze to see what had captured his attention. *Great. Round two.* Natasha wasn't in the mood to deal with his ex-wife again, and Antonio's expression said the same. Dressed in another expensive designer outfit and her makeup looking as if it had been professionally done, she strutted down the street like she was on a runway. For a split second Natasha's self-doubt reared its ugly head, but she quickly forced it down. She was done with listening to that stupid inner voice.

"What is she still doing in town?" Antonio muttered angrily.

Lori's jaw tightened when she saw them. Her gaze drifted down to Natasha's and Antonio's entwined hands and back up. Natasha just hoped the woman would pass by and keep it moving. She'd already been the subject of gossip in the last two months more often than she cared to be, but a confrontation on Main Street would guarantee to be a front-page headline. And she didn't even want to think about the news making it to her mother. "Looks like she's headed to the same place as us." *Unfortunately.*

"We can go someplace else if you want," he said, concern lining his features.

"Nope. I have my taste buds set on some of Ms. Ida's fried catfish. I've been craving it since I had it when Serenity and I had lunch a few weeks ago." Besides, after hearing Antonio declaring that she was the only one who mattered to him, she was *not* going to let one more woman get in her ear.

"Then let's get your fish, baby." Antonio kissed her hand and opened the door to the restaurant.

"Well, who do we have here?" Ms. Bernice said, beaming. "You two eating in?"

Natasha shook her head. "Hi, Ms. Bernice, and yes."

She retrieved two menus and led them to a table on the side of the spacious room that had a partial view of the mountains in the distance.

Antonio seated Natasha, then rounded the table and took the chair across from her. "Thanks, Ms. Bernice."

"You two, enjoy."

232

"Oh, and, Ms. Bernice," Natasha said with a teasing grin, "can you not call my mother and tell her anything other than we had dinner this time?"

A look of embarrassment crossed her face, and she let out a little giggle. "Sorry about last time. I'll be sure to keep it straight this time." Ms. Bernice gave them an exaggerated wink and pranced off.

"Or she could've said she wouldn't call at all." She sighed and picked up the menu.

"Look on the bright side. At least she has to wait until she gets off to call. My mom will probably know before our entrées hit the table," he said wryly.

She burst out laughing. "Yeah, you have a point. Maybe we should record the dinner to show our parents. That might be the only way the truth will be told."

"Probably." He leaned forward and clasped his hands on the table. "What do you think about us sharing the seafood family platter? It has your catfish as well as shrimp."

"I say you've got yourself a deal. It comes with three sides and either rolls or cornbread. My nonnegotiables are the mac and cheese and cornbread."

A grin curved the corner of his mouth. "Then it's good those are mine, too. We should make it look good and get at least one vegetable. I vote for the green beans."

"Works for me. Since we're going all out, might as well get fries. And there's only one option for a drink."

"Sweet tea," they said at the same time.

Natasha loved that they had so many things in common. Despite the years they were apart, it seemed as though that area of their relationship stayed intact.

SHERYL LISTER

After the server came and took their order, Antonio asked, "How did your day go? Any more problems with your co-worker?"

"No. Apparently, George convinced her to take some time off. I have no idea how long, but it was nice not to hear her snippy comments during our meeting. I just hope when she comes back, she'll leave all the animosity at home. Did you get a lot done? There's a lot of buzz going around now that you guys started on the condos."

"I only spent about two hours out there because I had to take care of some things at the office."

"Which killed you, huh?" She knew how much he enjoyed the hands-on process of a building taking shape. It had to be hard having to be in the office so much.

"You know me well. But it's okay. I'll be out there a lot more once the actual frame starts going up."

She gave him a sensual smile and said quietly, "And I'm going to make sure I get a front-row seat to watch those glorious muscles in action. Just like I did those summers when you worked for Mr. Davenport." Natasha leaned closer. "Maybe you can give me a preview when you follow me home after dinner."

Desire lit in his eyes. As Antonio opened his mouth to respond, the server returned with their food.

"Mmm, this looks and smells so good." She glanced up and found him still watching her. "What?"

"You like tempting me, don't you? And I already told you how much I like it when you tell me what you want."

Natasha shrugged as she added portions of everything onto a plate. "I like that you like it." He was the only man

234

she felt comfortable showing this side of herself. The few guys with whom she had been in a steady relationship with weren't particularly fond of her expressing her wants and desires—in and out of bed. Antonio, on the other hand, was the complete opposite. He actually encouraged her to share everything.

As he ate, he said, "I want to run something by you."

"Shoot."

"Remember when I mentioned wanting to build a memory care center here?" She nodded. "I reached out to a couple of guys I met at an engineering conference in LA some years ago. They own their family construction company now and said they might be able to take the project on."

"Are you *kidding* me? That would be so fabulous. Are they based in LA?"

"No, Sacramento."

Natasha grasped his hand. "Even closer. So when are you going to meet with them? I hope it's soon because I know how much this means to you."

"A couple of weeks, and I'd like for you to come with me. I want your input, too. And you still owe me a sleepover."

"I would love to go with you. Since Lake Tahoe is only a couple of hours away from Sac, can we go there?" She'd been trying to figure out some place for them to go and didn't want to go to Napa or the Bay Area. Lake Tahoe was a good choice, especially since the snow season had ended.

"I think I can make that happen," Antonio said between bites of mac and cheese. "There's one more thing."

"Okay." She popped a piece of cornbread in her mouth.

"What do you think about having your supper club crew over to my place this weekend for a little barbecue?"

"I say that's a great idea. Dana will be out of town, filling in at piano for an orchestra, though."

"That's pretty cool. I didn't know she still played. I'll call Gabe and see if he and Serenity are available. I don't have Jon's number."

Natasha waved him off. "I'll call Terri. I just hope Jon won't be working. He puts in way too many hours. I would volunteer to help, but my talents are limited to salad, store-bought rolls, and table decorating."

"Don't worry, baby. I got you, and I'd love for you to help me."

A shadow fell over the table, and Natasha glanced over her shoulder and saw Lori standing there. She groaned inwardly.

"I'd like to talk to you, Antonio," Lori said.

"I think we said everything yesterday, Lori."

She nodded. "I just wanted to let you know I'm going back to New York tonight. Again, I'm sorry for the way things turned out between us." Lori cut a quick glance at Natasha and let out a small smile. "I guess there's something to be said for a hometown girl, after all. I wish you both well."

"I wish you the same," Antonio said.

The woman gave Natasha an imperceptible nod and headed for the exit.

That wasn't what Natasha had expected Lori to say. Maybe the comment the woman had made yesterday hadn't been spiteful. She studied Antonio, who had his head down. "You okay?"

"Yeah, fine. I'm just glad I can close that chapter of my life, and we can both move on now. Hopefully, she can find someone who wants the same things she does because I have."

She paused, and her pulse skipped. Did they want the same things? He'd just given her the opening she'd been looking for. "Um . . . I heard what she said the other day about wanting children. Do you still want them, or is that something you've changed your mind about?" When he didn't say anything for a moment, her heart started pounding, making her wonder if it wasn't the right time to bring it up.

He set his fork down. "I haven't changed my mind. I know we talked about having two or three way back, and it's probably something we should discuss. I know we're not quite at that point yet, but what about you? Do you want to have children?"

Natasha nodded and released the breath she didn't realize she'd been holding. "I still want children but wondered whether it would actually happen."

Antonio reached for her hand. "Then we're in agreement."

They shared a smile and continued the meal while laughing and sharing their dreams.

When they finished, he said, "I'm glad Lori didn't ruin the evening."

She waved him off. "I wasn't going to let that woman mess up my date because aren't you supposed to be following me home?"

Antonio lifted his hand and signaled for the check. "Yep, and the sooner the better."

"Works for me." And she couldn't wait.

CHAPTER 24

Antonio's body simmered at a low boil as he drove to
Natasha's place, torn between passion and anger. More than
once over the past couple of days he questioned his judgment
in getting involved with Lori. For her to interrupt his dinner after their confrontation yesterday made him wonder if
she'd truly lost her mind. It had been all he could do to stay
in his seat and not personally escort her out. But then, that
would've created a scene he didn't want to have to explain.
His cell rang, and he held his breath, praying she wasn't calling, but relaxed when his brother's name popped up on the
car's display.

"Hey, Nate."

"Hey. I just wanted to make sure you're good after that
fiasco with Lori yesterday."

"Good probably wouldn't be the word I'd use at the
moment."

"Please don't tell me you and Tasha weren't able to
straighten things out. I know she was pretty hurt by all the
crap Lori was spewing."

"Nah, that's not it. She and I talked this morning, and

we're fine. Lori showed up at Ms. Ida's tonight while we were having dinner and all but demanded to talk to me privately, like she didn't see Tasha sitting there."

"Man, she has balls. What I don't understand is why she suddenly decided to show up after all this time."

Antonio released a deep sigh. "Apparently, now she wants all the things I was offering during our marriage."

Nate made a sound of disgust. "So, let me get this straight. She came *here* thinking what...that she could spout a few I've changed words and you'd just fall back into her arms? Un-*freakin'*-believable!"

"My thoughts exactly. Let me call you tomorrow. I'm on my way to Tasha's."

"Don't worry about calling. I was just checking on you."

Nate took his role as big brother seriously, and the older Antonio got, the more he appreciated it. "Thanks." He disconnected, then pushed a button. "Call Lorenzo, cell."

"What's up, Tony?" Lorenzo said when he picked up.

"Just wanted to confirm Tasha is coming with me. I know you guys offered your home, but she wants to take a trip to Lake Tahoe, so we'll probably head up there after meeting with you and Cedric."

"Actually, we can just take the meeting to Tahoe. We both own homes up there, as well as Ced's younger brother, Jeremy. Jeremy most likely won't be using his, so you guys could stay there, but I'll confirm with him just to be sure. Our places have enough bedrooms for you two, but I figure if you're taking this little trip, you're going to want a little privacy."

"You figured right." He wanted to be able to make love to

Tasha in any room without worrying about someone hearing or seeing anything.

Lorenzo chuckled. "I'll text you tomorrow with the dates and directions. Not sure if you have the flexibility to take Friday off, but it might be best if you could. That way you can leave early in the morning and miss all the weekend traffic. The other good thing is it'll be a couple of weeks before Memorial Day, when the season typically kicks off. It's less crowded."

"Thanks for the info." Antonio heard a little boy's voice calling for "Daddy."

"Come on, lil' man. Sorry to cut this short, but it's bath time."

"Go handle your business. I'll look for your text." He turned into Natasha's driveway as he ended the call and sat there a moment imagining what it would be like to have a little one calling him Daddy. Shaking off the yearning, he shut off the engine, got out, and sauntered to the porch to ring the doorbell.

"Took you long enough to get here," Natasha said when she opened the door. She pulled him inside and closed it behind him.

"It didn't take me long. Somebody's just a speed demon."

"Just tonight. I couldn't wait to have you to myself for a little while."

"And what exactly did you plan to do now that you have me?" She locked her arms around his neck and drew his head down for a kiss that shook him to his core. Her hands slid beneath his shirt at the same time. Antonio broke off the kiss, yanked the shirt over his head, and tossed it on the sofa.

"Mm-hmm...this is what I wanted to see. When did you get this?" Natasha asked as her tongue skated across his chest and over his tattoo. "It's exquisite."

A groan erupted deep in his throat. "Junior year of college. I took a couple of classes in African studies, got interested in the tattoos of different tribes and their meanings. This one is supposed to symbolize the transition to adulthood, so I thought it fitting for my twenty-first birthday." He could barely get the words out with her hands and mouth all over him.

"I'm sorry I wasn't there when you got it."

So was he. He gently grasped her hands and pressed a kiss to each one. "My turn." His hands went to the buttons on her blouse and undid them one at a time, kissing each newly exposed portion of skin. He removed the shirt and tossed it in the direction of where his landed. Antonio continued removing each piece of clothing, slowly and sensually, until her body trembled.

"Tonio, please."

"You don't ever have to beg me for anything, baby. I'll give you whatever you want. Don't you know what you mean to me?" As he carried her to her bedroom and laid her on the bed, he was so close to baring his heart, to telling her how much he loved her. But he couldn't, not yet. Not when he still had that corner of uncertainty and fear in his heart and until he knew for sure she was with him all the way.

"Are you going to stand there all night?"

"Not at all. Just admiring the beauty spread before me." Stepping back and with his eyes never leaving hers, he discarded the rest of his clothes and donned a condom. Antonio took his time caressing and kissing every part of her body. For him, this wasn't just sex. It had never been with Tasha. He loved her and wanted her to feel what his words could not tell her at the moment. His hand traveled over her smoother-than-silk skin, from her face to her neck, and finally settled on her breasts. He massaged the full mounds, then left her mouth, captured a pebbled nipple between his teeth, and tugged gently, drawing a sharp cry from her. "You like that, baby?"

"Y-yes," Natasha said on a ragged moan.

He slid down her body, hooked her left leg over his shoulder, and placed a kiss on her knee. He trailed his tongue along her inner thigh to her warm center, then mirrored his actions on her right leg. Antonio repeated the action until she trembled and writhed beneath him, then plunged his tongue into her slick, wet heat.

"Tonio," she chanted as his tongue moved faster and deeper. She arched her back and screamed his name again.

Lowering her leg and moving back up her body, he guided his engorged shaft inside her. He groaned as he sank deep within her tight walls. He lowered his head and kissed her, loving the way she fit in his arms, the way her mouth and body fit with his as if she had been created especially for him. "You take my breath away," Antonio murmured, thrusting in and out of her with long, languid strokes.

"Mmm, and you take mine away. You're mine, Tonio."

"And you're mine, sweetheart." He crushed his mouth to hers. The kiss was hot and demanding but filled with a sweetness that flooded his soul. Her breathless sighs and small whimpers of pleasure stoked his own, and he increased the pace. Antonio moved his tongue in and out of her mouth, imitating the movements of his lower body.

Natasha arched up to meet his deep strokes, while her hands moved up and down his back. "Don't stop." Her cries of passion filled the room. "*Yesssss!*"

Feeling her body start to tremble around him, he lifted her higher, stroking her harder, wanting to be as deep as possible when she came. She let out a scream that sent chills down his spine. He pulled out to the tip and surged back in. His orgasm exploded through him with a force that stripped him bare and left him weak and panting. Antonio dropped his head. *I have to keep her in my life.*

* * *

Natasha carried the platter holding grilled salmon inside to the counter laden with covered dishes of ribs, chicken, and a host of sides.

"Thanks for all your help, babe," Antonio said, coming to stand next to her and placing a kiss on her cheek. "I'm going to take a quick shower. If the doorbell rings, please answer it."

"Okay." She watched him until he disappeared around the corner. She could get used to being here like this. They were behaving as if they were a married couple, and Natasha realized she wanted that with him. She'd never enjoyed cooking—she'd much rather do all the table settings and create the ambience. This made the third time they had worked side by side in the kitchen, and she found herself looking forward to preparing meals with Antonio.

Speaking of table settings, since they were eating outside, Natasha had opted for a natural tablescape. She didn't want to cover the beautiful golden oak wood table and decided to use a sage-green runner instead. She added ivory square plates, champagne-colored napkins, and simple greenery for the centerpiece.

Natasha heard the doorbell and rushed inside to answer it. "Hey, Gabriel, Serenity. Come on in."

Gabriel dipped his head and placed a sisterly kiss on Natasha's cheek. "What's up? It smells good in here."

"Of course that's the first thing he'd say," Serenity said, hugging Natasha. "Girl, you're answering doors now. Guess that means things are pretty serious with you two. I'll be waiting for my wedding invite," she added sotto voce.

"Serious enough, and don't get ahead of yourself." Natasha couldn't deny that's where she wanted the relationship to go, but she was still afraid to hope. However, she planned to do everything in her power to make it work this time. Before she could close the door, she spotted Jon parking.

"I know you love him, Tasha."

"I love him so much, it scares me," she said softly.

Serenity gave Natasha's hand a gentle squeeze. "I understand, but it's worth every risk you'll take. And for the record, he loves you, too. His eyes give him away."

Natasha wanted to believe her friend. "I—" She cut herself off when she heard Antonio's voice.

"Welcome, welcome," Antonio said as he entered, greeting Gabriel and Serenity. He wore a pair of black shorts and a pale-blue pullover silk tee. The man made every piece of clothing he wore look amazing. Natasha didn't realize she was staring until Serenity elbowed her.

Serenity gave her the side-eye. "What's that you were saying about getting ahead of myself?"

Ignoring her, she waved Jon and Terri in. After the greetings were done, they all filed into the kitchen.

Antonio raised a hand to get everyone's attention. "Drinks are in the cooler outside—soda, water, and tea. Wine, in the bucket next to it. Help yourselves while Tasha and I bring the food out."

Natasha rolled her eyes when Serenity shot her another I-told-you-so look as she followed the others out. Before she realized it, she'd slipped into the role of hostess with no effort. And she liked it. A little too much.

"Everything all right, sweetheart?" Antonio asked, coming up behind her and sliding an arm around her waist. "You look like you're a million miles away." His lips moved over her neck and shoulder, which was bared by an off-the-shoulder top, while his hands roamed lazily over her hips.

Her head dropped back, and sparks shot to her core. "Mmm...I'm fine. I can't...We're supposed to be taking the food out." Natasha could barely get the words out because he had her body on fire.

"I know. Did I tell you how much I love having you in my home, in my kitchen...in my life?"

I love it, too. "I don't remember."

"Then let me go on record and *show* you how much." He spun her in his arms at the same time as his mouth came down on hers.

Natasha moaned and gripped the front of his shirt. The kiss was unhurried and infused with need and something else she couldn't identify.

Antonio locked his eyes on hers. "Do you feel it, Tasha? Do you feel how much you mean to me?"

In his beautiful eyes she saw passion, longing, and what looked like...love. Or maybe it was just wishful thinking on her part. "I feel it, Tonio." She felt it in every kiss, every touch. She wanted to believe he loved her, but he'd never actually told her.

He stroked a finger down her jaw and smiled. "Let's go enjoy our guests."

Our guests? Natasha followed him out with all the different platters and bowls, still trying to process his words, the kiss, everything. It took her a moment to get herself together and jump into the many conversations around the table.

"Antonio, with the spread you laid out here," Gabriel said, reaching for another rib, "it could be Supper Club Part Two."

"Nah, I'll leave that to the ladies and hope to get an invite every now and then. Speaking of the supper club, when's the next one?"

"Not for two or three weeks. Dana's out of town, and she pretty much threatened me if I had it without her. But when she returns, I'm thinking of doing an old Sunday dinner theme—fried pork chops, macaroni and cheese, candied yams, and collard greens," Serenity said.

Natasha pointed her fork Serenity's way. "If you're making greens, I know there had better be some hot-water cornbread with it. Antonio, I'm telling you it's to die for. So crunchy on the outside, tender inside...*So good*."

"Girl, you know I got you. You just can't eat all of it."

"Hey, you snooze, you lose." She bit into a rib and hummed because it was so good.

The conversation shifted to Antonio discussing how he'd beat Gabriel in a one-on-one basketball game.

"Man, I told you that was pure luck," Gabriel was saying.

"Nah, bro, like I told *you*, it's all skill. We can drive on over to the high school whenever you're ready. Jon, what about you?"

Jon laughed and held up his hands in mock surrender. "I ain't got nothing for you on a basketball court, but throw on some cleats and pads and I'll wear both of you out on a football field."

Everyone hollered.

"And then we're going to need some Bengay for all three of them," Serenity cracked. "Y'all are closer to forty than not."

Terri and Serenity exchanged a high five, and Terri said, "Exactly. Then you'll be coming into the ER for me to patch you up."

Natasha laughed so hard her side ached. "I can't believe you three. But I have to say, it might be kind of nice to see you out there playing if we get to see a little skin."

Serenity waved her fork. "Good point, good point. I vote for those little shorts the NBA players used to wear back in the eighties."

"Wait, wait," Antonio said with a laugh. "How did this turn into *that* kind of conversation?"

Natasha gave him a look of innocence. "I don't know what you mean. We're just talking about watching you all play ball, right?" She shrugged.

He leaned over and whispered, "I'll show you all the skin you want . . . *in private*."

She pretended to focus on her food. No way would she touch that comment, especially not here and now. Not when she wanted to find that private place.

"Uh-huh, that's what I thought." He winked and went back to eating.

Natasha glanced up and met Serenity's and Terri's gazes. Both wore knowing smiles, and Terri fanned herself. She mouthed, *Don't say one word.* Both women looked at each other and fell out laughing. "Some friends you are." They laughed harder.

Antonio reached for Natasha's hand under the table. When she turned his way, he said, "We should probably talk about us soon. I think Tahoe will be the perfect place. And don't look so worried. We're good, baby." He leaned over and kissed her.

"Aw, y'all are so cute."

"That's so sweet."

"That's what I'm talking about. Claim your woman."

Natasha looked at her friends, who were all smiling and making comments. "Oh, hush." Her heart started pounding, but she couldn't stop smiling or anticipating their trip to Tahoe.

CHAPTER 25

How are you doing over there, Grandma?" Antonio asked as they drove back home from the care facility. She'd been quiet for most of the drive.

"I'd like to say I'm fine, but I've never lied to you, and I don't plan to start now. I'm angry and sad that I'm going to lose him and that one day when I visit he won't remember me."

His heart broke at the anguish in her voice, and he couldn't find one word to say that would make it better or ease her pain, so he remained quiet. It made him more determined to get that facility done. He just prayed it wouldn't be too late.

"If you love Natasha, and I know you do, don't waste time, honey. Cherish each moment as if it's the last one because you don't want to ever look back and have regrets. Life is fragile, and just because she's here today doesn't mean she will be tomorrow. Never take that for granted. Say what you need to say, baby, then show her. Does she know you love her?"

"I hear you, and no, I haven't told her yet." She had to know he did, but he'd never actually said those three little words. However, he planned to tell her this weekend, because he wanted her in his life forever.

"What are you waiting for? You've loved that girl since you were fourteen," she added with a chuckle.

Antonio whipped his head in her direction and met her knowing gaze. He refocused his attention on the road. Had he been that transparent back then? "I plan to tell her soon."

She patted his knee. "Good. I always believed you two were perfect for each other."

I believe the same thing, he thought as he turned into his parents' driveway.

"Thanks, baby. I know you're busy these days, and I appreciate you taking time for this old lady."

"Never too busy for you, Grandma."

After walking her to the cottage, Antonio hopped back in the car, stopped to gas up, then picked up Natasha. His bag was already in the trunk. It would take four or five hours to get to Lake Tahoe, and he'd wanted to be on the road by eleven. Hopefully, they'd miss most of the traffic.

Natasha walked out the door as his foot hit the first step. "Good morning. I'm ready to get this party started."

Her bright smile and sparkling brown eyes hit him squarely in the heart, and he almost blurted the words then. *Stick to the plan.* "No more ready than I am." He eased the suitcase from her hand and brushed a kiss over her lips. It wasn't until they were back in the car that he noticed the two other bags in her hand. One was a small soft-sided cooler. "What's in there?"

"I figured we wanted to beat traffic, so rather than stop on the way, I brought us lunch. I took a chance that pastrami on a sweet roll with extra mustard and pickles was still your favorite."

Antonio leaned over and kissed her. "It is, and I can't believe you remembered after all this time."

She shrugged. "Like I told you before, I remember everything."

This added one more piece of evidence to a growing list that proved she was the one for him. He programmed in the directions and pulled off.

They spent the drive, laughing, talking, and eating—she'd also brought double chocolate chip cookies, which were another of his favorites. When they got close, he called Lorenzo to let him know they were about ten minutes away. His friend was standing outside as Antonio turned onto the cul-de-sac, which had only four exquisitely designed log cabins. Lorenzo, who stood with his arms around a woman, directed him to the driveway of the home next to his.

"If this is what's called roughing it, sign me up anytime," Natasha said. "They're gorgeous. I wonder how they found them. I'd love to find something like these to rent now and then."

"They bought the land and built them." Her mouth formed a perfect O, and he laughed. "Come on, baby. Let me introduce you." He climbed out of the car and took a moment to stretch before going around to help Natasha out. Cedric came out of one of the houses across the street, holding the hand of a woman.

"Good to see you. Hope the drive wasn't too bad," Lorenzo said, bringing Antonio in for a one-armed hug.

Cedric repeated the gesture.

"Not too bad. We ran into two small pockets of traffic, but otherwise it was smooth." Antonio urged Natasha forward. "Natasha, this is Lorenzo and Cedric." He pointed to each man. "And these beautiful women must be your wives." Lorenzo and Cedric introduced them as Desiree and Randi, respectively.

"It's really nice to meet you all," Natasha said. "And your homes are lovely."

"Let's get you guys settled, and then we can meet at my place to talk about what you need," Cedric said.

If he was impressed by the outside, Antonio was even more impressed when he entered the spacious two-story, three-bedroom, three-bath home. "You and Zo outdid yourselves with this place."

"Thanks. The master bedroom is upstairs. Just come on over when you're ready."

"Will you look at this place," Natasha said as soon as Cedric closed the door, spreading her arms. "I haven't taken a vacation in years, and I'm looking forward to this weekend." She jogged up the stairs, stopped halfway, and said, "Are you coming?"

Seeing her so excited made Antonio want to book a mini vacation every weekend for the next six months. "Yeah, I'm coming." He grabbed their bags and followed her enticing hips up to the second level.

"Do you consider Lorenzo and Cedric good friends?"

Antonio set the bags down and leaned against the doorframe with his arms folded. "Yes, why?"

She sauntered over to him and wrapped her arms around his neck. "You think they'd let us come back again soon?"

He threw his head back and roared with laughter. Lifting her off her feet, he swung her around and kissed her soundly. "I can ask. Let's head over." After retrieving his laptop, he and Natasha headed across the street. Cedric's place was slightly larger and similarly designed.

Randi looped her arm through Natasha's. "Natasha, while the guys are talking, you can hang out with us, so we can get to know you. And you can tell us how you two met. Don't worry, Antonio. I'll bring her back," she added with a grin.

Natasha smiled and gave him a little wave over her shoulder.

Lorenzo chuckled. "Man, you're as bad as we were." He gestured Antonio to the table, where Cedric already had his laptop open.

"What are you talking about?"

"Can't take your eyes off your woman—who is gorgeous, by the way," Cedric answered.

"I'm that obvious?" They were right. He hadn't been able to take his eyes off her since the day they met. Even when he saw her for the first time again and was still angry, he hadn't been able to dismiss her beauty.

Cedric slanted him a look. "That's a rhetorical question, I assume. So, tell us a little about what you're looking for."

Antonio powered up the laptop. "I initially mentioned wanting something like a small nursing-home-type facility, but while I was doing some research, I ran across something I think would fit much better." He told them about a facility that had been designed like a small community, with apartment-style rooms, paved streets, a grocery store, and a restaurant. "The medical personnel run the store and restaurant and dress in street clothes instead of uniforms." He showed them some photos of the original facility and his design for Firefly Lake.

"I've never even heard of this," Lorenzo mumbled as he scrolled through them. "Only one way in and out, twenty-four-hour surveillance, completely gated in . . . I know Desiree would love to have her mom in a place like this."

"We wouldn't need anything on this scale at home. I'm thinking eight to ten rooms, max. The restaurant could hold twenty-five to thirty, so families can dine with them."

"What about the grocery store?" Cedric asked, his fingers flying across the keyboard as he typed notes. "I can't imagine needing a full-on grocery store." He angled his head thoughtfully. "Maybe a place with toiletries, snacks, and basic stuff."

Antonio nodded and made his own notes. "I like that. I'd also like to include a park-like area." He thought about his grandparents taking the short stroll earlier. The three men went back and forth for another hour; then he moved the laptop aside. "The biggest hurdle will be financing it." He had a very nice portfolio and would use some of it to back the project, but there was no way he could finance the entire thing without wiping out his life savings. "We don't have the capital big cities enjoy."

Cedric and Lorenzo shared a look.

"What?"

"Let us make a call. Our family loves to get behind things like this."

He lifted a brow. "Zo, even if your family can contribute, we're talking somewhere in the ballpark of four to six million dollars, including start-up costs for equipment and salaries. Granted, that number is much smaller because the size of the facility is nowhere near what it would be in another place, and I plan to put some of mine behind it, but that's still a lot to ask."

"You didn't ask," Cedric pointed out. "We offered. Zo and I talked about it, and we'll be donating at least half the materials, so that brings the number down. Zo, call Brandon. He'll pass the word to the rest of the LA family."

Antonio's head was spinning. He lifted a hand. "Hold up. I—"

"Have you heard of Malcolm Gray?"

"The running back for the LA Cobras football team. Who hasn't? And didn't he recently announce his retirement? That still doesn't tell me anything."

"He's our cousin, just like Brandon Gray, who heads up Gray Home Safety."

He'd heard that the company was one of the largest of its kind in the country and doing exceptionally well. "Another cousin?"

"Malcolm's older brother," Lorenzo said with a wide grin.

Antonio's heart was so full, he couldn't speak. He listened while Lorenzo talked to his cousins. Other than his brother and Jeff—his college buddy in New York—none of his other friends had his back the way Lorenzo and Cedric were doing.

Less than an hour later, the call ended with the Hunter and Gray families having pledged donations that covered the remaining estimated costs, less the amount Antonio had allotted from his own savings. "I don't even know how to thank you two for this. If you ever need anything—and I do mean anything—you only have to call."

Cedric clapped Antonio on the shoulder. "Never doubted it. We'll be down in a couple of weeks to take a look."

"I'll set up a meeting with the mayor and town council. Just let me know what dates work best for you. My grandmother's going to want to adopt you," he added with a laugh.

"Works for me," Lorenzo said. "We made dinner reservations for later, if you and Natasha aren't too tired from the drive."

"I'm good, and I'm sure she'd be fine with it, but I'll ask." The three women entered as soon as he finished his statement. "Come here, baby." Antonio held his hand out to her. "We've got good news." He shared the details of the conversation.

Natasha brought her hands to her mouth. "Oh my goodness. That's fantastic. Mama Nora is going to be so excited, and I know the rest of the town will be as well." She leaned down and hugged him from behind, then whispered, "I'm so proud of you, baby."

Desiree and Randi agreed and said they couldn't wait to visit. Antonio promised to take them to Napa. "The guys made dinner reservations. Are you cool with that, or do you want to take a raincheck?"

"I'm absolutely cool with it. Gives me a little more time to chat with Desiree and Randi."

He nodded. The weekend was turning out to be better than he expected. Antonio hoped the rest went just as well.

CHAPTER 26

Natasha had the time of her life at dinner and getting to know the Hunters, especially their amazing wives. Randi, who was a former firefighter and fire investigator, had just started a career as an ATF agent. Desiree owned a bath and body shop and promised to send her some goodies, including some edible massage oil. She couldn't wait to try that out with Antonio, based on the stories the women had shared. With her owning a business, Desiree had allowed Natasha to pick her brain, and the woman had graciously offered some sound tips that Natasha planned to follow.

She'd picked up another two clients and was seriously contemplating talking to George about decreasing her work hours. She finished her shower, dressed, and went back to the master bedroom, which spanned the entire second floor. Natasha spotted Antonio standing on the balcony, leaning against the railing. Instead of approaching him immediately, she took the opportunity to study the man she'd fallen in love with all over again. Everything about him turned her on, from his giving heart, his intelligence, and his sexy body to his smoldering gray eyes and intoxicating smile.

Natasha eased farther into the room. As if sensing her presence, Antonio turned, and his gaze made a heated path down her body and back up. He slid the door open, bringing in a gust of cold air, then closed it behind him. She shivered and ran her hands up and down her arms. "How can you stand out there in shorts and a tee? It's freezing. And didn't you take a shower? You know what the old folks say about catching a cold because your pores are open." The daytime temperatures had been in the seventies, but they had dropped when the sun went down and now hovered near forty degrees. The cabin, however, was warm and toasty. They'd turned on the gas fireplace and dimmed the lights to their lowest setting, creating a romantic ambience.

"I didn't notice," Antonio said, coming toward her with a smile. "Nice blanket. Did you get it from one of the shops in town?"

"No. I hand crocheted it." She skipped the part about it being after that kiss at Ms. Ida's when they were barely on speaking terms.

"I like it."

"Thanks." Natasha had been cold when she first came out of the bathroom, but being near him heated her up, so she placed it on a chair. She frowned. "Are you okay?"

He nodded. "Just thinking."

"About the memory care facility?"

"That and other things." He stopped in front of her, leaving mere inches between them.

His intense gaze made her pulse skip. "I'm still in awe of what they did and how their families committed without even talking to you."

"They trust Zo's and Ced's judgment, so for them it was a no-brainer. I admire them."

"I think they're amazing."

Antonio caressed her cheek with the pad of his thumb. "And I think you're amazing. Beautiful, talented, intelligent, and mine."

Natasha's heart started beating double time.

"I love you, Tasha. I love you so damn much it scares me sometimes."

Her words stuck in her throat, and she couldn't stop the tears from cascading down her face.

He laughed softly and gathered her in his embrace. "I have to tell you, this is not how I envisioned the conversation going. Why are you crying, baby?"

"Because." His confessing his love and exposing his vulnerabilities at the same time made the tears fall faster. In his arms, she felt sheltered and loved, and she couldn't imagine being any place else.

"Because what?" Antonio cupped her face in his hands and kissed the tears. "Sweetheart, you're killing me here. You know I could never handle your tears."

"Because I love you, too, and I didn't know if I would ever hear you tell me again. I never stopped loving you, Tonio." It made her wonder if it had been her fault that none of her previous relationships had worked out. Had any of those men sensed that she'd held back a corner of her heart, the closed-off part that no other man had touched except her Tonio?

"I think you've always had a part of my heart. I just didn't realize it until I came home. But now my whole heart is yours and always will be."

When their lips met, Natasha didn't have to wonder if what she felt was love. She *knew* it, tasted it, absorbed it.

"Tasha. My sweet, sweet, Tasha," he whispered. "You are my heart." He whipped his shirt over his head and tossed it on the bench at the foot of the bed.

Natasha slid her hands over his broad shoulders, chest, and down to his tight abs. She loved his smooth skin and how the muscles contracted beneath her hands. Stepping back, she pulled the sleep shirt up and off, leaving her completely naked.

Antonio groaned. His hands feathered up her torso to her breasts, and he captured her lips again.

His tongue twirled with hers, sending waves of pleasure through her. Still kissing her, he walked her backward until her legs hit the bed. He followed her down and stretched his tall body over hers.

"Tonight I'm going to show you how much I love you, how much I adore you."

"Show me, Tonio. Then I can show you how much I love *you*." He made love to her slowly, tenderly, whispering passionate endearments. The way he moved inside her was unlike anything Natasha had ever experienced. She wrapped her legs around his back and gripped his shoulders. The sex between them had always been good, but tonight... The feeling was indescribable, and she cried out his name.

"Tasha." He called her name almost reverently.

He used a finger to trace her lips and gazed at her with such love, tears pooled in her eyes. He kept up the intense thrusts, his eyes never leaving hers. Sensations started deep in her belly and flared out to every part of her body. Natasha exploded with white-hot pleasure, shaking uncontrollably and screaming his name.

Antonio went rigid, then bucked inside her. He threw back his head and groaned out her name. "Baby, I love you."

Natasha held on to Antonio, grateful that they'd been given another chance.

* * *

Antonio stood on the town hall steps talking to Cedric and Lorenzo. They'd just left the meeting with the town's governing body, along with the hospital's medical director.

"I thought the mayor was going to run out and dance in the middle of the street," Cedric said with a chuckle. "I wish we had this kind of support from our political officials." Mayor Brewer had been beside himself with excitement, particularly when he found out the entire cost was already covered. The only stipulation was that the Hunters and Grays remained anonymous. He'd readily agreed and stated he would announce it at the next town hall meeting.

He smiled. "The beauty of small-town living. I'm sorry you two won't be able to hang around for the weekend, as planned." There had been a hiccup at one of their work sites, so the two men were heading back to Sacramento.

"We'll make sure we can do it next time." Lorenzo clapped Antonio on the shoulder. "Either Ced or I will give you a call to confirm the start date. Because the land is already leveled and paved in places, it'll cut down on the building time."

"I hope so. Thanks again for everything, and please pass along my thanks to your family." Even with the land already leveled, it would still take close to a year to finish the project. When the mayor heard the plan, he and the council voted to donate the land adjacent to the hospital on the old grocery store lot. With the hospital being located near the outskirts of the town, the owners had wanted a more central location for people to shop.

"No problem, Tony." Cedric glanced down at his watch. "We'd better hit the road." He gave Antonio a brotherly hug. "Go on over and give your grandmother the good news."

"Drive safely, and tell Randi and Desiree that wine tasting is on us when you come back." Cedric and Lorenzo headed to the parking lot, and Antonio started up the street to pick up Tasha from her office. He wanted her with him when he told his family. It had been two weeks since Tahoe, and they'd grown closer each day. And as soon as they left his parents' house, he had a surprise for her.

Antonio spoke to the receptionist and waited in the lobby while she called Tasha. Minutes later, the woman he loved strutted out. His heart nearly beat out of his chest with pride. In her, he'd found everything he'd always wanted, and the connection they shared was unlike anything he had ever experienced.

"Hey, handsome." Natasha leaned up to kiss him. "Ready?"

"I'm always ready for you, love." He held the door open for her.

She called out a good night to the receptionist, then paused and said softly over her shoulder, "It's a little early in the day for sweet-talking, isn't it? Unless you plan to—"

"Don't start," he said with a shake of his head. He didn't think he'd ever get used to her flirting. "I don't know what I'm going to do with you, woman." He'd parked at her office earlier to save time. He led her to the car and helped her into it.

"How did the meeting go?"

Antonio merged into the light traffic. "It went very well. Mayor Brewer was more excited than with the condo project." He gave her the particulars.

"Wow. I can't wait to see the look on Mama Nora's face when you tell her about the facility."

"I just hope my mother can keep the information to herself until the town meeting in a couple of weeks."

"Good thing it's not *my* mother. I'd wait, and she would find out when everybody else did."

He laughed. "That is a thought. But since I already told her I had something to tell the family, she'd hound me until I did."

Joining in his laughter, she said, "Good point. Maybe your dad can help her keep a lid on it. Oh, and can we do dinner later tomorrow? I'm going over to Serenity's after work. We're going shopping."

"Of course. I'll change the reservation to seven, instead of six. Will that be enough time?" While preparing meals together had become a special time for them, he still wanted to go out as well. Tomorrow they'd decided on the steakhouse in town.

"Plenty, thank you. And guess what? I'm meeting with another potential client." She did a little squeal. "This is the fifth one. George has already approved me going down to thirty-two hours a week."

Antonio grinned. "Congratulations, baby. I'm so happy you're getting all the new business. Pretty soon you'll be looking for office space for your own business." He kissed her hand but didn't let go. If he had his way, it would be someplace near his. But if she couldn't find what she wanted, he'd build it for her. He'd do anything for her. Now that the house was finished, he didn't see her as often during the weekdays, and he missed her.

She let out a satisfied sigh. "That would be something. It feels like those dreams we talked about in your fort all those years ago are finally coming true. And as I said before, I don't plan to let anything stop me this time."

She was the best part of that dream for him by far. He parked in front of the house and reached into the back seat for his laptop case.

"Okay, let's do this." Natasha almost beat him to the door.

His father answered the doorbell and pulled Natasha into a bear hug. "Hey, Tasha. How's it going, son? You two come on in. Your mother is driving me crazy, wondering what this is about."

"She'll find out in a minute," Antonio said. As soon as he rounded the corner to the family room, his mom leaped up from her favorite recliner with a huge grin on her face. "Hey, everybody."

Her gaze went from Antonio to Natasha and back to him again. "I hope this is the news I've been waiting for."

"Exactly what news is that?" He knew exactly what she meant, and if all went as he planned, that would be the next bit of news he'd share.

She swatted him on the arm. "Don't play with me, Antonio Jamal Hayes."

Nate chuckled.

Antonio hugged her. "That's not it, Mom. This is something else."

Her face fell, and Natasha said, "It'll be just as good, trust me." Natasha hunkered down in front of his grandmother while he opened the file to the 3D image of the proposed facility.

"When I took Grandma to visit Grandpa, she said something to me that got me thinking." He turned the computer around so she could see it. "This is going to be the new memory care facility here in Firefly Lake. It'll be built on the old grocery store plot next to the hospital."

Grandma Nora gripped his hand, and tears filled her eyes. "How did you . . . ? When . . . ?" She shook her head.

His family bombarded him with questions, which he patiently answered. "It will resemble a neighborhood, instead of an actual medical facility."

"The common dining hall will be a restaurant-type building, and there will be a small store and a park area with a walking path," Natasha finished, staring up at him. "This grandson of yours is incredible, and I am so proud of him."

Her words made Antonio feel as if he could do anything and filled his heart until it overflowed.

His father shook his head. "Son, this is a huge undertaking. How are you going to manage this and the condo project? The company isn't that large, and as much as I love this idea, I don't want you to spread yourself too thin."

"That was my question, too," Nate said. "Along with who's going to put up the finances."

Antonio and Natasha shared a smile. He said, "It's all been covered—they wish to remain anonymous—and some friends of mine who own a construction company in Sacramento will build it. Their company is much larger, and it will cut the time down considerably to what I could do." He turned back to his grandmother. "I just hope Grandpa gets to be part of it."

His mother rushed over and engulfed him in a crushing hug. "Oh, baby, I'm so very proud of you. And, Natasha, you were right. This news is just as good. I'm still holding out for the other news, though."

Antonio groaned. "One last thing. This conversation can't leave the room. The mayor will make the announcement at the next meeting." He chuckled when all eyes went to his mother.

"What?" she asked, affronted. "I'm not going to say anything."

"I love you, honey, but you can't hold water." His father slung an arm around his wife and kissed her cheek, while everyone else laughed.

"Antonio, this is the best gift I've ever received," Grandma Nora said. "And even if it turns out to be too late for my Fred, it will give me peace knowing that others will be able to experience being close to their loved ones." She hugged him and patted his cheek. "You make me so proud."

His emotions rose swiftly and nearly overwhelmed him. "Thanks, Grandma. That means a lot." He cleared his throat and stood. "Tasha and I need to get going."

"Ooh, a hot date," April, who had been content just to listen until now, said.

"Something like that." After a round of goodbyes that took way longer than he wanted, they finally got out.

Thankfully, because it was almost June, the days were longer and the weather stayed warmer later.

"Exactly where are we going? You never said," Natasha said as he drove.

"You'll see in a minute."

"We're going to our special spot."

"Yep. I thought a picnic dinner would be nice."

She craned her neck, trying to see the back seat.

"Go on and turn yourself around because it's not there." Knowing he didn't have to worry about anyone finding the area, Antonio had come earlier to set everything up.

He hung back a bit when they got to the inlet because he wanted her to see it first.

"Oh, Tonio, it's beautiful. But when did you have time to do this?"

"Before the meeting." He had erected a canopy with sheer panels on each corner in her favorite blue color and spread pink rose petals on the blanket. "Have a seat."

Natasha slowly lowered herself onto the blanket and fingered one of the petals. "I love this. I love you."

"I love you, too. We haven't done this in a long time, and I thought it might be nice." He pulled out the charcuterie board he'd done, plates, glasses, and a bottle of wine. They talked, laughed, and fed each other.

"I hope you brought dessert, too," she said, popping a grape into her mouth.

"Of course I brought dessert." He'd called Serenity and asked her to make a few of the chocolate-dipped strawberries Natasha loved so much, complete with champagne and whiskey. When he showed her the container, the smile that spread across her face could have lit up the sky. He removed the lid and offered them to her.

She bit into one and moaned. "Ooh, this one has whiskey. Here, taste it."

She held it out to him, and he bit into it. The flavors exploded on his tongue. "You're right. This one is a little more potent, but it's so good."

Natasha polished off the rest and reached for another one. "See, I told you. It's the perfect pairing." She let him take the first bite, then finished it.

"I agree. Just like us."

A shy smile played around the corners of her gorgeous lips. "Yeah, like us."

Antonio leaned over and slanted his mouth over hers, kissing her until she lay flat on the blanket. He wanted to be with her this way for the rest of his life.

CHAPTER 27

Natasha tried on another pair of sandals and stood in front of the mirror turning her foot one way, then another. "What do you think about these?" The navy-blue three-and-a-half-inch high heel had a slim toe strap, one that crisscrossed over her instep and around the ankle. Now that she had actual dates, she needed to upgrade her wardrobe.

"Those are cute," Serenity said. "Are you thinking of wearing them tonight for your date?"

"Only if I can find a nice dress to go with them. I really like these."

"Then get them. We only have about an hour before we need to head back. You can't be late. And speaking of dating, you and Antonio seem to be getting pretty serious."

"We are. He told me he loved me when we went to Tahoe." She removed the shoes and put them back in the box.

Serenity whirled around and planted her hands on her hips. "What? And you're just now telling me? I thought I was your BFF, and you're out here holding out on me."

Natasha chuckled. "We haven't really had a chance to talk."

She came and sat next to Natasha. "We're talking now, so come on, I need details. Wait." Serenity held up a hand. "*Most* of the details, like where were you, was it an after-good-sex confession, pillow talk? You can skip the X-rated version."

"I thought you said you didn't want all the explicit details. Those last two definitely qualify. But it was neither of those. I'd just gotten out of the shower, and we were standing in the middle of the bedroom. Did I mention that the master bedroom takes up the entire second floor? Girl, it was *gorgeous*. But anyway, I think I said something about the room being amazing, and he said I was amazing, too. And beautiful, intelligent, and *his*. Then he told me he loved me."

Serenity pretended to swoon. "That is so romantic. I know you told him the same."

"After bawling my eyes out." It still touched her that he felt comfortable enough to share his fears with her. Truth be told, loving him as much as she did scared her, too. The young love they'd shared didn't hold a candle to this new deep, emotional connection, which seemed to be growing daily. "It's better than last time."

"I should hope so." Serenity let out a laugh. "You both are adults, not teenagers, and have had some life experiences, some good, some bad."

"Yeah, that's true. I never told you that his ex showed up again at Ms. Ida's when we were having dinner."

"What did she want?"

"She told him she was headed back to New York, apologized for how things ended again, and wished us both well. I was shocked but glad."

"Me too. At least Antonio has some real closure now."

"I agree." Everything seemed to be falling into place this time.

Serenity stood. "Now we need to find a dress to go with those shoes. I think I'm getting these gray sandals."

Laughing, Natasha picked up the box holding the blue sandals and another one with a pair of low-heeled casual ones, and they went to pay. Afterward, they power shopped for a suitable dress.

"Tasha, girl, I think I've found it." Serenity waved around a navy and white contrast sleeveless bodycon dress with a front slit. "Antonio is not going to know what hit him when he sees you in this dress."

"I think you might be right," she said with a slow grin. She tried it on with the shoes and had to agree that the combination worked perfectly. And with the late-spring temperatures climbing into the eighties, it wouldn't be too cold. She added that to her purchases for the day.

She had less than forty-five minutes to get ready when they returned, and after a quick shower, she applied light makeup and stepped into the dress. Tonight she wanted Antonio to know how much she loved him. She went to the closet for the container holding her memory items and took out the black velvet box she'd placed there almost eighteen years ago. The ring was too small for her finger now, so she strung it on the chain with the heart and fastened it around her neck. Fingering the treasured jewelry, she recalled his words: *I know we're too young for marriage right now, but this is my promise that we'll be together when we graduate from college.* They'd lost so much time, and she couldn't help but wonder if she'd see the promise realized this go-around.

Natasha was putting on her shoes when the doorbell rang. She quickly fastened the last strap on her shoe on her way to the door. "Hi." The word came out breathier than she'd planned, but it was the best she could do as she stared at Antonio in his charcoal-gray suit that nearly matched his eyes. But then, she wasn't the only one. He didn't say anything for the longest time, but the banked heat in his eyes told her everything she needed to know. She'd have to let Serenity know the dress had done exactly what she had hoped. "So, are you going to stand there all night staring at me?"

"I just might. Baby, you are stunning, and I'm about two seconds from canceling those reservations and having a private dinner right here."

Laughing, she hooked her arm in his and pulled him inside. "I don't think so. I bought this outfit specifically for tonight."

"Then I don't want to disappoint you." Antonio kissed her softly.

Nothing about the man disappointed her, and she could kiss him all night long. The way his tongue tangled with hers had her almost canceling the dinner herself. Natasha saw the moment he noticed the necklace.

He gently ran his finger along the chain, then lifted the heart charm and ring. "You wore it."

The tenderness in his expression nearly took her breath away, and if she hadn't already been in love with him, she would have fallen at that moment. "It means everything to me. *You* mean everything to me."

Antonio rested his forehead against hers. "And you mean everything to me."

They managed to leave a few minutes later and got to their reservation on time. Natasha rarely dined at By the Lake and didn't know that the expensive restaurant had been remodeled. The color scheme had been changed to beige with black and chocolate-brown accents. Combined with the dim lighting and candles on the table, the owners clearly had romance on their minds.

As they ate, Antonio asked, "Have you gotten any offers on the Ward home yet?"

"A couple, but both were below the asking price, so Chase and Mike want to wait a bit longer to see if they can get a little closer."

"They should. With all the new upgrades, it's definitely worth more now." He ate another bite. "I can't get over how beautiful you look tonight."

"Thank you. I can say the same about you."

Shaking his head, he said, "Men aren't beautiful."

"Okay, then handsome, fine with a capital F . . . Take your pick." He dropped his head. "Aw, are you blushing?"

"No. Men don't blush, either, so let's move on to another topic."

Natasha took a sip of her wine. "That's not what those red cheeks are saying right now." She couldn't believe he was embarrassed.

Antonio eyed her over his glass. "I thought we were changing the subject."

Smothering a giggle, she held up her hands in mock surrender. "Okay, okay, moving on. Or back to our previous conversation. Have you decided what you're going to do about your housing?"

"I pretty much decided on buying."

"As much as I want to represent you, I think I'd better pass it off to Brett. Don't want anybody accusing me of favoritism."

His brows knitted in confusion. "Why would it be favoritism?"

"Seriously? We're dating. And if it's one of my listings, that would be a whole other potential mess because I'd be representing you as the buyer and the other person as the seller."

"Dual agenting isn't illegal if both parties agree, Tasha."

"I know that, but I'd be taking a risk that sometime down the line either one or both parties might wonder if I lowballed their selling price to help you out. Or I increased yours to help them out."

"True, but everybody and their mamas know everybody else in this little town, so there's no way to get around it."

She scooped up the last bite of the fluffy mashed potatoes. He had a point. It was hard not to sell to a friend or family member living in a town like this one.

"When I'm ready, I'll let you know, and you can decide then what you want to do." Antonio nodded toward her plate. "Do you want to get dessert?"

"No, but if you want to order some, go ahead."

"I'm good. If you're finished, I can take you home and do what I've wanted to do all day."

Check, please! "Take me home." She started to ask what he wanted to do but decided she didn't care, as long as they were together.

They made the drive in companionable silence, interspersed

with soft conversation. As soon as they entered the house, Antonio pulled Natasha into his arms. "I've wanted you in my arms from the moment I woke up this morning."

He held her close, his hands idly roaming up and down her spine. Natasha closed her eyes and listened to his heart beating. The strong rhythmic sound comforted her and made her feel safe. No words were exchanged. They didn't need any. She slid her hands inside his suit coat and wrapped them around his middle.

At length he eased back. "There's something else I've wanted to do."

"What's that?"

"Dance with you."

She smiled up at him. "We haven't danced since Grandma Nora's party." Come to think of it, he'd held her much the same way that night. "I can put some music on."

"I've got my own playlist," he said close to her ear, his voice low and sexy. "I just need to sync it to your speaker."

No other man had made a specific playlist just to dance with her. She retrieved the speaker and waited while he synced it. A moment later, the first notes of Luther Vandross's "If Only for One Night" filled the room.

He drew her into his arms again and tenderly kissed her. "I love you, baby."

He started a slow sway, and they danced to song after song. From Luther and India Arie to vintage Earth, Wind & Fire and Michael Jackson, he'd selected songs that gave her a glimpse into his heart. "I love you, too, Tonio." *Forever.*

* * *

Antonio could hold Natasha all night long. Being with her brought back all the dances they'd shared during middle and high school, in his fort and at the inlet. He recalled having to endure teasing from his buddies, who said Antonio was so into Natasha that no one else existed. They hadn't been wrong then, and they wouldn't be wrong now. His gaze went to the necklace she wore. She'd mentioned once that she preferred white gold over yellow, and he'd made sure both pieces of jewelry reflected her desires. He took in the barely visible diamond solitaire in the ring's center and smiled in remembrance of how he had painstakingly searched through every ring in the case to find the perfect one. And one he could afford. Antonio hadn't been able to keep his promise then and prayed he would get the opportunity this time.

Cherish each moment as if it's the last one because you don't want to ever look back and have regrets. Life is fragile, and just because she's here today doesn't mean she will be tomorrow. Never take that for granted. Say what you need to say, baby, then show her. His grandmother's words sounded in his mind. He wasn't going to take their love for granted, and he planned to show her.

"You're quiet. What's going through that head of yours?" Natasha's voice drew him out of his musings.

"You. Us. Let's sit." Antonio paused the music, and they sat on the sofa. He draped an arm around her shoulder and pulled her closer until their bodies touched.

Leaning her head against his shoulder, she asked, "You care to share?"

"Where do you see this going?" He knew what he wanted, but he needed to know whether they were on the same page.

Yes, she loved him, but did that include working toward something more permanent?

She seemed to contemplate her next words before speaking. "I've tried not to think about it too much because I don't want to jinx anything. But I do know I don't want us to end up where we did before."

He lifted the heart charm and ring. "Neither do I. I'm in this for the long haul, Tasha. I want us to do all those things we dreamed about." Antonio stopped short of mentioning marriage. While he intended it to be his end goal, he still had a few things he needed to work out first. The admission was freeing in a way. All those years when he'd been angry and thought he was over her, she remained somewhere in the dark recesses of his heart, occupying a space no other woman could claim, not even his ex-wife.

Natasha sat up and searched his face. "Are you talking about us starting a business together?"

"Not sure how realistic that would be, but having our offices near each other sounds good to me. However, I can't say how much work I'd get done because I'd find every excuse to steal a few minutes with you each day."

She smiled. "You're pretty distracting yourself. And yeah, not certain how that whole business would work."

"But that's not what I'm talking about. I meant the dreams we had as they related to us." His cell buzzed in his pocket, but he ignored it.

Natasha leaned over and checked her phone. "That must have been your phone. Aren't you going to see who it is?"

"If it's something important, they'll call back. I have to

leave soon, so I want to spend these last minutes without interruption. Whoever it is can wait."

She snuggled closer to him. "That's one of the sweetest things a guy has ever said to me. I think I'm going to keep you."

Chuckling, he kissed her forehead and let out a sigh of contentment. He planned to keep her, too. Until the end of time.

CHAPTER 28

Antonio didn't get around to checking his messages until the next morning. He had one from his brother with a photo attached of a grinning Noelle holding another drawing she'd done. Smiling, he replied that he'd stop by later to pick it up. At this rate, he'd have a wall by the end of summer, but he didn't mind. He loved that little girl.

Antonio finished his smoothie and left to meet Gabriel. They tried to get together every couple of weeks or so to shoot around on the basketball court or go running. Today they planned to do both and had invited Jon to join them. He sensed Jon and Terri might be going through something, but he didn't know for sure.

Gabriel was waiting at the start of the trail when Antonio arrived but stood at Antonio's approach. "Jon canceled. He said something about going to the Bay Area with Terri."

"I'm not mad at that. She's the priority. You stretch yet?" Antonio asked as he went through his own routine.

"A little."

"Ah, you might want to do a little more, old man. I don't want Serenity to blame me when you come home hurt."

"Who're you calling old?"

He chuckled. "You're two years older than me, and there's no one else around." He made a show of looking around the area. "So..."

Gabriel snorted. "I see you're starting early. Let's see if you can back it up. Midnight Hills Trail?"

"Easy." They started on the path at an easy jog, then increased the speed until they'd reached a sprint. The slip slap of their running shoes hit the pavement in a steady, coordinated rhythm. "Taking the hill?" Antonio asked. There was an alternate route for people who didn't want to climb the hill.

"Yeah," Gabriel said, winded.

Because he'd been running the hill almost daily for the past three weeks, Antonio had no problem with the incline, but Gabriel lagged behind a few steps until they started back down on the other side. It took about half an hour for them to make the complete loop.

Gabriel gestured to a picnic table near the lake. "I need to catch my breath."

Antonio took a moment to do a few stretches, then dropped down on the opposite end of the bench. He leaned back and rested his elbows on the table.

"You and Natasha seem to be doing well. Are you in love with her yet?"

"I've always loved her. Now I want more, though."

"Let me know if you need some help with anything. Natasha helped me when I was ready to propose to Serenity, so I want to return the favor." Gabriel shared the details of how she'd helped to set up a private picnic and brought Serenity to the spot under the guise of needing to take photos for her portfolio.

He laughed. "My baby goes all out for others." Natasha had a big heart, and Antonio loved that about her. "I'll let you know if I need some assistance."

Gabriel's cell rang. "Let me answer this. It's Nana."

"Tell Ms. Della I said hello."

Chuckling, he said, "You sure you want me to do that? Hey, Nana."

On second thought, maybe not. All he needed was more interference from her and his grandmother. He already had some idea about how he wanted to propose, but he was wisely choosing to keep the details to himself and only share them with his brother or Gabriel. The thought of taking another trip down the aisle made him a little anxious, but then so did not having Natasha in his life. Antonio had to believe they'd been given this second chance and it would be better than before.

"I'm going to have to skip basketball. Nana's sink is stopped up, and I need to go check it out." He slowly stood, groaning.

Antonio laughed. "I told you to stretch. Man, ain't no snap back after thirty."

Doing a few twists and bends at the waist, Gabriel said, "No lie." They walked back to their cars. "Oh, and Nana wanted me to ask if you knew anything about the special town hall meeting next Friday."

A grin tugged at the corner of his mouth. "Maybe." He unlocked the car by remote and opened the door.

"Wait. That's all you're going to say?"

"Yep. Later."

"You're cold, my brother. Later." He shook his head, slid behind the wheel, and drove off.

Now that Antonio had some extra time, he texted his brother to see if they'd be home so he could stop by and pick up his picture from Noelle. After receiving a thumbs-up, he headed in that direction, stopping at home first to shower.

As always, Noelle's exuberant greeting made Antonio feel special. "Hey, Noelle." He caught her up in his arms and hugged her as tightly as she did him. "How's preschool going?"

"Good. I can count to ten and I know my colors and I played with Rachel outside and we had fun," Noelle said without taking a breath.

"Wow, all that. Sounds like you're pretty busy at school." She nodded. "Uh-huh."

He finally spoke to Nate and April, who stood by smiling as their daughter barely let Antonio get a word in edgewise, let alone greet anyone else first.

"I feel like a second-class citizen in my own home," Nate said with a chuckle. "You've been here for five minutes, and we're just now getting a measly hello."

"I can't help it if I'm Noelle's favorite. Right, baby girl?" Antonio tickled her, and she giggled. He set her on her feet. "How about you go get my picture."

She sprinted out of the room.

April hooked her arm in Antonio's. "Okay, now that little ears are gone for the next ten seconds, how are things with you and Natasha? Do you need some help planning the wedding? And *please* tell me your crazy ex-wife took her behind back to New York." She leaned back to check down the hall-way. "Hurry up and answer."

He couldn't stop the laughter that poured out of him. "Thankfully, she's gone, and Natasha and I are good."

"You skipped a question, dear brother-in-law, which means you're close." She let out a whoop and did a little dance. "I can't wait," she said in singsong.

"I didn't even say anything."

"You didn't have to," Nate said. "The look on your face says it all, and I'm happy for you two."

Antonio held up his hands. "Wait. No. We're not... I haven't—"

"Here's your picture, Uncle Tony," Noelle said, skipping into the room. "I cut it out all by myself."

He squatted down, and she shoved the paper close to his face. Gently moving it back, he smiled at the shapes that had been cut out using different colored paper to make a house, grass, and sun. "Thank you. I have to stop at the store to buy a frame for it."

"Ooh, goody! I wanna go with you."

"Baby, Uncle Tony might have things to do today," April said. "Maybe you can go with him next time, okay?"

"Okay," she said with her lip trembling. A fat tear rolled down her cheek.

She turned her big brown eyes on Antonio, and he heard himself say, "She can come with me." He didn't care about the cleaning he'd planned to do, washing his car and truck, or mowing the lawn. He couldn't disappoint his niece. Some of his friends and co-workers in New York had nieces, neph-ews, and grandchildren who loathed spending time with them. Antonio was blessed that even though he'd rarely seen Noelle for the first four years of her life, she knew him, loved him, and wanted to spend time with him. He couldn't—wouldn't—deny her. Everything else could wait.

April shook her head. "Your uncle is such a big softie. Come on, let's put your shoes on. And you are *not* spending the night this time, little missy," she added as she ushered Noelle to her room.

"I cannot wait until you have your own. We'll see how fast you become immune. Just pitiful," Nate said.

Antonio merely smiled. "I'll bring her back in a couple of hours. We may go to the park and get ice cream."

"You have her spoiled rotten, Tony."

He clapped Nate on the shoulder. "That's what favorite uncles do."

Nate shrugged the hand off his shoulder and muttered something about having irritating little brothers as he went to get the car seat.

After getting Noelle strapped in her seat a few minutes later, Antonio drummed his fingers on the steering wheel. He wanted to invite Natasha to go with them.

"Let's *goooo*, Uncle Tony," Noelle called from the back seat.

"In just a moment. I'm going to call a friend to see if she wants to hang out with us." Noelle clapped, and he smiled. Because Natasha's greetings weren't always kid friendly, he made the call before starting the car, so it wouldn't come through the speakers.

"Well, hello, sexy," Natasha said when she answered.

His point exactly. "Hey, baby. Are you busy right now? I

wanted to invite you to hang out with Noelle and me for a couple of hours. She made me another picture, and I have to pick out another frame."

"Aw, she's such a sweetheart. Actually, I'm free, and I'd love to go with you two."

"Great. I'll see you in a few minutes." Ending the call, he pulled off. He'd downloaded the soundtrack to *Encanto* and started the music. Noelle's happy screams filled the interior of the car, and she immediately started singing. He had no idea how she memorized so many of the words to each song, but she belted them out like she was part of the cast.

Antonio paused the music when he arrived at Natasha's house. "We'll start it again in a minute."

"Okay."

As soon as he stepped out of the car, Natasha came out and rushed down the stairs.

"Hey." Natasha leaned up and gave him a short kiss. "I didn't want you to have to take Noelle out and then have to go through all that trouble strapping her back in."

"Hey, baby. Thanks. I'm still working on getting her in and out in less than fifteen minutes." He closed the door behind her, rounded the fender, and slid behind the wheel. "Noelle, do you remember Ms. Baldwin?"

"Hi, Noelle," Natasha said.

"Hi. You came to dinner at Gramma's house."

She shifted in the seat so she could see in the back. "I sure did. You have a good memory."

"I go to school."

Noelle proceeded to give Natasha the same rundown of

her activities she'd given Antonio, and he smiled. Watching Natasha interact with Noelle told him she'd be a wonderful mother. He had his two favorite girls, and life couldn't get any sweeter.

* * *

Natasha enjoyed seeing Antonio with his niece as they searched for the perfect picture frame. The two couldn't be closer, and he displayed the patience of a saint as they picked up and discarded frame after frame.

"Do you like it?" Noelle asked, holding up a dark-blue frame.

"I think this matches perfectly, Noelle." The picture had been done on light-blue construction paper.

The little girl beamed, then said to Antonio, "This one."

Antonio smiled and eased it from her hands. "Your picture is going to look great in here. I have to go pay for it." He took her hand and started toward the cash registers.

Noelle stopped and reached for Natasha's hand. "Come on. We have to go together."

She skipped happily between them, and Natasha's heart filled to near bursting. Several people shopping in the store scrutinized them as they passed, some sneaking glimpses and others more obvious. One woman even outright asked if they were practicing for their own. Natasha took her cue from Antonio, who didn't comment.

Back in the car minutes later, he covered her hand. "You okay? I was so anxious to spend time with you that I didn't think about how it would look or what people would say."

"I'm fine. What we do is our business." Natasha shifted in her seat to face him. "And you know what else? If I decide to kiss you in the middle of Main Street, I'm going to do it."

"We can absolutely make that happen, but I'll just take one here for now." Antonio leaned over and touched his mouth to hers.

Noelle giggled. "You kissing like Mommy and Daddy."

Natasha and Antonio glanced at Noelle in her car seat wearing a big grin, then at each other, and burst out laughing. "I think we should get going."

"Probably, before you get us in trouble."

Her mouth fell open. *"Me?"*

"Yes, you, Miss-I'll-kiss-you-in-the-middle-of-Main-Street."

She fell back against the seat and clamped her jaws shut since she didn't have a comeback for that one, rolling her eyes when he chuckled.

They stopped to get ice cream before going to the park. After enjoying the sweet treat at one of the picnic tables, they took Noelle to the playground. Natasha had as much fun as Noelle on the slides, climbing structures, and swings.

Antonio stood behind Noelle and pushed her on the swing, then moved to the next one and did the same for Natasha.

"Go higher, Uncle Tony," Noelle said.

Natasha leaned her head back and echoed the little girl. "Yeah, higher, Tonio." He laughed and kept alternating between them, being careful not to let Noelle go too high. As Natasha's swing came back toward him, he caught it, snuck in a quick kiss, and sent her sailing again.

A few minutes later, Antonio said, "Okay, last time. Then we have to go."

"Aw," Natasha and Noelle chorused.

Natasha slowed her swing and jumped off like she'd done as a kid. "This was the best time ever. I could do this forever." Being with him and Noelle today made her long for a family of her own.

He swung Noelle up on his shoulders and dipped his head to kiss Natasha. "And we will."

She froze. *What did that mean?* It was the first time he'd hinted at something more permanent. Natasha had been afraid to hope, but maybe this time they'd get it right. *She'd* get it right.

CHAPTER 29

Monday, two weeks later, Natasha sat in her office with a smile on her face. It had been a permanent fixture on her face since her outing with Antonio and Noelle. And to add icing to her decadent cake, Kathleen had come back last week and had basically kept to herself, taking the tension in the place down to zero.

She opened an email from a prospective buyer who had made an offer on the Ward home and sighed. Their loan had been denied, and they had to withdraw. Natasha replied, then sent a text to Chase to let him know she'd be going back to the drawing board.

Her cell rang, and she frowned at the display, not recognizing the number or the area code. "Hello," she said tentatively, hoping it wasn't a spam call. There had been an increase in everyone around town getting them.

"Is this Natasha Baldwin?"

"May I ask who's calling?" Natasha didn't give out any personal information unless necessary, particularly when she didn't know the identity of the caller.

"Yes. This is Ana Webb, calling from Yarbrough Technologies. Ms. Baldwin was referred to us by Daphne Lockett, and I was hoping to speak to her about an interior design project."

She bolted upright in her chair. "This is Natasha." Daphne had mentioned passing her name along, but she figured that meant to people around town. Natasha had never heard of this company and did an immediate search. "How can I help you?" The company name popped up and was located in Los Angeles.

"Our company frequently brings in analysts and programmers for extended stays, depending on the project. We've recently purchased a ten-unit apartment complex that has been renovated and now needs the next step to make it a home away from home."

Her heart pounded in excitement. "Are you looking for simple or minor changes or a complete overhaul, including furniture?"

"Complete overhaul. Do you have a few minutes to meet with us right now on video? We'd like to get to know a little about you to determine whether you'd be a good fit for what we need."

"I . . . yes." Inside, she did cartwheels.

"Great. What's your email address? I'll send you a link."

Natasha rattled it off, then after a few more instructions, ended the call. She leaned back in the chair and took a few deep breaths to calm herself. Was this the opportunity she'd been waiting for? She gave herself a pep talk. "You can do it. You've got this. You know the information like the back of your hand." Her computer chimed with an email, and she quickly sat up and opened the message. Good, she had ten minutes to get herself together.

At the listed time, she clicked on the link and was more than pleased by the diversity of the six people on the screen. It made her even more excited about the potential of doing business with them. After a round of introductions—the CEO himself ran the meeting. Natasha answered every question, and all the nervousness she'd initially experienced disappeared. This was her area of expertise, and by the time the meeting ended, they knew it, too.

"Ms. Baldwin, I'm very impressed by your knowledge and passion and would like to offer you the position," Mr. Yarbrough said.

Wait. What? Just like that? Shouldn't she take time to think about it and discuss it with her girls, Antonio? Mr. Yarbrough's voice cut into her thoughts as he outlined the salary. *On second thought, I can just tell them later.* "I'd love to work with your company and bring your vision to life."

"Wonderful. We'd like for you to come to LA within the next week. You and Ms. Webb can finalize the details."

"Ms. Baldwin, if you could stay on, we can take care of the logistics now."

"That would be fine." Her voice stayed calm, but inside she was a jumbled mess. Everything was happening so fast, it left her head spinning. And who did Daphne know at the company? Once the details were hashed out, Natasha would fly to LA on Thursday for an overnight trip. At the end of the conversation, a thought popped into her head. "Ms. Webb, would I need to be on-site during this entire process?" She'd gotten so excited, she had totally forgotten about the locale.

"I believe that's the plan. We'd put you up in one of the corporate apartments for the next few months until the project is completed. Will that be a problem?"

Yes! I finally got a second chance with the man of my heart, and now I'm supposed to leave? Not to mention my current job. Her heart plummeted. "There may be an issue, as I'm currently employed. However, I'm hoping we can work something out that will satisfy both parties."

"I'll let Mr. Yarbrough know, and we can discuss it when you get here later this week. I won't hold you, Ms. Baldwin. Please look for an email with your travel itinerary by end of day."

"Thank you so much." When the call ended, Natasha did a little shimmy in her seat. She'd been dreaming about an opportunity like this.

She picked up her cell to call Daphne. "Daphne, this is Tasha," she said when the woman answered.

"Hey, girl."

"I'm calling to thank you for the referral to Yarbrough. Who do you know there?"

Daphne screamed. "Yes! I had hoped they would call you. My cousin is an executive there and mentioned the company was looking into purchasing temporary housing for their consultants because they were spending so much contracting with other companies. Tasha, please tell me you're going to do it."

"They asked for a meeting, so I'll be doing that." She didn't want to give too much information yet.

"Girl, I know you're going to knock their socks off."

"Thanks for the vote of confidence. I can't tell you how much I appreciate you doing this."

"Please. I've gotten so many compliments on my bedroom, you're lucky I haven't given your name to every one of my family members spread across the country."

Natasha laughed. "Whoa. Let's take it slow and see how this goes first. I have to get going, but I owe you, girlfriend."

"That's what friends do. Talk to you later."

She disconnected, placed the cell on her desk, and smiled. *Yeah, friends.* Picking up the phone again, she sent a group text to her besties with a dancing GIF. She cracked up at their responses as they trickled in over the next several minutes. Each one had included its own emojis and GIFs expressing excitement. Serenity said they needed to celebrate. Natasha agreed but decided to just invite them over for a celebratory drink for tonight. They'd party once she actually got the job. It would also be a good time to talk to them about her dilemma.

Natasha sent a text to Antonio, telling him she needed to talk to him.

Thirty minutes later, he replied: *Hey, babe. Late call tonight with Ced and Zo. If I get home early enough, I'll call. Otherwise, I'll walk down to your office tomorrow morning.*

She sighed. Of all the people she told, he was the one she wanted to talk to most. He'd always been there to help her sort things out. Turning back to her desk, she finished all the tasks on her to-do list, said goodbye to her co-workers, and left.

When she got home, she changed into a pair of shorts and

a T-shirt. The early-June temperatures had soared to nearly ninety. At this rate, they would be in for a hot summer. Natasha got one of the bottles of Moscato she'd purchased after the wine tasting and stuck it in the refrigerator. She still had an hour or so before her girls arrived, so she sat and ate the rest of her chicken Caesar salad from lunch while sorting through her mail. Not seeing anything important, she tossed the pile aside and finished her dinner.

Natasha still had a few minutes and decided to call her mother. "Hey, Mom."

"Hey, Tasha. How's it going, honey?"

"Pretty well. I have some news to share."

"You and Antonio are engaged?" her mother asked excitedly.

She rolled her eyes. "How did I know that would be the first thing out of your mouth? No, we aren't. I just received an offer for a huge interior design project."

"Oh my goodness! That's wonderful."

"But it's in Los Angeles." Natasha really hoped she'd be able to do her job remotely.

"Oh."

"Yeah, oh. I don't know what I'll do if I have to move there."

"I can see how that would complicate things."

Complicated didn't even begin to describe her problem.

"But I'm sure you'll figure out what's best."

"That's all you're going to say?"

Her mother's chuckle came through the line. "Exactly what do you want me to say? You're a grown woman, Natasha, intelligent, and very capable of making decisions."

Her mother usually had an entire monologue of advice and suggestions, but this time, when she needed it most, she had absolutely nothing. "I guess," she mumbled. The doorbell rang, cutting off whatever she had planned to say. "Mom, someone's at the door." She headed to the front and let Serenity in. Natasha hugged her friend, then mouthed, *My mom.*

"Okay. Keep me posted."

"I will. I'll talk to you later. Tell Dad hi." She disconnected. "Sorry about that."

Serenity waved a hand. "Oh, girl, please. How're your parents doing?"

"They're fine."

"Good. I was going to try to get all the details as soon as I walked in the door, but I guess I'll wait for Terri and Dana so you don't have to repeat yourself more than once. I'm so happy for you. I remember all the time you spent in college praying for this kind of opportunity."

She smiled. "I did." Poor Serenity had to endure Natasha asking her opinion on one design or another almost daily. "And you were such a good sport, listening to all my dreams."

"You did the same for me." The doorbell rang, and Serenity said, "I got it. You pour the wine." She shooed Natasha toward the kitchen and crossed the living room toward the door.

Natasha laughed and went to the kitchen. She had the glasses and the wine on the counter when Serenity came back with their other two friends. The women greeted each other with hugs.

"Girl, I was so happy to see both of them at the door. Now

we can get all the juicy details." Serenity rubbed her hands together and wiggled her eyebrows.

After the wine had been poured, Terri held up her glass. "To Tasha. May this be the first of many successes in your interior design career and the start of a new business."

"Congrats, sis," Dana said.

"I second that," Serenity added, lifting her sparkling cider.

They touched glasses and sipped. "I'm still trying to process all this." Natasha told them about Darlene's referral, the video meeting, and that the company was flying her down on Thursday. "It's all so fast, and the pay is more per hour than I expected."

"What did Antonio say when you told him?" Dana asked.

"I haven't had a chance to talk to him yet. I think they're getting ready to start work on the memory care center, and he's talking with the Hunter cousins tonight." The town had been more than a little excited about having a place here in town, and Natasha had laughingly told Antonio he was getting closer to having that key to the town, if all the applause had been any indication. "There's something else. I think they're expecting me to live in LA for the next several months until the project is done." She placed her glass on the table. "There's no way I can do that, not with the way things are going with Antonio. I walked away the last time, and now that I've gotten a second chance with him, I refuse to mess it up."

"I see your point," Terri said. "Is there anything you can do?"

She massaged her temples. "I don't know."

"A good portion of designs are done digitally these days, so I'm sure you'll be able to work something out," Dana said.

"True." Natasha wanted this job, but she wanted Antonio, too. She just hoped she wouldn't have to choose.

* * *

It was all over town about Natasha's interior design offer. Before Antonio made it to his office Wednesday morning, he'd gotten texts from his brother and godfather and a call from his mother. He and Natasha had been playing telephone tag for the past two days. He'd had another long day at the job site yesterday and had driven to the Bay Area for some supplies rather than wait two days for them to be delivered. The unplanned trip meant that he'd been unable to meet her. Then she was out of the office when he called later. He'd talked with Ced and Zo again last night and wished he had called Natasha afterward, despite the late hour.

He couldn't be happier for her, but one piece of the news gave him pause. If the "rumors" were correct, it meant that she'd have to move to Los Angeles for who knew how long. Where did that leave them? And once she finished that one and was presented with another opportunity, would she take it and decide to stay in Southern California for good? Growing up, that had been all she talked about—becoming a designer to the stars.

Staring out his office window, Antonio had no idea what to do. He couldn't deny her this chance, but for him, it felt like déjà vu all over again, like with his marriage. They had to talk, and soon. He sent her a message, asking if she had a few minutes this morning. She replied almost immediately with one word: *Yes!*

After signing the documents Leah left for him, he took the folder to her desk. "Here's everything. I'm going to walk over to see Natasha for a few minutes."

"Okay." Leah leaned forward and gave him a bright smile. "Isn't her news *fabulous*?"

"It is. Be back in a little while." As he meandered up the block, two more people stopped him to talk about Natasha's great opportunity and how she's making her hometown proud. By the time he made it to her office, he had resigned himself to the fact that he was going to lose her again. His steps were heavy as he approached her door.

"Come on in," Natasha said when he knocked. She rounded the desk, met him halfway, and slid her arms around his neck. "You're a hard man to catch these days."

"I'm not the only one." Antonio held her for the longest time, not wanting to let go for fear it might be the last time.

"I am so sorry I didn't have a chance to talk to you before all this blew up. I made the mistake of calling my mother and forgot to tell her to keep it to herself. The next thing I knew, it had spread like wildfire."

He released her and propped a hip against her desk. "I'm proud of you, baby."

"Thank you. It still doesn't feel real." She told him about the call and that she'd be going to LA tomorrow.

"How long will you be gone?"

"Just overnight."

"For now. They're going to need you to be there for the next several months, I imagine."

"She mentioned that, but I'm not sure I want to be gone for so long. I *can't* be away from you all that time."

Antonio reached for her hand and pulled her back into his arms. "Sweetheart, you can't pass up this opportunity. You have to follow your dream. I don't want you to look back years from now with regrets." He struggled to get the words out, and each one felt like a dagger to his heart. "It would..." He paused, trying to keep his emotions under control. "It would kill me if you woke up one day and resented not taking this chance." If she resented *him* for staying.

She searched his face and gripped the front of his shirt. "What are you saying, Tonio?"

The hardest thing he'd ever have to say. He placed a lingering kiss on her lips. "I'm saying you have to go." Her phone rang.

"Hang on a minute. Let me tell whoever it is I'll call back." Natasha checked the display. "It's Mr. Yarbrough's office. I have to take this."

Antonio kissed her again. "I love you. Go follow your dreams, baby."

"Antonio, wait." She grabbed his hand.

"You'd better get that." Letting her go was even more difficult this time around. With a bittersweet smile, he brought her hand to his lips, then walked out, his heart breaking all over again because he didn't know how they'd make it work if she had to move.

CHAPTER 30

Natasha walked through the small one-story apartment complex on Friday morning and thought the layout was genius. Not only was it located within walking distance of the company, but each room had a terrace that overlooked lush gardens. Each one-bedroom unit had a kitchenette with a stove, microwave, and refrigerator. The rest of the place lay bare like a blank canvas waiting for an artist's splash of color. Excitement raced through her veins, and she couldn't wait to get started.

"Do you have any questions, Ms. Baldwin?" the efficient Ms. Webb asked.

"No. I think they've all been answered, but I'll let you know if I think of something else."

"Please do. We'll head back so you can fill out some paperwork before your flight this afternoon."

As they walked the one block, Natasha surveyed the neighborhood. Yarbrough Technologies was situated in an area with both residential and commercial properties, along with a park that had a walking trail. Once at the office again, she finished all the paperwork and handed it back to the executive assistant.

"I think this about does it. We have you scheduled to return two weeks from now. Your office will be ready by then."

"Thank you, and I really appreciate the flexibility to do this remotely." She had been nervous about asking for a schedule that would allow her to travel to LA two or three times a month as needed but utilizing videoconferencing and emails for the bulk of the job. Natasha understood that there would be times when she had to stay a little longer, especially once the materials arrived and the setup began, but she couldn't have been happier to know she wouldn't have to leave Firefly Lake—and Antonio—for an extended period of time.

Ms. Webb picked up the phone receiver, spoke into the handset for a minute, then hung up. "Your car is waiting downstairs."

Natasha thanked the woman again, gathered her bags, and took the elevator to the ground floor. The black town car sat at the curb, while the driver stood at the open back door. *I could get used to traveling like this.* Being closer to the Long Beach airport meant avoiding the mess of LAX, and she breezed through the security checkpoint with time to spare for her noon flight.

After landing in Oakland, she still had to drive home, and depending on traffic, it could take two to three hours. Since it was still earlier in the day, she, fortunately, missed most of it.

Her first order of business was finding Antonio. She hadn't talked to him since he walked out of her office two days ago. It had taken her much of the day and night to realize that he was willing to sacrifice their relationship in order for her to realize her dreams. It made her love him even more, but she was also determined to have her cake and eat it, too, as the saying went.

As soon as she was within a few miles of town, she engaged the Bluetooth and called his office. "Hi, Leah. It's Natasha."

"Hey, Tasha. How was your trip?"

Natasha shook her head. She still couldn't believe her mother had spread her business like that. One call to Ms. Bernice and the news had spread like a lit fuse attached to a stick of dynamite. Next time she'd either wait to tell her mother or ask her not to say anything. "It was fine. Is Antonio around?"

"He's out at the condo site. Come to think of it, he's been out there working since before eight this morning. Same thing as yesterday."

"Um...thanks, Leah. I'll try him there."

"Oh, okay. See you later."

She hit the button to call and ask him to stop by her place when he got off so they could talk but disconnected. Natasha didn't want to wait that long, especially because she knew he would dig his heels in about her not blowing the opportunity. However, he had no idea about the arrangement she'd made. A smile played around the corner of her mouth. *But he's about to find out.*

Natasha spotted him on the partially done roof of one of the buildings as soon as she parked. If he saw her, he gave no indication because he never looked up from working. She got out, leaned against the car, and just observed the play of muscles in his sculpted arms with every movement. As if sensing her scrutiny, he lifted his head and his surprised gaze met hers.

Smiling at him, she started in his direction. "Hey, handsome."

"Hey. How was the trip?"

"Good. Very good."

A pained expression crossed his features, and he turned away for a split second.

Her heart swelled with emotion. How she loved this man.

"What are you doing here?"

"We need to talk."

"We'll talk later," Antonio said quietly.

"This can't wait. I won't take up too much of your time."

"Tasha—"

"Are you coming down, or should I come up there? Makes no difference to me." She stepped out of her low-heeled pumps and braced her hands on the ladder. If he thought she was going to leave without setting him straight, he had another thing coming.

* * *

When Antonio had seen Natasha at her car, it had taken everything in him not to jump off the roof and haul her into his arms to show her how much he'd missed her. He knew they needed to talk, but he wasn't sure he wanted to hear what she had to say. The love he felt for her consumed every

303

part of his body, mind, and soul. All this time, he'd believed that receiving her letter ending their relationship had been the worst thing that had ever happened to him. But if he had to actually *hear* the words from her lips, he didn't think his heart would ever be whole again.

"Ah, boss."

He turned to see where Todd was gesturing, and his heart jumped to his throat. "Tasha, baby, what the hell are you doing?" She was halfway up the ladder, and Todd rushed over and held it.

"Since you decided to revert to being a butthead and won't come down, I'm coming up to you. I'm not leaving until we talk."

This woman. "Just stop before you get hurt. I'll come down." If she fell, he would never forgive himself. Antonio's heart rate didn't slow until she was safely on the ground. He carefully climbed down. Before his feet touched the ground well, she was in his face.

Natasha jabbed her finger into his chest. "Listen to me, Antonio Jamal Hayes, and listen good. I know you think you're being all noble and whatnot by thinking you can let me go out into the world and realize my dreams, and I love you for it." She cupped his jaw. "But, baby, don't you know you're the biggest part of that dream? Don't you know how much I love you?"

He removed his gloves, stuck them in the back pocket of his jeans, and grabbed her hand. "You're going to put a hole in my chest."

She snatched her hand away and planted it on her hip.

She was his dream, too, but still. "My wanting you to take

this job has nothing to do with me not loving you—because I do, more than my own life. But—"

Natasha scowled up at him. "But nothing. I'm *not* giving you up for any job, no matter how good it may be. I walked away from us the first time, but I'll be damned if I do it again."

Is she saying she turned the job down? Antonio placed his hands on her shoulders. "What are you talking about? Tasha, you can't pass up this opportunity." Being tasked with such a large job so early in her career was akin to winning the lottery.

"I'm not passing on the opportunity."

Was she thinking about them engaging in a long-distance relationship? He didn't have a problem with doing something like that, but if she decided to stay in LA permanently, it wouldn't work unless he gave up the construction company. Just like he didn't want her to let go of this contract, he knew she wouldn't ask him to do that. "Then please explain it to me."

She placed her hand on his heart. "I am not going to move to LA. True, years ago, I said that was my ultimate goal. But I realize I can still have my dream job without sacrificing the most important person in my life—you. I'll travel to Southern California a couple of times a month and may have to stay two or three days at a time, but my home is *here* . . . with you, Tonio. I don't want to be anywhere else."

Antonio crushed his mouth against hers, relief flooding his body. "I love you so much, baby. But how?"

Natasha smiled. "I explained my dilemma to the company president, who apparently is a die-hard romantic. He's been married for almost forty years and, according to his executive assistant, still dates his wife, buys her flowers for no reason, and goes out of his way to make sure she's happy. Anyway, he said love was a precious gift and not something that should ever be taken for granted or tossed away and readily agreed to my proposal to pretty much do the job remotely." She slid her hands around his neck. "So that means you're stuck with me."

"I can't tell you how much I love hearing this. You'll never know how hard it was to walk away from you, but I'd do anything for you, even if that means letting you go. I want you to reach and exceed every goal you set."

"And I appreciate that. Oh, and speaking of the whole letting me go thing. If you ever try to break up with me again, I'm going to hurt you."

He threw his head back and laughed. "No need to get violent. Like you said, you're stuck with me." *Forever.*

"Good. I love you, Tonio."

He swung her up in his arms and kissed her with all the love in his heart. Whoops, claps, and whistles sounded around them. Antonio lifted his head and found his entire crew viewing the exchange with wide grins and fist pumps. He shook his head. "Go back to work."

Natasha buried her head against his shoulder and laughed. "Can't wait to see how this kiss will end up after traveling around town. By the end of the day, it'll probably turn into a kiss, a proposal, and a wedding."

Antonio chuckled. *This time they won't be wrong.*

CHAPTER 31

A week later, Natasha sat with her three friends at Brenda's Bake Box, enjoying mouthwatering cinnamon rolls and tea, and telling them about her LA trip. They'd been so busy, it had been difficult to schedule a time when all of them were free.

"How many units did you say there were, Tasha?" Dana asked.

She finished chewing the warm sweet roll. "Ten. There is literally nothing in them except kitchen appliances. I almost did a happy dance, knowing I'll be able to put my stamp on every detail."

Serenity took a sip of her tea. "That is so cool, and I'm betting you already have a few ideas."

"Girl, you know me well. I just have to make sure I don't cross them with the condos here." She had already started a file of designs for the apartments with neutral colors that would appeal to both men and women and finished two potential condo designs. "I'll be going back to LA next week for a couple of days for an update meeting and to take some measurements."

"You mentioned they wanted you to stay down there until the project is complete. Are you going to take a leave or quit working for George?" Terri asked.

Natasha leaned forward and said conspiratorially, "I've already talked to George, and he's allowing me to work part time for now. And I'm not moving. I'll be staying here and only traveling when necessary."

"Oh my goodness. That's fabulous. I know a certain some-one is probably going to be *really* happy about that."

She smiled at Serenity and wiped her hands. "He is. I didn't get a chance to tell you all, but right before I left, Antonio sort of ended our relationship." She held up a hand when they all started to speak. "It came from a good place, so y'all don't go harassing my baby. He thought I would have to move down there and was basically going to sacrifice us so that I could chase my dreams."

Serenity brought her hand to her heart. "That is so roman-tic and selfless. I know he loves you, and for him to say that had to be so hard."

"Yeah, it was a sweet gesture, but I told him I'd hurt him if he ever tried to break up with me again." The women howled with laughter. "Shoot, got me out here working hard for this second chance, and he's acting up," she added with a mock pout, which only made the women laugh harder. After they'd gotten everything straightened out, they had taken a walk by the lake and talked about how they would navigate her being gone. Antonio would fly down and meet her some weekends when it came time for her to be gone for longer stretches of time. "But we're straight now."

"So, that must have been when the famous lip-lock

happened." Dana chuckled. "Girl, you and Tony are keeping this town on its toes with this soap opera love affair. You know folks are taking bets that you two will be engaged by the end of the year." She polished off the last piece of her cinnamon roll.

Natasha's mouth fell open. "Are you *serious*? I heard a few comments, but I didn't know anything about bets." She shook her head. "These people need to find something else to do."

Terri snorted. "It's a small town, Tasha. I've learned over the past few years that people here take their amusements where they can get them. And a rekindled love affair that started when you two were teens is big news. So, is it considered something like insider trading if I ask you how close you are to a proposal, then place a bet?"

She swatted at her friend. "Just hush. He hasn't said anything about us getting engaged anytime soon." Antonio had hinted at them being together long term at the park that day, but the subject of marriage had never come up. Not that she wouldn't marry him in a heartbeat if he asked, but despite it feeling as if they had been together a lifetime, in reality, it had only been about three months.

Serenity narrowed her eyes and pointed a finger at Natasha. "Well, since we're your BFFs, I expect us to get inside information *before* the masses."

"And before my mother," she cracked. When Natasha called her a few days ago, her mother hadn't been apologetic one bit and said, "Of course I had to brag on my baby."

"I am so glad my parents didn't grow up here," Serenity said.

Terri lifted her hand for a high five. "Same, my sister."

"I think I'm going to skip the whole dating thing, then," Dana said. "My entire family is here, and my mother is as bad as yours."

They shared stories about their mothers embarrassing them, and then the conversation shifted to tomorrow's supper club. "What time are you thinking for dinner tomorrow, Serenity?" Natasha asked.

"Probably around three. That way we'll have plenty of time to relax afterward, and no one has to rush since Monday's a workday."

"Works for me." Natasha's cell rang, and she checked the display. "This is Chase. Let me see what he needs." She connected. "Hey, Chase."

"Hey, Tasha. I hope I didn't catch you at a bad time."

"Oh, no, you're fine. I'm just hanging out at the Bake Box with my girls. How's your mom adjusting?"

"Not too badly. Your finding and sending the photo albums helped a lot. But that's not why I called. I know it's Saturday and you're off, but I received a call with an offer that's above the asking price."

"That's fantastic. If you send me the name, I'll get in touch first thing Monday morning."

"Actually, the party is wondering if you'd be able to meet at the house today around two."

Natasha took a quick peek at her watch. That was only forty-five minutes from now. "Sure. It shouldn't take long to walk them through and start the preliminary work. If it turns out that they want it, do you want to accept the offer?"

"Absolutely. Thanks, Tasha."

"You're welcome. I'll call you later this afternoon and let you know how it goes. I am kind of curious as to why they didn't just contact me if it's someone who lives here."

"I have no idea. Gotta run. I'll let them know you'll be there."

"Okay." She disconnected and frowned. Was it someone close to his family? That might explain why they went directly to him. Whatever the case, she'd find out when she got there. "As you heard, there's a potential buyer for the house, and I need to meet them out there in a little while."

"Keeping my fingers crossed this one will be the one," Dana said.

Natasha finished up her food, stood, and hugged her friends. "I'll see you guys tomorrow. Serenity, if you have anything specific in mind for table decorations, text me."

"Will do. Now go sell that house, girlfriend."

Laughing, she weaved her way through the tables to the exit. Natasha made a quick stop at her office to pick up the information packet she had put together, then drove over to the house.

What's Antonio doing here? His truck was parked in the driveway when she pulled up. She thought he'd finished all the renovations. Unlocking the front door, she called his name. No answer. Natasha retraced her steps and walked around the porch to the back. She spotted him leaning against the big oak tree at the far edge of the yard with one foot bent and resting on the trunk and his arms folded. He seemed deep in thought. The pose was so sexy, she pulled out her phone, zoomed in, and hit the camera button to take a picture.

She descended the deck steps and crossed the yard. "Hey,

Tonio. What are you doing here? Is there something wrong with the house?"

Antonio straightened and kissed her softly. "Hey. No, the house is fine. It's peaceful here."

"Yep, my favorite place to be." And next to where he'd been leaning, she could still see where he'd carved their names inside a heart. Her hand involuntarily went to the spot. "Well, we won't be able to come here much longer. I'm meeting a buyer, and Chase has already given the okay to take the offer if the client likes the house." Natasha frowned, still staring at their names. "I don't remember the word forever being here."

"I added it earlier. And the client loves the house."

She eyed him, trying to process him adding the word below their names. "You added it? Wait. And how do you know what the client likes?"

Instead of answering her, he tucked her hair behind her ear and walked her toward the lake. "Have I told you how much I love you?"

"You might have mentioned it a time or two," she said, fighting back a smile. "But you still didn't—" She stopped walking when she saw red rose petals in the shape of a heart. He walked her inside the heart, lowered himself to one knee, and gently took her hand. Her pulse skipped, and her heart started pounding.

"My sweet Tasha. You are everything I've ever wanted in a friend, woman, and lover. I never thought we would be here like this, but I'm so grateful for this second chance with you." He bowed his head briefly before continuing. "I know it's been only a few short months, but I don't need years to know that we will always be a perfect pair. Seventeen years ago, I made a promise to you."

Natasha fingered the ring on the chain around her neck. She hadn't taken it off since that first night. Her hands shook, and she could feel the tears stinging her eyes. Antonio retrieved a small black velvet box from his pocket and opened it. The diamond solitaire caught in the sunlight and nearly blinded her. "Oh my goodness," she chanted.

"It's been a long time coming, but I love you, Natasha Leigh Baldwin, and I want to spend the rest of my life with you. I added the word *forever* on the tree because that's what I want with you. Will you marry me?"

"*Yes!*" she screamed. He slid the ring on her finger. She was so excited, she launched herself at him, and they both tumbled to the ground. His laughter rang out as he held her tight. She rained kisses all over his face. "I love you, Tonio."

"I love you too, baby. I do have one request, though."

"What's that?" She couldn't stop looking at the beautiful ring on her finger. The princess-cut stone had to be close to two carats.

"Can we have a short engagement? I've been waiting for you for almost two decades, and I don't want it to be another two."

Natasha burst out laughing. "We can get married *tomorrow* for all I care! I just want to be your wife." She was all for a short engagement. Two, three months, tops. She'd get together with her girls for their help to pull it off. She gasped and scrambled off him. "Oh, shoot. I'm supposed to be meeting a client." Natasha tried to smooth down her hair and brush the grass and stray rose petals off her crop pants.

Antonio pulled her back down and banded his arms around her.

"Antonio," she whined. "I can't let my client catch me out here rolling in the grass like a horny teenager."

"Sweetheart, you don't have to worry about that."

She stopped struggling in his arms, not like it did any good because it was like trying to move steel. "What do you mean I don't have to worry about it?"

"I'm the client."

She blinked. "Wait a minute. What do you mean you're the client? I thought you weren't ready to buy a house."

"I couldn't very well tell you that I was going to buy this house."

"And why not?"

"Because I hadn't proposed, and you hadn't accepted. This is my wedding gift to you. Remember when I told you I'd do anything for you? You have loved this place since you were a kid and dreamed of living here one day. This is just the beginning, baby. I plan to make every one of your dreams a reality if I can, because you mean that much to me."

Natasha couldn't utter a word. When she finally got her mouth to work, the only thing she managed before the tears started was "You are my heart, Tonio." She didn't think she could love Antonio any more than she already did, but he'd just proven her wrong.

* * *

"I can't stop looking at it," Natasha said Sunday afternoon as Antonio drove them over to Gabriel and Serenity's house.

He slanted her a glance. "I'm glad you like it. I wanted to get something a little bigger than the first one." He'd teasingly told her yesterday after proposing that he was trading the old one for the new one. The look on her face had been priceless. She told him in no uncertain terms that she wasn't trading anything.

"It's bigger, all right. I have to keep my shades on in the house now." She did a little shimmy in her seat. "Did you know people were taking bets on when we would get engaged?"

"Yeah. Leah tried getting some information out of me the other day, and Nate basically said that since I'm his brother, it wouldn't look good for him to lose the bet."

Laughing, she said, "That's the same thing my friends said. Speaking of family, when do you plan to tell them?"

"We can call them tonight. I wanted at least one day of peace before the town gets in our business."

"Amen to that. I say we wait two days. But I would like to tell our friends today."

Our friends. When he moved back, he never expected to develop new friendships so quickly. But in a short time, he had bonded with Gabriel and Jon and looked forward to hanging out with them. "I'm cool with that. I don't think they'll have a problem keeping our secret."

"Not at all. In fact, I can see them running out Monday morning and placing those bets and acting like they don't have a clue."

Antonio smiled over at her. He parked in front of the house. "Looks like we're the last to arrive."

"That's good, because I don't know how long I'm going to be able to keep this to myself."

"Didn't you say you wanted to wait until after dinner?" he asked with amusement.

"Yeah, I know. I'm just so excited. Okay, okay, after dinner."

"You don't have to wait if you don't want, Tasha."

"No, no. I'm going to wait." She turned the ring around so that the solitaire was facing her palm. "I'm ready."

He helped her out of the car, eased the tote from her hand, and with a hand at the small of her back, guided her to the door.

"About time you two got here," Serenity said, pulling Natasha inside and hugging her. She repeated the gesture with Antonio.

"You said three, and it's five till," Antonio said with a little laugh. They followed her out to the back deck, where the table sat beneath a canopy. Two outdoor air coolers were placed at opposite corners. With July right around the corner, summer was in full effect.

After all the rounds of greetings, he went inside to pour himself and Natasha glasses of wine while she set the table. "It smells so good in here." The counter was lined with platters of fried pork chops, mac and cheese, candied yams, greens, and Serenity's hot-water cornbread. His grandmother was the only one who could make the little oval pieces of bread, so he hadn't eaten it in years. "You two need help with anything?"

"Nah, man, we're good. As soon as Natasha is done, we can eat," Gabriel said.

Antonio nodded and took the wine outside. He stopped short at the sight of Natasha bending over the table. The shorts she wore stretched tight across her rounded backside, and he took a big gulp of the wine to keep himself from doing something crazy like stepping behind her and caressing every inch of it.

Jon came and stood next to him with a knowing smile. "Problems, my brother?" When Antonio didn't answer, he chuckled. "We've all been there."

The conversation halted when everyone joined them outside. Antonio seated Natasha and placed her wine in front of her, then took the seat next to her. Plates were filled, lively chatter ensued, and he had to admit that Serenity's hot-water cornbread was the best he'd ever tasted.

He must have groaned because Natasha said, "I told you." She bit into hers and pretended to swoon. "It's so good, huh?"

"It is. Just like everything else." Antonio raised his glass. "To Serenity. You outdid yourself with this meal."

"Thanks, Antonio. Although my wonderful husband did help." She smiled at Gabriel, and he placed a tender kiss on her lips.

Antonio and Natasha shared a secret smile, and he went back to his plate.

After everyone had finished first and second helpings, Natasha said, "That was so good, Serenity. I'm definitely going to let my food settle before I get a piece of that cake. But in the meantime, y'all wanted to get the inside details, so *bam*!" She whipped her left hand out and waved it around.

All four women screamed. Terri, seated closest, grabbed her hand. "You did good, Antonio. It's amazing."

Serenity and Dana rounded the table and alternated checking out the ring and hugging Natasha.

"Now, that's what I'm talking about," Gabriel said, extending his hand for a fist bump. "Welcome to the club."

"Thanks. I've waited a long time for my girl."

Serenity bounced up and down. "We have to make a toast. Gabriel, fill everybody's glass."

"I will, but I need you to slow your roll with all that jumping." He stood and placed his arm around her shoulder, gently rubbing her belly.

She waved him off. "I'm fine. Hurry up."

Gabriel poured wine for everyone and sparkling cider for Serenity. He held his glass up. "Antonio and Natasha, you two went through a lot to get to this point. May your love continue to grow always. Congratulations."

They all touched glasses, and Antonio lowered his head and kissed his future wife. She was his first, his last, his forever love.

EPILOGUE

Two months later.

Natasha walked toward Antonio on her father's arm, and it was all she could do not to hike up her dress and sprint the rest of the way. She'd waited her entire life, it seemed, for this day. His beautiful eyes radiated love, and it took her breath away. A sexy grin tilted the corner of his mouth as his gaze made a lingering path down her body and back up. He mentioned liking her dresses that showed her curves, so she'd chosen a one-shoulder dress that hugged every one of them.

She glanced around at how their backyard had been transformed into an outdoor wedding venue. Their love affair had started in this place, and she thought it fitting that they start their new life in the same spot. And it was a wonderful way to christen their new home. Her father stopped, kissed her cheek, and placed her hand in Antonio's.

"Take good care of my baby girl," her father said.

"I will, sir."

They faced the minister, recited their vows, and fifteen

minutes later, he said the words she'd been waiting to hear for a lifetime.

"You may now kiss your bride."

Their first kiss as husband and wife filled her with a joy she had never experienced. It was unhurried and so infused with love, she could feel it clear down to her toes.

"I love you, Mrs. Hayes."

"I love you, too, Tonio."

Antonio leaned close to her ear. "You know what it does to me when you call me that."

Natasha knew exactly what it did, and she looked forward to every day with him. He was the first and last man to hold her heart, and just like he'd said, they were a perfect pairing. And she planned to love him from now until eternity.

Don't miss Sheryl's next book,

COMING IN FALL 2024

RECIPES

Natasha's Shortcut Peach Cobbler

- 1 29-ounce can plus 1 15-ounce can sliced peaches in heavy syrup
- 1¼ cups sugar (plus more for sprinkling on top)
- ½ teaspoon nutmeg (plus more for sprinkling on top)
- 1 teaspoon pure vanilla extract
- 1 teaspoon butter
- dash of salt
- 2 tablespoons flour
- 4 tablespoons water
- Pillsbury Refrigerated Pie Crusts (2 in box) (let come to room temperature for 15 minutes before using)

Preheat oven to 350°F.

Add peaches, sugar, nutmeg, vanilla, butter, and salt to a 4-quart pot and stir to mix. Bring to a boil. In a separate small bowl, whisk flour and water together until flour dissolves. Add slowly to fruit mixture while stirring to prevent clumping. Boil for one minute and remove from heat.

Spray an 8x8 glass baking dish with nonstick cooking spray. Unroll first crust and arrange in dish, cutting where necessary to cover entirely. Pour fruit mixture into pan, being careful not to overfill. Cut second crust into 1-inch strips and cover in a lattice pattern. If desired, sprinkle sugar and nutmeg on top of crust. Bake for 30–40 minutes or until crust is lightly browned.

Hot-Water Cornbread

- ½ to 1 cup water
- 1 cup yellow cornmeal
- ¾ cup flour
- 1 teaspoon salt
- 1 tablespoon Crisco shortening
- vegetable oil for frying
- small bowl of cold water

Set kettle of water to boil. While water is heating, mix together the cornmeal, flour, and salt until combined. Cut in shortening until it resembles crumbs. Add just enough boiling water to your mixture to make a very stiff dough.

Add about a half inch of oil to a skillet and heat on medium-high. When the oil is hot (pops a little with a few drops of water), wet hands with cold water, scoop about two tablespoons of the mixture, and form into an oval. Press down slightly in the center (should be about a half inch thick) and carefully place in grease. Repeat, wetting hands in between each piece. Fry over medium heat about 4–6 minutes or until golden brown, flip to other side, and repeat. Drain on paper towels and enjoy!

ACKNOWLEDGMENTS

My Heavenly Father, thank you for my life. You never cease to amaze me with Your blessings!

To my husband, Lance, you continue to show me why you'll always be my #1 hero! I couldn't do this without you. Twenty-five years and counting...

To my children, family, and friends, thank for your continued support. I appreciate and love you!

A special thank you to the authors, readers, bloggers, and reviewers I've met on this journey. You continue to enrich my life. Your support is everything!

They always say to find your tribe, and I've found mine. They know who they are. I love y'all and can't imagine being on this journey without you. Thank you for keeping me sane!

A special thank you to my Forever team.

A very special thank you to my agent, Sarah E. Younger. I can't tell you how much I appreciate having you in my corner.

ABOUT THE AUTHOR

SHERYL LISTER is a multi-award-winning author who writes sweet, sensual contemporary romance featuring intelligent and slightly flawed characters who always find love. She is a former pediatric occupational therapist with over twenty years of experience and often says she "played" for a living. A California native, Sheryl is a wife, mother of three daughters and a son-in-love, and grandmother to two special little boys. When she's not writing, Sheryl can be found on a date with her husband or in the kitchen creating appetizers.

Find out more, at:

SherylLister.com
Facebook.com/SherylListerAuthor
Twitter @SherylLister
Instagram @SherylLister